HOT TIME

HOT TIME

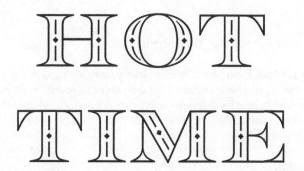

A Mystery

W. H. FLINT

ARCADE
CrimeWise

An Arcade CrimeWise Book

First Edition

This is a work of fiction. Names, places, characters, and incidents are either the products of the author's imagination or are used fictitiously.

Arcade Publishing books may be purchased in bulk at special discounts for sales promotion, corporate gifts, fund-raising, or educational purposes. Special editions can also be created to specifications. For details, contact the Special Sales Department, Arcade Publishing, 307 West 36th Street, 11th Floor, New York, NY 10018 or arcade@skyhorsepublishing.com.

Visit our website at www.arcadepub.com.

10 9 8 7 6 5 4 3 2 1

Library of Congress Cataloging-in-Publication Data is available on file.
Library of Congress Control Number: 2021949494

Cover design by Erin Seaward-Hiatt
Cover photography © Grant Faint/Getty Images

ISBN: 978-1-950994-31-1
Ebook ISBN: 978-1-950994-45-8

Printed in the United States of America

To Teresa and Nick

HOT TIME

ONE

Sunday, August 9, 1896

BY THE TIME Otto Raphael reached the great pile of brick and brownstone known as the Union League Club, on the corner of Fifth Avenue and Thirty-ninth Street, he could already feel the sweat trickling between his shoulder blades. His shirt was plastered to his ribs, and the sleeves of his suit coat were clinging to his arms. The sun had set two hours ago, but it must still be close to ninety degrees.

He stopped beneath the clubhouse's iron and glass marquee and lifted his brass watch and chain from his pants pocket. Five minutes to nine. He glanced up and down the airless roadway. There wasn't much traffic at this hour, and the few animals in sight were lathered and laboring. Headquarters had been flooded with complaints about the hundreds of horse carcasses rotting on the city's streets. He blew out a sigh. How much longer could New York endure this hellish weather?

He heard a metallic *click* behind him. Turning, he saw a liveried doorman eyeing him from the topmost step. Finally, the man asked, "May I help you, sir?" Raphael thought he heard an unkind emphasis on the final word.

Before he could answer, a black hired brougham rattled to a stop at the curb. Two men climbed out. One was in his late thirties, with close-cropped brown hair and the burly build of a wrestler. The other, a decade older, had the thinning gray hair, drooping mustache, and gold spectacles of a schoolmaster. Both were wearing black tailcoats with white vests and black satin bow ties.

Raphael approached the younger man. "Good evening, Commissioner. Mr. Riis," he added, without a glance toward the other.

"Evening, Rafe," Mr. Roosevelt replied. "Warm enough for you?"

The doorman hurried down the steps and took the leather grip from the commissioner's hand. "I'll have that, sir."

"Put the bag in my room, will you, Hennessy?" Mr. Roosevelt said. "We're going to get something to eat. I'm famished." The commissioner had just come back from Oyster Bay. With Mrs. Roosevelt and the children staying out on the island during the hot wave, he would be spending a few nights at his club.

Hennessy held the door. As Rafe followed the others inside, he felt the doorman's gaze on him again, not so much hostile this time as curious. Mr. Roosevelt had instructed Rafe not to wear his uniform, but now he felt underdressed even in his gray serge suit. He had read of the elegant banquets held within these walls, in honor of governors and presidents, but before the commissioner's invitation he had never thought of passing through the heavy iron doors. He suspected that, if the members knew who he was, he wouldn't be welcome tonight, even as Mr. Roosevelt's guest.

They entered a spacious foyer with paneled walls and a tall carved ceiling, then climbed a grand staircase surmounted by fluted columns. Passing an array of marble busts and gilt-framed portraits, they came to the dining room. Rafe took in the soft lighting, the gentle clink of porcelain, the bass hum of hushed male voices. As the maître d' showed them through the long, high-arched room, he recognized the faces of industrialists and politicians he had read about in the pages of the *New York Sun.* The trio took their places at a square, white-clothed table near a window. The sash was thrown open in the hope that a breeze might stir, but the velvet curtains hung straight as a carpenter's plumb.

"No need for menus," Mr. Roosevelt told the maître d'. "We're working tonight, and we're in a hurry, aren't we, boys? We'll have the veal with truffles, I think. With petit pois—and some of those potatoes I like."

"Pommes parisiennes. Would the commissioner care to see the wine list?"

"Not tonight."

On their way in, Rafe had noted the wineglasses and champagne flutes dotting the tables. He knew that Mr. Roosevelt enjoyed the occasional glass of white wine but rarely indulged in anything stronger. Rafe suspected it had something to do with Elliott. The commissioner never discussed it, of course, but everyone knew that his beloved younger brother had passed away a few years ago after a long bout with alcoholism. It had been in all the papers.

But even if he wasn't imbibing himself, the other diners had nothing to fear from the police commissioner, even on a Sunday night. Despite Mr. Roosevelt's shocking decision to enforce state law, a man could still get a legal drink seven days a week in New York City—as long as he was dining at a private club or hotel restaurant. The commissioner was right, of course. The law must be enforced. Especially since his corrupt predecessors had reaped more in bribes for overlooking the Sunday closing rules than they had received in the department's official budget. The crackdown was part of Mr. Roosevelt's long-overdue reforms, along with a restructuring of the detective department, competitive exams for promotions, and firearms training for every officer, although patrolmen didn't generally carry sidearms. He'd even outfitted a bicycle squad, which was proving particularly useful in corralling runaway horses. Altogether, the changes made for the most sweeping transformation in the history of the N.Y.P.D., and Rafe felt honored to be a part of it. Even so, he was hard-pressed to explain to his neighbors on the Lower East Side why rich goyim could get a drink on the Christian Sabbath and they couldn't.

The reforms weren't popular in other parts of the city, either. Uptown, the swells were still blaming Mr. Roosevelt for the Republicans' drubbing at the polls last November. In Albany, the assembly had even tried to legislate his job out of existence. This past May, the city comptroller had challenged Mr. Roosevelt to a duel with pistols—and the commissioner had accepted, before cooler heads prevailed. On the four-man police board, Mr. Roosevelt had only one ally, the young Mr. Andrews, whose inexperience made him a weak partner at best. Even a newcomer like Rafe could see that, with so few friends in the department and in his own party, the commissioner was in a hard place.

Mr. Roosevelt's eyes settled on a table in the far corner. Following his gaze, Rafe made out the dark features and celebrated glower of J. P. Morgan. Not the richest man in America but, they said, the most important. The man who financed corporations like General Electric and American Telephone & Telegraph, who controlled most of the country's railroads, who just last year had personally saved the federal government from default. But apparently, America's preeminent banker was taking dinner alone tonight.

"Morgan lost his sister Sarah last month," Mr. Roosevelt murmured to his companions.

Riis nodded and stroked his mustache.

Rafe said, "There was a piece in the *Sun* last week, when her body came back from Germany."

Mr. Morgan raised a brandy snifter to the commissioner, but Rafe couldn't tell whether it was in deference or in mockery of the unpopular closing law.

Rafe let his glance wander up to the richly carved ceiling. As if sensing his unease, Mr. Roosevelt said, "You know, when I was first nominated for membership here, back in eighty-one, I was blackballed. They didn't want me." He clacked his oversized teeth at the absurdity of the idea. "Well, on the other hand, maybe they don't want me now, either. Ha!"

He turned to Riis. "Jake, what do you have on tap for us tonight?"

"I thought we might go down by the Brooklyn Bridge," Riis said in his raspy Danish burr. "We haven't been over there yet."

For the past week, the pair had been touring the slums to see for themselves how the poor were coping in the deadly heat.

Although the city had opened the floating public baths in the East and North Rivers for twenty-four hours a day, people were still dying. Especially in the unventilated tenements, where temperatures could reach 120 degrees. Workers were collapsing on piers, in stables, behind pushcarts; skinny-dipping boys were being swept away in the current; nightshirted sleepers were rolling off rooftops, where they'd gone hoping for some relief. According to this morning's *Sun*, eighteen people had died in New York and Brooklyn yesterday alone. Unless the heat broke soon, they said, hundreds more would perish.

For Mr. Roosevelt the nightly visits were part of his official duties. As president of the board of police commissioners, he also sat on the board of health, which had a clear responsibility in the hot wave. And as head of the police, he saw the violence that could erupt when human beings were forced to endure the unendurable. For Riis the visits were more personal. Coming from Denmark at the age of twenty-one, he'd lived in the tenements and worked as a carpenter and a flatiron salesman before getting his start in journalism. Now, as star police reporter for the *Sun*, he still spent his days and nights in places the affluent knew only by their unsavory reputation. His book exposing the desperate conditions of the poor, *How the Other Half Lives*, had caused a sensation when it was published several years ago.

Mr. Roosevelt had been among those moved by the work, and, after he'd come back to New York to take over as police commissioner, he had called on Riis to offer his help. Now Riis called him a brother, and Mr. Roosevelt called him the best American he knew. Rafe couldn't help but admire Riis's reforming zeal. But when he'd picked up a copy of *How the Other*

Half Lives, he had barely recognized his Irish and Italian neighbors in its pages. And he certainly hadn't recognized the Jews. "Money is their God," Riis had written of Rafe's people. "Life itself is of little value compared with even the leanest bank account." Riis meant well, but how could the man believe those shopworn slanders about his fellow immigrants?

Tonight was the first time Rafe had been invited on one of these excursions. About noon last Friday, Mr. Roosevelt had come out of his office holding Rafe's report on arrests for violation of the Sunday closing law. "That's fine, careful work," the commissioner had told him. Then, as Mr. Roosevelt had turned away, he'd called over his shoulder, "Jake and I are going out again Sunday night. Why don't you join us?" Rafe was flattered by the invitation, but he still wasn't sure why he had been included. Should he take it as a sign of Mr. Roosevelt's rising confidence in him?

A waiter brought their food, and the table grew quiet as the commissioner and Riis enjoyed their veal. Rafe sipped from his water goblet, nibbled on a roll, lifted a few peas on his silver fork. As Mr. Roosevelt came up to wipe the gravy from his mustache, he glanced at Rafe's plate. "What's the matter, not to your taste?" he asked. Then as soon as he'd said it, he realized. "Why didn't you say something?"

"I'm fine," Rafe told him.

"We'll get you something else."

"No, thank you." His tone was polite but definite. The last thing he wanted was a scene.

Riis looked puzzled at the exchange. "I forgot," Mr. Roosevelt explained. "Rafe here keeps kosher. I admire that in a man. Religious devotion, I mean."

Rafe opened his mouth but then closed it again. How to explain the tangled ties of culture and family, more potent even than belief?

Mr. Roosevelt jabbed a slice of potato onto his fork and pointed it at Riis. "Did I ever tell you how Rafe here came to be my assistant?" He had, but he didn't wait for Riis's answer. "Last year, a tenement—where was it, Rafe?"

"Allen and Hester."

"Yes, that's it—a tenement caught fire in the middle of the night. Rafe and his father live down the street, over the family meat market. Still in their nightclothes, they ran into the building, banging on doors, waking people, saving every soul in that part of the tenement. Didn't you, Rafe?"

"Anyone would have done the same," Rafe said.

"Not everyone. No one went into the other side of the building, and a dozen people died. Not long after, I was invited to give a talk at the Young Men's Institute on the Bowery. Some proud neighbor took the opportunity to introduce me to Rafe. Or Otto, as they called him. I was the one who started calling him Rafe." He took a deep swallow from his water goblet. "Anyway, I could see he was a powerful fellow, with a good-humored, intelligent face. From talking to him I could tell he was sober and resolute, with a strong will to improve himself. He was still working in the meat market, but I encouraged him to take the police examination. Out of nearly four hundred applicants, don't you know he earned the highest score on the physical test and tenth-highest on the mental portion. So this past December I offered him a job in my office. Oh, and he's a champion boxer. Every Wednesday afternoon, he condescends to spar with me. My fighting Maccabee I call him, don't I, Rafe?"

Rafe smiled unconvincingly. Despite the admiration and gratitude he felt toward the commissioner, he wouldn't mind if he never heard that story, or the nickname, again.

"Not many of your people on the force," Riis said.

"No." Rafe had never known a Jewish cop, had never dreamed of becoming one before his chance encounter with Mr. Roosevelt. But when the possibility presented itself, he leapt at the opportunity to get out of the meat market. The pay was better, but there was more to it than that. Like everybody in his neighborhood, Rafe had known the violence and injustice faced by the poor, and he liked the idea of standing up for those who couldn't stand up for themselves. He and Mr. Roosevelt were alike in that way, he figured. Sometimes policing even felt to Rafe like a civic duty, a kind of mitzvah.

He threw himself into the work, learning all he could, doing all the commissioner would let him. And as the months passed, and Mr. Roosevelt was generous in his praise, he began to feel maybe he had an aptitude for it. He began to think of it not only as a job but as a career, maybe even as his family's way out of the Lower East Side. After all, he told himself, somebody had to be the department's first Jewish detective.

A waiter handed Mr. Roosevelt a note. Opening it, he looked once again toward the table at the rear of the room. Rafe could see his mind working, but even the president of the board of police commissioners didn't refuse a summons from J. P. Morgan. Mr. Roosevelt took a final bite of veal. "Blast!" he said as he pulled himself up from his chair and tossed his napkin aside. "I'll be with you quick as I can."

Rafe watched him glide from table to table, slapping a back here, shaking a hand there, like the veteran politician he was. In a few minutes' time he had reached Mr. Morgan.

⁘

Morgan didn't rise from his seat or extend his hand, but Roosevelt wasn't taken aback by the reception. The banker's brusqueness was legendary, and Roosevelt had known him too long to expect anything else. The man must be nearing sixty, Roosevelt calculated as he pulled out a chair. The banker's hair had gone white, but the great arching brows and the brush-like mustache were black as ever. So were the eyes, which he would fix on a man like a snake studying its prey. He'd been a handsome man, Roosevelt recalled, until he'd been struck several years back by a bizarre skin disease that had left his nose a swollen, purple mass. He was fiercely self-conscious about it, Roosevelt knew. As far as anyone could tell, it was his only vulnerability.

Roosevelt perched on the front of the chair. "My condolences on the death of your sister," he said.

Morgan set down his crystal snifter. "Do you know a creature by the name of William d'Alton Mann?" There was a lifetime of cigars in his voice.

"No," Roosevelt answered. "Should I?"

"He's the publisher of *Town Topics*."

"The society magazine?"

Morgan picked a cigar from the ashtray and relit it. "The scandal sheet, you mean. A sewer of innuendo."

"I can't say I've ever seen it." His voice had the superior tone of a man who had never done anything of interest to gossips.

Morgan blew out a cloud of acrid smoke. "None of the Four Hundred admits to reading it, either. I guess that makes it the best-circulated, least-read magazine in the country. No one subscribes for the poetry and essays, I can tell you. The real attraction is a filthy little column called 'Saunterings.'" He gauged Roosevelt down the long black barrel of his Cuban cigar. "Mann pays a servant for information of a . . . personal . . . nature. Then the next thing you know, a note arrives asking if the scoundrel may see you on 'a matter of considerable importance.' If you don't respond, scurrilous hints begin to appear in print. Such as, 'Why does the wife of a certain wealthy man always go to Europe about the time he returns home, and vice versa?'"

Roosevelt recognized a description of the Morgans' routine.

"Or he'll make some seemingly innocuous mention of a prominent husband and wife, then in the space directly opposite, he'll print the name of a . . . friend . . . of the husband, say. Everyone understands what he's doing. It's a parlor game. And the articles continue until he receives a check."

"How large a check?"

"Until recently, twenty-five hundred dollars was the going rate. You'd be shocked if I told you the men who have written checks like that."

Roosevelt rubbed his finger over the crisp white tablecloth. "Blackmail is still a felony in New York State," he said.

Morgan coughed out a dry laugh. "But not so easy to prove when no direct demand is made. Mann claims he's selling stock in the company, of all the preposterous fabrications. Besides, who could afford the publicity of a trial?"

Roosevelt nodded. Who would put his wife and children through that? Not to mention his bank. Roosevelt knew nothing of finance, was so bad with money that Edith had to pin a twenty-dollar bill inside his pants pocket every morning, and at the end of the day he couldn't tell her how he'd spent it. Yet even he understood how these things worked. Morgan could move millions of dollars on his say-so, without so much as a signature. More than cash, more than the myriad corporate boards he controlled, his most valuable asset was his own good name. Scandal, even of the purely domestic variety, was bad for business.

Morgan ran his starched napkin over the beads of perspiration on his forehead. "Last year I wrote such a check myself," he said. "And the articles stopped. But then this past week they began again. Mrs. Morgan and I were named across from a pointed reference to—"

Roosevelt raised his hand. He didn't need the particulars of Morgan's most recent conquest.

But Morgan had apparently decided to tell him everything. That's when Roosevelt realized he was about to be asked for his help. "To Mrs. Douglas."

Adelaide Townsend Douglas. Roosevelt knew the name. She and her husband, William, had an estate on Long Island's Little Neck Bay, twenty miles west of the Roosevelts' house, Sagamore Hill. There were a couple of children, he recalled.

The older man took the cigar from his mouth. "Theodore, there is more at stake here than the humiliation of two families. I don't need to remind you, of all people, that we are in the midst of the most important presidential election in decades. I know McKinley wasn't your first choice for the nomination, but now you're on board. I had Hanna in the other night. Your help is much appreciated."

Roosevelt wasn't surprised that McKinley's campaign manager had been to see Morgan, after the millions the financier had raised from his Wall Street cronies. "If people think times are bad now," Roosevelt said, "wait until that fanatic Bryan gets in the White House."

Morgan leaned closer, as though about to utter a curse unfit for the halls of the Union League Club. "Eliminating the tariff, debasing the currency with *silver*." He spat out the final word like an epithet. "I'm telling you, we will have a disaster on our hands that will make last year's crisis look like a summer shower. I'm doing all I can, but as you know, I'm not exactly popular with certain elements right now."

Joseph Pulitzer's *New York World* had been particularly brutal, Roosevelt remembered. Morgan had never been a favorite of the common folk, especially the western and southern farmers drawn to William Jennings Bryan's populist streak. They were the borrowers, not the lenders of the world, and they blamed Morgan and his ilk for the depression the country had been suffering for the past three years—the worst economic decline of the century, they said. Then last winter, after Morgan had rescued the federal government by issuing sixty-five million dollars in gold bonds—sixty-five million!—ungrateful demagogues like Joseph Pulitzer could only complain about the size of the banker's commission. Earlier this summer, Morgan had even been hauled before a congressional committee to defend himself against charges of profiteering in the deal.

As police commissioner, Roosevelt could hardly condone blackmail, but in this case neither could he advise against it. *What is twenty-five hundred dollars to you?* his expression asked. *And what is any of this to me?*

"What I don't need right now is someone dragging my name in the gutter," Morgan went on in a low voice. "Or Mr. McKinley's, for that matter."

He leaned closer across the table, and Roosevelt tried not to stare at the famously purple, pathologically swollen nose. Now he understood. Though McKinley needed Morgan's money, he couldn't afford his notoriety. If Morgan were tainted by scandal now, the Democrats would seize on it as yet another example of the unholy alliance between Wall Street and Washington. In a close election it could be enough to tip the balance.

"Have you been to see Mann?" Roosevelt asked.

"This afternoon. At Delmonico's."

"And?"

"The price has gone up. 'A simple case of supply and demand,' the bastard told me. To keep my name out of his . . . publication . . . he wants five thousand dollars a month between now and the election."

"So much?" *Such are the wages of sin*, he wanted to add. But he said, "I'm sorry, Morgan. You know I don't get involved in personal cases."

Morgan sat back and tapped the ashes from his cigar. "Theodore, do you remember when your father and I signed the charter for the American Museum of Natural History in your family's parlor on Twentieth Street?"

How could he not remember? As a ten-year-old boy besotted with nature, he'd found it the most thrilling moment of his young life. He'd even presented the museum with his treasured collection of bird and mammal specimens, all mounted with his own hands.

"And then the next year, Theodore Senior and I were founding members of the Metropolitan Museum of Art. He was always raising money for some charity or other—the Newsboys Lodging House, the Children's Orthopedic Hospital. No wonder they called him Great-Heart. I was always glad to contribute. Such a good man."

Roosevelt pressed his lips together then said, "He was the best man I ever knew."

"And do you remember, in eighty-one, when you were running for assemblyman?"

He had been waiting for that. Morgan had been among his earliest donors, at the start of his political career.

"We go back a long way, your family and mine. Don't we, Teedie?"

Roosevelt chafed at the use of his childhood nickname. "Morgan—"

"It's not just myself I'm thinking of, you understand. It's the Republican Party. The party of your father. The party that elected you to the assembly. The party that took you back after your ranch out in the Dakotas went bust. The party that ran you for mayor of New York in eighty-six."

"I had no interest in running—"

"The party that appointed you to the national civil service commission and now to the board of police commissioners. You're a young man, Theodore. Who knows where your career might take you next?"

Roosevelt glared at him.

"And who knows what form Mr. McKinley's gratitude might take? It's not as though things have been easy on the police board lately, especially with all this folderol over the Sunday closing law." He gave a rare smile. "I should thank you for that. They say you've eclipsed me as the most despised man in New York. But how much longer do you think you can hang on? Don't you think next spring might be a propitious time to return to Washington? Maybe to the Navy Department. That would suit you, I imagine. But of course, only if McKinley is elected. And only if he has reason to extend his gratitude." He took a folded slip of paper from his vest pocket. As he handed it across the table, it occurred to Roosevelt that their meeting tonight might have been more than coincidence. "Talk to Mann, Theodore. That's all I'm asking. Have him into the office for a little chat. What can it hurt?"

⁓✽⁓

Rafe was glad to see Mr. Roosevelt returning to their table, if only to fill the awkward silence that had descended between him and Jacob Riis. But as the commissioner drew nearer, Rafe made out the sour look on his face. "Come," he muttered without breaking stride. When Riis and Rafe caught up in the carpeted hallway, Mr. Roosevelt turned to his assistant. "Do I have anything on the agenda for tomorrow morning?"

"Just the board meeting at ten." The board of police commissioners met every Monday, Wednesday, and Friday at that hour.

He shoved a sheet of crumpled stationery into Rafe's hand. "Telegraph this individual first thing tomorrow. Say I want to see him at eleven-thirty."

The brougham was halfway down Fifth Avenue before the commissioner's expression began to clear. Rafe knew how it went. Mr. Roosevelt might be quick to anger, but he was also quick to regain his customary bonhomie. That wasn't to say he didn't harbor a grudge, and it was Rafe's fervent hope that he never found himself in the commissioner's bad graces.

At Twenty-sixth Street, they passed Madison Square Park. To the east Rafe could make out the high tower of Madison Square Garden, topped by the celebrated copper statue of Diana, her bow drawn, her gilded body naked except for the wisp of fabric wafting from her shoulder. In the white glare of the park's arc lights, he could see wooden benches crowded with New Yorkers of all classes, hoping to catch a breath of air. But he knew that if anyone dared to stretch out and fall asleep, one of Mr. Roosevelt's officers would draw his nightstick and give him a good rap on the soles of his feet.

Under the arching elms, cyclists of both sexes were tracing loops around the curving paths, luxuriating in their manmade breeze. Even Mr. Roosevelt's young stenographer, Minnie

Gertrude Kelly, had embraced the bicycle craze, buying one of the machines on the installment plan. Rafe could imagine her diminutive frame balanced on the leather saddle, her knees pumping, her long black hair floating on the wind.

At the park's southern end, they veered east onto Broadway. Even on this hot Sunday night, the city's principal artery was clogged with traffic and the sidewalk was dotted with strollers peering into the display windows at Brooks Brothers and Lord & Taylor. Then the carriage turned onto the Bowery, and the department stores gave way to threadbare theaters, music halls, dime museums, beer gardens. Shifting closer to the window, Mr. Roosevelt scrutinized the saloons, satisfying himself that all were dark tonight, as the law required.

On the corner of Delancey, two city workers had opened a hydrant and were standing on their wagon, training a canvas fire hose on the street. Rafe had read about the plan in the paper, but this was the first he'd seen it in practice. The idea was to bring some relief to the neighborhoods by cooling the pavement. Tonight a dozen squealing children, stripped to their under-clothes, were running this way and that in the bracing stream.

The farther south they traveled, the more dilapidated the buildings, the more rubbish in the streets, the rougher the characters slouching in the shadows. With every breath Rafe took, the rarefied atmosphere of the Union League Club was replaced by the old, familiar odors of rotting garbage and open sewers. The brougham crossed Hester Street, where even now, a few blocks to the east, his father, brother, sisters, and little nephew would be settling down for the night in the tiny apart-ment he shared with them.

His eyes trained out the window, Jacob Riis said, "Rafe, did you know there are seventy thousand unemployed in New York, most of them immigrants? And even the ones with jobs don't earn enough to support their families."

I know all too well, Rafe wanted to say.

"Look at how they live," the commissioner put in. "It's a powder keg. I just hope the hot wave doesn't provide the spark." It wasn't the first time Mr. Roosevelt had voiced his fear of so many poor immigrants packed in unnatural, combustive proximity. "Who knows what men are capable of when they're pushed too far?" the commissioner asked. Especially if they were poor and foreign.

It wasn't that the commissioner was a hypocrite. Rafe knew his concern for the poor was genuine. That, along with his utter incorruptibility, was part of the reason he admired him so. But to Mr. Roosevelt, with his estate in Oyster Bay, and to Jacob Riis, with his fine house in Brooklyn, the Lower East Side was a social problem to be solved, a threat to be neutralized. For Rafe it was home, and a place to escape.

The driver opened the hatch and called down, "Are you sure this is the way, sir?" Mr. Roosevelt took out his round silver badge and held it up for him to see. Reassured, the man let the hatch fall shut again.

With the massive stone piers of the Brooklyn Bridge rising before them, they turned onto Roosevelt Street. "The nearer the river, the nearer to hell," went the saying, and it was easy to see why. But it was hard to imagine that this swarming slum, notorious even by the standards of the Lower East Side, had once been a bucolic estate belonging to one of the commissioner's forebears. Tumbledown dwellings now lined the street, and it seemed that if one fell down the others would topple of their own accord. Built for single families, the structures had long ago been divided into the worst class of tenements, where a dozen souls might be packed into a kitchen and a bedroom. No wonder the Lower East Side was said to be the most densely populated place on earth. Milling on the sidewalk, lounging on the stoops, dressed in as scanty attire as decency would allow, were knots of the Jewish immigrants who were fast pushing the more affluent Germans uptown.

Jacob Riis knocked twice. "Wait for us," he called up.

"Here?" Even through the hatch Rafe could hear the alarm in the driver's voice.

As they climbed down, a circle of sweaty faces closed around them. But the commissioner was unperturbed. "Good evening," he announced in his reedy, patrician tones. "I am Theodore Roosevelt."

The crowd gaped at his evening clothes and gold watch chain. But Rafe noticed that, toward the edge of the circle, a few young men began to drift away.

"I've come to see how everyone is faring in the heat. As you may have heard, I'm hoping to distribute some ice through the local precinct houses."

A young girl pushed to the center of the crowd. Mr. Roosevelt grasped her slender chin between his meaty thumb and forefinger. "Wouldn't you like some ice, so your mama can keep your milk nice and fresh?" She pulled her hands behind her waist and rocked from side to side.

A man's voice called, "What I'd like is a nice cold glass of beer!"

A laugh ran through the crowd. Rafe glanced toward the back but couldn't identify the wit.

Mr. Roosevelt pretended not to hear. "Have any of your neighbors been prostrated by the heat?" he asked.

"On Friday they came and took Mr. Rosen away," one old woman offered. "Right out of his apartment."

"Where was that, back through here?" Without waiting for an answer, the commissioner cut through the crowd, toward an alleyway so narrow he could have reached out and touched one wall with each palm. Rafe maneuvered himself into the lead. Inching up the dark opening with his hands stretched before him, he kicked what sounded like an empty wooden box. In another few feet, his shoe stubbed against a soft object. "Hey!" shouted the obstruction. Rafe stepped over the man, and the others followed. The farther they penetrated, the worse the smell, until even Rafe had to will himself not to hold his nose.

They reached a cramped courtyard where a second tenement had been thrown up behind the first. Candlelight seeped out a few dirty windows, revealing a ramshackle wooden porch four stories high. A tangle of clotheslines spun out from the banisters, and through the unpainted slats Rafe made out dozens of human forms in various angles of repose. In the center of the yard a lone water pump jutted from the hardpacked earth. Directly behind was a closed wooden door where three people in their nightclothes queued outside.

Riis lifted his chin in their direction. "One latrine for two hundred people." That would account for the stench.

Placing their feet carefully, skirting the mounds of trash, they crossed the yard until they came to the porch. Down its length, children were spread out on the wooden floor. A mother was rocking a squalling infant. His back pressed against the clapboards, an old man struggled for breath. The commissioner had seen enough. "Mr. Rosen won't be the last one they take out of here before the heat breaks," he muttered.

They inched through the dark passage again. By the time they reached the street, the crowd had wandered back to their gutters and stoops. Mr. Roosevelt turned to address them. "I want you to know that I am going to direct that an official from the health department come here tomorrow and make a thorough inspection to ensure that all laws and regulations are being met," he said. The residents received the news impassively, but behind the commissioner a ragged cheer broke out. Turning, the visitors spied a dozen newsboys gathered around the carriage. All were wearing their unofficial summer uniform of dingy white shirt, woolen knickerbockers, and wool tweed cap.

"Why, hello, boys!" the commissioner called.

"We knew it was you, Mr. Roosevelt!" one boy answered. "Who else has the nerve to bring a carriage down here at this hour?"

"But why ain't you at the lodging house tonight?" another asked. He meant the Newsboys Lodging House, a few blocks away, on the corner of William and New Chambers, where homeless boys could get a hot meal, a wash, and a clean bed, all at rates even they could afford. Like his father, Mr. Roosevelt served on the home's board, and like his father, he was in the habit of visiting on Sunday nights.

"How are you boys doing in the heat?" the commissioner asked. "I couldn't make it tonight. Not that you would have seen me if I had. Why aren't you all at the lodging house yourselves?"

"No use paying six cents for a bed in this heat," someone answered. "We'll sleep rough tonight," said a tall boy.

As Rafe and the others headed back to the brougham, he noticed a thin boy standing apart from the others beside the carriage door. From his size he seemed to be ten or so, though his face looked young for his age. Thick blond hair poked from his gray cap. He was barefoot, like the others, but his clothes were better made. Rafe guessed he hadn't been homeless for very long. There was something familiar about him, and as Rafe waited for the commissioner and Riis to climb into the carriage and retake their seats, he realized what it was. The boy wore the same lost expression that Rafe had seen on his nephew Harry, Sarah's young son. But for his salary from the police department, who knows what would have become of Harry and Sarah after her husband died?

As he climbed into the carriage, he gave the boy a reflexive pat on the head. "What's your name, son?" he asked.

The boy gazed up with big hazel eyes. "They call me Dutch. What about you?"

He smiled at the boy's cheekiness. "They call me Rafe."

Before Rafe could settle himself in the jump seat, the driver flicked his whip, and the brougham sailed up Roosevelt Street, toward the next port in Riis's archipelago of misery.

❧

Dutch watched the carriage retreat. The big man with the dark hair and the kind dark eyes was with Mr. Roosevelt, so the boy would have figured him for a policeman, but he wasn't wearing a uniform. Dutch had seen the commissioner at the Newsboys Lodging House, and he seemed nice enough. But no copper, not even Mr. Roosevelt, had ever given him a pat on the head before, just a swat of his club and an order to move on. Was the stranger a newspaperman then, like the famous Mr. Riis?

The brougham made the corner, and the newsboys began drifting off in groups of two or three to find their beds for the night. But Dutch stood alone. Just a few months ago, Dutch—or William, as he was known then—used to pass gangs of newsboys on his way to school or church. Dirty, ragged, foul-mouthed, they would be crying the headlines in a language he could barely understand—"Extry! Getcha *Woild* heah!"—and he would cross the street. Now, even though he lived among the newsies, he hadn't lost his wariness of them, and he kept to himself as much as he could. Mistaking the reason for his aloofness, the other boys called him stuck-up, made fun of his grammatical English and middle-class clothes, and bullied him off the prime selling corners. None of which worked to temper his opinion of his fellow entrepreneurs. It didn't matter, he told himself, because soon he would be home again, restored to his rightful place, like the boy heroes in *The Prince and the Pauper*.

Like the other newsies, Dutch turned to the question of where he would sleep tonight. There was a coal chute on Hester where he sometimes went, and some cellar doors on Cherry that were generally left unlocked. But lately, owing to the heat, he'd been tending toward a place he'd discovered off Rose Street, around the corner from the Newsboys Lodging House. He ambled in that direction, keeping to the gutter and kicking a stone with his bare foot.

Farther up Roosevelt Street, he saw a cluster of women lingering under a gas lamp. They turned painted faces in his direction. Then, seeing it was just a boy, most of them turned away again. "Come here, big man!" a tall blonde called, and the others laughed. But Dutch didn't see the particular face he was looking for, and he kept moving.

Several blocks later, he came to the brick headquarters of the Rhinelander Sugar Company. Behind it was an alley, and halfway down, along one wall, a stack of wooden packing crates. He climbed until he reached the top, about six feet off the ground. Then he lay on his back, studying the narrow patch of sky between the buildings. Cloudy tonight, no stars.

He hated the night. During the daytime, there were people on the street, and he heard all the familiar city noises, the *clop-clop* of horses' hooves, the clanging of streetcar bells. At night, the few sounds that reached him were strange and alarming—a woman's nervous laugh; a man's drunken shout; a sharp, faraway *crack* that might have been a gunshot. But even worse were the times in between, when no other living being made its presence known. Then he would pray for sleep, and daylight.

Tonight he was tired. After a while he gave a yawn and rolled onto his side. He settled himself on the crate's thin slats. Unfastening a shirt button, he pulled out a small, folded handkerchief. In the darkness, he ran his thumb over the threads of an embroidered violet. He held the fabric to his face. If he breathed deeply, he could still catch her scent, a blend of rose water and talcum powder. Turning toward the brick wall, he clutched the scrap of cloth to his cheek. As he drifted off, he thought he heard the roll of thunder.

TWO

Monday, August 10

RAFE AWOKE TO the rumble of the elevated train. The sun was well up. Taking his watch from the small table beside the bed, he saw it was past seven o'clock. The sheet was in a tangle at the iron footboard, and his brother, sixteen-year-old Harry, was still stretched out beside him. Across the tiny room, their father's bed was empty. Rafe rolled onto his back and rubbed his eyes.

Last night, after leaving Roosevelt Street, Riis had conducted them to another, even grimmer tenement on Cherry Street, where ten ragpickers and all their wares were crammed into a one-room basement apartment. Afterward, the three men were driving down South Street, along the river toward the Fulton Market, when a violent wind came up and sheets of lightning lit the western sky. The commissioner called through the brougham's hatch, and the grateful driver reversed his course.

It was still blowing and thundering when they let Rafe out on Allen Street. He jiggled the lock on his father's meat market, then climbed the unlit stairs to the second story. After visiting the water closet on the landing, he turned toward the family apartment. The transom was dark; everyone was in bed. He slipped in his key and let himself into the kitchen. The smell of chicken fat still hung in the warm air. He draped his clothes on the wire hook beside the door and stole into the bedroom. The wind was gusting through the only window, and Rafe lay for a long time, sweating and listening to the thunder. Maybe the hot wave was about to break at last. But the breeze died and the clouds passed without yielding a drop. It was long after midnight before he fell asleep.

Now, standing before the pine wardrobe, he slipped on a clean white shirt but left it unbuttoned. In the kitchen, Sarah, his older sister, was standing at the sink with her broad back to him. Their father, Raphael Raphael, was seated at the plain table in the center of the room, only his graying hair visible above the pages of the morning's *Sun.* Without glancing up, he asked in Yiddish, "So did your hero Mr. Roosevelt save any lives last night?"

"Morning, Papa," Rafe answered in English.

His father read the lead headline: "'34 Killed by the Heat.'" He looked up and went on, also in English, "That's one day. In Manhattan they took over fifty people to the hospital. Even your Mr. Roosevelt can't do nothing with that."

Rafe sighed. "He's a good man, Papa. He's trying to help people."

"I told you before, Otto. He's your boss, not your friend. With all his money, what does he care about the poor?"

Rafe took his pants from the hook near the door and pulled them on. "How did you sleep?"

"Who can sleep in this weather, with his business going down? Ice is so high, nobody buys meat. Me and Harry stand at the counter all day and look at ourselves. I can't hardly afford ice neither. If I don't get ice, my meat goes bad."

Rafe hiked up his suspenders. "The heat has to break sometime. The customers will come back. They'll want their chicken soup again."

"I wish you was still in the market with me. Harry goes back to school soon. Then what?"

Rafe studied his father's thin, dark face and waited for him to return to his newspaper. But Raphael Raphael's black eyes were fixed on his son. Finally, Rafe inclined his head toward Sarah and whispered, "Papa, you know we can't all live on what the market brings in. With the thousand dollars they pay me, Sarah doesn't have to take in piecework. Harry can stay in school. After I get a promotion, maybe we can get a place uptown and you can open a market up there."

Raphael Raphael let the paper fall to the table. "And when they give your Mr. Roosevelt the boot? They say he fights with the other bosses and they can throw him out anytime. Then what? Who's going to promote you then? You know the Irish, they don't want you there."

Rafe slumped in his chair. "Then I guess you'll get your wish, and I'll be back at the meat market. Though God knows what we'll live on." He added silently, *And God knows how I'll survive.*

Sarah came to the table and set a glass of water in front of him. She hadn't pinned her hair up yet, and it hung beyond her shoulders in a frowsy tangle. "It's so hot, I didn't light the stove for coffee," she told him. "There's some bread and butter."

"Who can eat?" Rafe said.

She went to the other bedroom to look in on her ten-year-old son, also named Harry, and her and Rafe's little sister Nellie, just seven. Rafe moved to the chipped enamel sink and took a bar of soap from the shelf along the wall. After he finished washing and shaving, he combed his hair in the little mirror hanging over the sink, then pulled on his woolen police coat. As he fastened the long row of brass buttons, he thought of the poor patrolmen. It was bad enough having to work outside in the relentless sun all day, just tending to normal police business. But now they also had to ferry the hot wave victims to Bellevue Hospital, and they were even being called on to cart away the hundreds of stinking horse carcasses that clogged the city's roadways. Every day some officers' names appeared in the newspaper lists of the prostrated. No wonder there had been so many fights in the precinct locker rooms.

He put on his helmet and picked up the paper lunch sack that Sarah had left on the table. He didn't need to open it; there would be two hard-boiled eggs inside. As he closed the door behind him, he took a last glance at his father. He thought, *Oh, how we miss you, Mama.* "Papa," he said, "don't worry so much."

His face buried in the paper, Raphael Raphael didn't answer.

As Rafe made his way down the steep flight of stairs to the street, he shook his head. The only thing worse than his father's stubbornness was the guilt Rafe always felt after one of their arguments. The squabbles had grown more frequent since Rafe joined the police force. But even before that it was always, "Be careful of the Irish, be careful of the Italians, be careful of the Americans." Sometimes Rafe wondered how his father had gotten up the nerve to leave Poland.

Out on the sidewalk, it seemed that last night's bogus storm had only added to the humidity. The sun was streaming across Allen Street, and Rafe guessed the temperature was already well into the eighties. Some housewives had draped their sheets over the fire escapes for airing, and even at this hour some of the shops had set out their barrels and crates of produce. On the flagstone sidewalk, a few mothers tugged at whining children, hoping to finish the day's errands before it got even hotter. The egg lady, Mrs. Kulesh, was in her usual spot in front of the meat market. Rafe raised his hand to the brim of his helmet. "Gut morgn," she called.

Farther up the block, Mr. Abramov was building a pyramid of deep-purple plums. Rafe chose two from the pile.

As he took Rafe's money, Mr. Abramov asked in Yiddish, "Think we'll get some rain today?"

Rafe dropped the plums into his lunch sack. "From your lips," he answered in English.

At the Bowery, he crossed under the elevated tracks, grateful for a moment's respite from the sun. His usual newsboy was on the corner. Brown hair stuck out from under his woolen cap, and he stood with a habitual hunch, like a stray dog wondering whether the next passerby was good for a handout or a boot in the ribs. The boy sold the *Sun* and the *World*, and he made it his business to remember which of his customers took which. Recognizing Rafe, he folded a copy of the *Sun* and held it out. Rafe realized that, although he had bought a paper from this boy every working morning for the better part of a year, he had no idea where he came from or where he went at night. Just another of the city's fifteen thousand homeless children. Rafe fished a nickel out of his pocket. The boy had his three pennies' change ready, but Rafe waved him off. "Bless you," the boy said.

As Rafe walked west on Hester, the Hebrew lettering in the shop windows was replaced by Italian, and the street vendors' carts became piled with tomatoes, peppers, onions, and fava beans. He turned onto Mulberry, passing store windows showing cheap clothing and used furniture. Two young men in a doorway were arguing in Italian, but on seeing his uniform they grew quiet and began to take an uncommon interest in the sidewalk. Except for the newsboy, he hadn't heard a word of English since leaving the house.

Between Houston and Bleecker, he came to an unassuming four-story limestone building. Across the flat facade was carved: CENTRAL HEADQUARTERS OF METROPOLITAN POLICE. Rafe mounted the long flight of granite steps to the entrance, then crossed the lobby to the central staircase. But instead of climbing to Mr. Roosevelt's office, on the third floor, he trotted to the basement, where, along with jail cells, patrolmen's lockers, and the police museum, the departmental telegraph office was located.

The note the commissioner had given him last night listed two addresses for the publisher, home and office. Not knowing the man's schedule, Rafe decided to send his message to both places. He took a slip of paper and a stub of pencil from the counter and wrote:

Mr William d'Alton Mann, the Kenmore, 353 W 57th St
"Town Topics," 17 Madison Ave
Dear Mr. Mann
Commissioner Theodore Roosevelt requests that you
appear in his office at Police HQ, 300 Mulberry St, at
11:30 this morning, Aug 10.
Sincerely
Otto Raphael, Asst to Commr Roosevelt

He handed the sheet to the operator. Then as he darted into the
hallway, he walked directly into the path of two plainclothesmen. The closer and bigger of the two, a beefy Black Irishman
named Gallagher, drew himself up. "Look, Jimmy," he glowered, "it's Roosevelt's pet." Gallagher generally wore a pinched,
put-upon expression, as though the world owed him something
and was behind in its account.

Jimmy Walsh's face split into a bony grin. "Not for much longer he ain't. That's one job we'll be getting back, huh, Tommy?"

After the commissioner was forced out, he meant. "I sure miss
you boys around here," Rafe told them. In January, Mr. Roosevelt
had transferred most of the plainclothesmen out of headquarters
and assigned them to the various precincts. But since the new chief
of detectives, forty-five-year-old Captain Stephen O'Brien, kept
his office at 300 Mulberry, the other plainclothesmen still showed
up here on a regular basis. There were two kinds of cops, Rafe
had learned, those who welcomed the commissioner's reforms,
embracing professionalism and integrity, and those who clung to
the corrupt ways of the past. From all appearances, Gallagher and
Walsh were in the latter category.

Like most of their colleagues, they had been appointed by
Captain O'Brien's predecessor, Thomas Byrnes, probably the
most famous detective in the world and inventor of harsh techniques like the third degree. But after being promoted to superintendent, Byrnes had somehow amassed a personal fortune of
$350,000 on his policeman's salary. Mr. Roosevelt had forced
his retirement last year, and since then, Byrnes's minions had
been directing their fury not only at the commissioner but at
anyone working for him, especially if he happened to be Jewish.

Under Mr. Roosevelt, Rafe told himself, men like Gallagher
and Walsh would never have been promoted to New York's celebrated detective force, the pinnacle of the profession, the envy
of police departments around the globe. Yet Captain O'Brien
didn't seem to notice the problem. More than once he'd called
Gallagher his hardest worker, his best man. Rafe saw the weekly
reports, and it was true, Gallagher had more arrests than any
other detective. But Rafe wondered, did he get them through
the unorthodox techniques he'd learned from Thomas Byrnes?

"Not to worry, Raphael," Gallagher was saying. "We're only
at the Fourth, just a few blocks away, so we can still drop by and
pay our respects anytime, can't we, Jimmy?"

Jimmy Walsh gave a choking laugh. Then he said, "You
know, Tommy, it's just like Mr. Ward was saying—"

Gallagher's grin turned to ice.

"You know, last night—" But Gallagher's look kept him
from going on.

Rafe shook his head. That would be Robert DeCourcy
Ward, the climate scientist who had joined with some other
Harvard alumni to found the Immigration Restriction League.

Rafe had seen in the *Sun* that Ward was in town to spread some of his pseudoscientific hatred. Anglo-Saxons were genetically superior to Southern and Eastern Europeans, he believed. As immigrants, these inferior creatures brought poverty and took jobs from Americans. Ergo, they must be excluded. Rafe was hardly surprised that Gallagher and Walsh had been in the audience.

Gallagher poked Walsh in the ribs. "Come on, Jimmy. I don't want to keep Captain O'Brien cooling his heels, now do I?"

The pair edged past Rafe and headed up the stairs. "Dirty Jew," Rafe heard, though he couldn't be sure which one had said it. As he watched them go, he unclenched his fists and shook his head again. Not only had Rafe's kind made the mistake of getting here a few years after Gallagher's family, they had the poor judgment to speak a different language and practice another religion.

He began the long climb to the third floor. With each step the temperature in the building rose, until by the time he reached Mr. Roosevelt's office Rafe had removed his helmet and was reaching for his handkerchief. In the anteroom, he found Minnie at her typewriter, her head bent over her stenographer's notebook, her white pleated shirtwaist already wilting in the heat.

"Morning," he said, going to the desk across from her, just outside Mr. Roosevelt's office. "I see the commissioner has been dictating." Rafe was often the first one in, but after the late night he was running behind today.

Minnie looked up. "Oh yes, we got an early start." She nodded toward the circular iron staircase leading to the floor below.

"He just went down to speak to Commissioner Andrews. Then he said he was expecting Captain O'Brien at nine thirty."

"That's not on the calendar," Rafe said. "He must have spoken to the captain this morning." He set his helmet on the filing cabinet. "How was the streetcar?"

"Crowded. And hot." She grinned. "Did you hear? It's so bad the bees are taking off their yellow jackets."

Rafe groaned. It was a running gag between them. She would tell an awful joke, and he would feign disgust. Then she would chide him for being so serious. "Otto the Solemn," she called him.

She rolled a sheet of paper into the typewriter, and the keys began their staccato clatter. Rafe started to open the morning mail, but every so often he felt his glance drifting over to Minnie's fine features, intense blue eyes, and straight, jet-black hair, gathered this morning into a loose bun to keep it off her neck. She lived with her mother up on East Eighty-first Street. But every day she left her comfortable neighborhood and came down here to work this job.

After the commissioner hired her last May, Minnie Gertrude Kelly had become something of a celebrity, and profiles of her had appeared in some of the papers. Under Commissioner Roosevelt, the force had finally hired a couple of dozen matrons to look after female prisoners. But Minnie, just nineteen years old, was the department's first woman stenographer. Her salary was twelve hundred dollars a year—more than a starting patrolman—and she had taken the place of two men, who between them had been making twenty-nine hundred. Rafe reckoned she was worth twice what they were paying her. A girl like Minnie wouldn't have had trouble finding more genteel work closer to home, and he knew she hadn't taken the job just for the money.

But even her Irish surname hadn't guaranteed her a warm reception at headquarters. If it was hard being a Jew in a mostly Irish police department, Rafe knew it must be that much harder to be a woman among four thousand men. Yet she never seemed daunted. During one of their quiet lunches sitting at their desks, she'd even confided that she hoped to make a career of it. When one of the other cops asked him what it was like working with a woman, Rafe would just smile. He hoped she would make a career of it.

Just then Minnie felt his glance and looked over her machine at him. He turned back to his paperwork. But before long he felt his gaze wandering in her direction again.

At 9:25, Mr. Roosevelt burst into the anteroom. He had changed last night's tailcoat for a gray business suit, and under his arm he was carrying a jumble of papers. "Is O'Brien here yet?" he asked without breaking stride. As he disappeared into his office, he called, "When he comes, send him in."

A moment later Captain O'Brien strode through the door. Rafe was about to say that the commissioner was expecting him, but he froze on seeing who was by his side. So that was what had brought Gallagher to headquarters this morning. But what business could he have with Mr. Roosevelt? Some breach of discipline, most likely. The pair went in and shut the wooden door behind them.

❧

The commissioner was still standing at his wide mahogany desk when Captain O'Brien appeared in his doorway. Roosevelt was surprised to see Detective Sergeant Gallagher with him. When O'Brien had sent a note early this morning asking for some time, he hadn't mentioned that anyone would be joining them.

The captain closed the door, and the commissioner gestured toward two cane-backed chairs in front of his desk. O'Brien perched on the seat of one. Gallagher slumped into the other and crossed a leg.

"You know Detective Sergeant Gallagher," O'Brien said in his gruff brogue.

Roosevelt eyed the detective sergeant. He knew enough of Gallagher to appreciate that he was one of Byrnes's favorites and, he suspected, one of the ringleaders against reform.

O'Brien went on, "As you know, the detective sergeant here is one of my best men. That's why we put him on the anti-terror squad. He's been attending anarchist meetings, earning their trust, trying to find out what mayhem they're plotting next. He's come across some intelligence I thought you should hear for yourself."

As O'Brien praised Gallagher, Roosevelt watched the man puff and preen.

The detective uncrossed his legs and leaned forward. "Over the past week," he began, "there's been a change in the anarchist meetings. Bigger names are showing up, like Emma Goldman and Johann Most. And the speeches are getting more violent, like they're trying to whip up the crowd. Like they're working up to something."

Despite his dislike of the man, Roosevelt sat up a little straighter. He shifted his gaze from the detective to the captain and back again. Finally, he asked, "Why now?"

"The election campaign," Gallagher answered. "They want to use it for their propaganda. The election is the biggest story of the year. Think of the reaction if they pulled off an attack right in the middle of it all."

"'The propaganda of the deed,'" Roosevelt said. The evil idea that spectacular acts of violence would demoralize the rich and incite the masses to revolt. "But what would be the target?"

Gallagher shrugged. "Don't know yet. But something is going to happen. I can feel it."

O'Brien spoke. "As you know, Gallagher is our only man to make any progress at all with the anarchists. I've told him to go ahead with his surveillance and report anything out of the ordinary."

Roosevelt looked from one to the other. Could it be true? He wished the intelligence had come from a man he had more confidence in.

"There's something else," O'Brien said. "Involving the department." He motioned to Gallagher.

The detective leaned farther forward, until his face hovered over the commissioner's desk. In a hoarse whisper he told them, "The anarchists have spies here at police headquarters."

Roosevelt sat back in his chair. "I don't believe it."

"There's a network of terrorists in this building," Gallagher said.

"How could that happen? Who would be capable of such a thing?"

Gallagher leaned closer still. "It's the Hebrew element." *The ones you added to the force*, his look seemed to add.

Roosevelt slammed his palm on the desktop. "What evidence do you have?"

Gallagher was already reaching into his breast pocket. He pulled out a folded sheet of white stationery, opened it, and handed it across the desk. "I found this on the floor in the locker room."

Roosevelt adjusted his pince-nez and examined the sheet. At the top was the familiar letterhead, *Metropolitan Police Headquarters, 300 Mulberry Street*. Below, a message was written in blue ink. He looked up at Gallagher. "I see that it's Hebrew or Yiddish, but I can't tell you what it says."

"I had one of my connections translate it," Gallagher told him. "It says, 'Meeting tonight, 8:00, Schultz's saloon. Death to the capitalists. Long live anarchy.'"

Roosevelt studied the inscrutable script. He could feel O'Brien and Gallagher watching him, waiting for a response. He eyed them. Then he refolded the sheet and slipped it into his suitcoat pocket. "Not a word of this to anyone," he said.

❧

The commissioner's door opened, and Rafe lifted his head. Judging from Gallagher's mocking grin, he hadn't been there on a disciplinary matter after all. If anything, he was strutting more brazenly than ever.

Not long afterward, the commissioner stepped into the conference room adjoining his office. When he emerged, his face suggested that the board meeting had been the usual purgatory.

"Is Mann here?" he asked.

"No, not yet," Rafe told him.

"Show him in when he arrives." He went into his office and shut the door with a decisive *click*, just short of a slam. Minnie gave Rafe a questioning look. He shrugged.

The office clock was chiming eleven thirty when a portly figure appeared in the doorway. "I am Colonel William d'Alton Mann," he announced in a well-bred baritone. "I am here to see Commissioner Roosevelt."

Colonel Mann wore long white hair tucked behind his ears and an unruly white beard and mustache. He was dressed in a blue blazer and striped gray trousers, with a flaming red vest and matching bow tie. In one hand was a black plug hat, in the other a heavy, carved walking stick. Among the hundreds of people who had come to call on the commissioner, Rafe had never seen such a getup, which seemed to have been chosen especially for its power to offend. Colonel Mann was the first person Rafe had seen in a week who didn't seem to be sweating.

He showed him into the commissioner's office and closed the door. As he retook his seat, Minnie said, "I always wondered what Santy Claus wore on his day off."

But Rafe wasn't smiling. He was remembering the dark look on Mr. Roosevelt's face after his talk with J. P. Morgan last night, as he'd stalked back to the table clutching the bit of stationery with Mann's name on it. He couldn't say why, but he doubted the colonel's visit this morning was a subject for levity.

❧

Roosevelt couldn't help but stare at the spectacle standing before him, the luxuriant, stark-white hair and whiskers, the outrageous choice of wardrobe. Finally, he said, "Mr. Mann."

Mann bowed from the waist. "Colonel Mann, if you please. Seventh Michigan Cavalry. Second Bull Run, Gettysburg."

Roosevelt grunted. As much as he admired military service, he couldn't abide men who made a show of it.

Mann gave his cane a playful flick. Far from betraying any nervousness, he was beaming like a schoolboy out for a cruise to the Locust Grove Picnic Ground. Apparently, he'd even dressed for the occasion. As he came closer, Mann gazed frankly about the office, taking in the wide, cluttered desk, the tall pendulum clock on the mantel, and the faded oriental carpet laid over the wooden floor. To Roosevelt he had the appraising eye of an auctioneer.

Mann asked, "How may I be of service, Commissioner?"

Roosevelt wasn't in the mood for preambles. "Colonel Mann, I have recently become aware of your activities ..."

Mann put a hand to his scarlet vest. "My 'activities'? And what might they be?"

Roosevelt glowered. "I'm talking about your method of funding *Town Topics*."

Mann gave a little laugh. "Oh, you mean my stock plan." Before Roosevelt could answer, he went on, "Wherein prominent members of society are invited to purchase shares in my business."

"In convenient increments of twenty-five hundred dollars."

"That used to be the standard purchase, yes. But due to high demand, I'm pleased to say the price has risen."

Roosevelt leaned toward him. "Look, here, Mann—"

Mann arched his unruly brows. "Is it now a crime in the city of New York for a business owner to sell stock in his own company?"

"Worthless stock at overblown prices."

If Mann had known Roosevelt better, he might have noticed the telltales of building rage—the rising pitch of his already reedy voice, the whitening knuckles as his hands gripped the arms of his chair. But the colonel continued in a blithe tone, "Hardly worthless, sir. On the contrary, I am performing a great moral agency. My ambition is to reform the Four Hundred by making them too disgusted with themselves to continue their silly, sinful ways. I assure you, what I do, I do for the sake of the public."

Roosevelt grunted. What did this pretender know or care about the cream of New York society, except as a source of ill-gotten cash? As he spoke, he struggled to keep his voice level. "And you don't do too badly out of it yourself. Last night, I had a conversation with one of your 'investors,' a prominent banker—"

"That could be one of a dozen men," Mann observed with a smirk. "Many financiers have chosen to invest in my publication. And industrialists and businessmen." He inclined his head toward Roosevelt. "And many politicians—of all persuasions. It seems evildoing and hypocrisy know no party affiliation." He pointed to one of the caned armchairs. "May I take a seat?"

When the yelling began, Minnie ceased her typing and Rafe threw down his papers. Although they couldn't make out the words through the heavy door, it was Mr. Roosevelt's voice they heard. Rafe rushed to the door and gave a hurried knock. When there was no answer, he swung it open. Mr. Roosevelt was leaning over his desk, supporting himself on his hands. His cheeks were flushed, and even from across the room Rafe could see the veins pulsing in his forehead. He had stopped shouting and was sputtering in amazement and rage. Then, as Rafe watched, he sent his oak swivel chair spinning against the wall and he charged to the other side of the desk. Seizing Mann by the lapels of his blue blazer, he hauled him out of his seat and heaved him across the desktop. A pile of books thudded to the floor, followed by a flurry of papers.

The commissioner was leaning into the colonel's face. "You listen here, you evil little man! If you do any such thing, you'll regret it, you hear? You have no idea what I'm capable of." He pinned him for another few seconds, peering into his stunned blue-gray eyes. Then, with a glance toward Rafe, he released his grip and backed away. He took a breath. "Now you get out of my office, before I lose my temper."

With as much dignity as he could muster, Mann straightened himself and smoothed his coat. He collected his hat and walking stick from the floor and retucked his long white hair behind his ears. The grin had finally deserted him. When he reached the doorway, he turned to the commissioner.

"You won't want to miss our next edition," he said. And then he was gone.

Mr. Roosevelt slumped into his chair. Rafe went to retrieve the mess on the carpet, but the commissioner waved him off. "Close the door on your way out," he told him.

Minnie was wide-eyed as Rafe took his seat again. "Who was that?" she whispered.

He turned up his palms. "A friend of J. P. Morgan's, I think." It wasn't the first time fisticuffs had threatened to erupt in Mr. Roosevelt's office, but the target was usually Commissioner Parker or Chief Conlin, not a member of the public. Rafe and Minnie sat wordlessly for another minute before turning back to work.

THREE

AT NOON, THE commissioner opened his door and announced that he was leaving for lunch. An hour later Minnie went to meet a friend, and Rafe found himself alone with his hard-boiled eggs as he assembled the agenda for that week's disciplinary hearing. There were cases of roundsmen sleeping on their beats, patrolmen overusing their nightsticks, a detective accused of investigating a brothel with undue diligence. Nothing out of the ordinary.

Just before two o'clock, Rafe heard footsteps in the hallway. He thought it must be Minnie, but when he glanced up, he saw only a perspiring middle-aged man dressed in a black frock coat and silk hat.

"Is Mr. Roosevelt in?" he panted.

"No, sir. May I help you?"

"When will he be back?"

"I really can't say. Would you like to leave word?"

The stranger took a calling card from his pocket. "Give him this. Tell him it's urgent."

"Very good, sir."

"Urgent. I must speak to him today."

"Will the commissioner recognize the name?"

"Yes."

"I'll make sure he gets it."

The man hurried out. Rafe read the card, but it meant nothing to him.

Ferris Appleby
316 Madison Avenue

Minnie came in from lunch not long after, her shirtwaist drooping and her straw hat pushed to the back of her head.

"Did you see a man coming down the stairs just now?" he asked.

She shook her head. "Not that I noticed. Why?"

He handed her the calling card. "He wanted to see the commissioner. Said it was urgent. Does the name mean anything to you? Has the commissioner written him lately?"

She read the card, then passed it back. "Never heard of him." She went behind her desk and set her purse in the chair. As she unpinned her hat, Rafe could see fine beads of sweat strung out just below her hairline. She saw him looking. "What?" she smiled. "Do I have mustard on my cheek again?"

Rafe could feel his face reddening. She knew she had no mustard on her cheek.

Roosevelt had found J. P. Morgan where he knew he would, in his mahogany-paneled office in the rear of 23 Wall Street, the white-marble cathedral to commerce he had erected across from the stock exchange. Hat in hand, Roosevelt was standing before Morgan's carved desk, which was empty except for a telephone, a huge enamel ashtray, and the gold fountain pen used to sign the sheaves of documents that came his way. To one side, through a beveled glass partition, several men were beavering away in the firm's partners' room. Lord only knew how many millions were changing hands in there.

"You might say the meeting didn't go precisely as planned," Roosevelt said. "Mann is determined to go ahead. He claims to have incriminating information not only on you but on a number of other prominent Republicans. Apparently, he has raised his prices to capitalize on the election campaign. And he's threatening to run something in the next edition."

Morgan stubbed out his Cuban cigar, one of the dozens he smoked daily. "There's absolutely no talking him out of it?" he asked.

"I'm afraid not."

"Then we must see Hanna. He's staying at the Waldorf-Astoria during the campaign."

Roosevelt didn't answer. He was busy calculating how the Mann business would affect his odds of finding something for himself in a McKinley administration. Finally, he nodded.

"Now," Morgan said.

He made a brief telephone call then ordered his carriage. "The Waldorf-Astoria," he told the driver.

Uptown traffic was heavy, and they sat and sweated for the better part of an hour before the carriage finally jerked to a stop at the corner of Fifth Avenue and Thirty-third. As he climbed down, Roosevelt glanced up at the enormous sandstone-and-brick building before them. He remembered when George Boldt built the Waldorf Hotel, just a few years ago, on the site of the old Waldorf mansion. When Boldt expanded into the Astoria Hotel next door, people said he was mad to sink five million dollars into the world's largest hotel. He would never fill 450 rooms, they said. The rooms were too expensive, they said. It was too far from Wall Street, they said. But it turned out that Boldt knew better than they did. It would seem that if you built the most elegant hotel in the city, with private baths and electricity in every room and a fine restaurant to rival Delmonico's or Sherry's, the well-heeled would find you. There was a lesson in that, Roosevelt reminded himself. Don't listen to the naysayers. Don't trust anyone's judgment but your own.

He and Morgan entered under the iron and glass marquee and passed through the crowded lobby, with its frescoed ceilings and European antiques. They continued down the main corridor until they came to an alcove where the elevators were located. Morgan stepped in and requested the twelfth floor. They rode in silence. On leaving the car, Morgan turned to the right. He seemed to know exactly where he was going. At the end of the carpeted hallway, he knocked on a door.

It opened right away, and they were shown in by a self-possessed young man whom Roosevelt didn't know. "Good afternoon, gentlemen," he said. "Mr. Hanna is expecting you." He led them through the foyer to the handsome sitting room, then bid them good day and slipped into the hallway. In another minute, Mark Hanna came out of the adjoining room.

Roosevelt took him in like a boxer sizing up an opponent. Though about Roosevelt's height, he was heavier and softer. His round cheeks were unlined, and he looked younger than his sixty years, save for the dark, puckered circles under his eyes. His remaining hair, mostly gray, was oiled and combed unconvincingly over the top of his head. The necktie was a natty check, and the suit looked expensive, as befitting an iron and coal magnate. He'd inherited the company from his father-in-law, Roosevelt recalled, but he'd managed it well, the way he managed everything. For the past decade he had left the business increasingly to others, while he devoted himself to a different sort of industry—the political advancement of his old friend William McKinley.

McKinley had served several terms in Congress before being gerrymandered out of his seat. Then five years ago, under Hanna's tutelage, he had been elected governor of Ohio. A year later, when the crash had left McKinley in a financial embarrassment, Hanna and some others had stepped in with $100,000 to rescue his honor. It had been an act of friendship, but so much more. Finally, all the time and money Hanna had invested over the years was about to pay off. With the Republican nomination in hand, McKinley was poised on the verge of the presidency. Roosevelt couldn't imagine what that must feel like.

They were an odd pair, the kingmaker, as shrewd as he was coarse, and the candidate, as upright and anodyne as a Methodist preacher. They said Hanna shuffled and dealt McKinley like a pack of cards. One thing was clear: If, God willing, the Republicans won in November, it would be Hanna whispering in the president's ear and doling out jobs in the new administration. Roosevelt looked into the man's coal-black eyes. He saw that Hanna would do absolutely anything to get McKinley elected.

Morgan extended a wary hand to Hanna, as though afraid he might not get it back. Word was that Morgan and his friends had invested a stunning seven million dollars in the campaign, but only after extracting Hanna's personal commitment to support the gold standard, the most important issue to the financiers and industrialists. Now Morgan had to hope that Hanna made good on his promise. Just because the two men were united in common need, Roosevelt knew, that didn't mean they were bathed in mutual trust and affection.

"We're so glad to have you on board, Theodore," Hanna greeted him in his flat Ohio accent. "We want to get you out west for some barnstorming, out in your old stomping grounds, the Dakotas, out that way. How does that sound?"

Both men knew the pro-business, anti-silver McKinley was a hard sell out west. But Roosevelt said, "I'm honored to do whatever I can. Anything to keep that anarchist Bryan out of the White House." Then, realizing how that might sound, he added, "McKinley is a good man."

If Hanna noticed the gaffe, he didn't let on. He waved his visitors toward an embroidered French sofa and chairs.

They had agreed that Morgan would do the talking. "We have a minor problem," he began after they'd situated themselves. "With a certain publisher, William d'Alton Mann, of *Town Topics*. Ostensibly, it's a journal of the arts, but no one buys it for the short stories or theater reviews. There's a gossip column that exposes the peccadilloes of the prominent. It's utter blackmail. If you want the innuendo to stop, you have to pay."

Roosevelt gauged Hanna's expression, but the man showed no surprise at this intelligence. Maybe he knew the publication.

Morgan went on to describe Roosevelt's meeting with the publisher, how he'd claimed to have incriminating information on an array of prominent Republicans.

"Who?" Hanna wanted to know.

Morgan inspected the oriental carpet, then admitted that he himself was among their number.

Roosevelt was half-expecting an outburst, but Hanna only sat for a moment, resting his chin on his knuckles and taking Morgan in with his sharp black eyes. Finally, he asked, "He can't be persuaded?"

Morgan shook his head. "Theodore tried, in the most persuasive terms." He thought it best to omit the part about throwing the publisher across his desk. "But Mann is threatening to print something in the next issue. You understand, it's not my own reputation I'm concerned about, but the effect it would have on the campaign. Bryan is already making hay out of my support for McKinley."

"This Mann must be stopped," Hanna said.

"And quickly," Morgan put in.

"I'll take care of it."

"What will—?" Morgan began.

"I said I'll take care of it," Hanna snapped. Roosevelt wondered how many men had the grit to speak to J. P. Morgan in that tone. He stole a glance at Morgan's face, but his expression revealed nothing. Then Hanna stood and ushered the callers into the hallway.

They strode down the quiet corridor. As they reached the elevator, Roosevelt asked, "Do you trust him to 'take care of it' before it's too late?"

Morgan stabbed the black call button with more force than was strictly necessary. "As my late, sainted father used to say, 'Trust the dealer, but cut the cards.' Don't worry, I know someone who may be able to help."

❦

By five o'clock, Rafe was concluding that the commissioner wouldn't be coming back this afternoon. He and Minnie were used to Mr. Roosevelt's irregular hours, especially when the family was in Oyster Bay. He might be at his desk by 7 a.m., attend meetings outside the office all afternoon, have dinner at one of his clubs or at Delmonico's, then prowl the streets with Jacob Riis until all hours. Sometimes when Rafe got in at eight, he would find the commissioner, still in his evening clothes, stretched out on the divan in his office. Even so, it was unusual for him to be gone all afternoon without sending word.

As if reading Rafe's mind, Minnie said, "I wonder what became of the commissioner."

Just then a familiar Danish accent wafted through the doorway. "Is the commissioner in?"

"Mr. Riis," Rafe said. "No. I thought maybe he was with you."

"I haven't seen him all afternoon."

"Neither have I. Will you make the rounds with him tonight?'

Riis gave him an impatient look. "That's what I was hoping to find out."

"If you see him, would you tell him I have an urgent message?" Rafe jotted a note, sealed it in an envelope, and handed it to the reporter.

Riis slipped it into his breast pocket. "I'll be across the street for a while yet." He motioned toward the dilapidated brick building that served as the bureau for all the police reporters.

When he'd gone, Minnie asked, "You're not concerned about the commissioner, are you?"

Rafe shook his head. If Mr. Roosevelt could prowl the worst parts of the city all night with impunity, he figured that nothing was likely to befall him in the middle of the day. "No, it's that message from Appleby," he said.

Minnie understood. It was a loose end, and Rafe didn't like loose ends. She finished typing her letter and slipped it into the folder with the others. Then she covered her machine and collected her things. "Good night, Rafe," she said. "Stay cool." She laughed at the improbability of that. "Well, have a good night anyway."

Rafe watched her disappear into the hallway, then went back to his papers. At seven o'clock he wrote a note and placed it with Mr. Appleby's card on the commissioner's desk. On the way out, he stopped in the telegraph room and sent the commissioner a wire in care of the Union League Club. He wondered, should he take a trolley up to the clubhouse? No, if

Mr. Roosevelt were there he would get the telegram, and if he weren't Rafe could do nothing but leave him another message anyway. Figuring he'd done all he could, he headed up the stairs for home. Still, it bothered him.

❦

"We are here because we are hungry. We are hungry because the capitalists give us no work. I tell you, they are no better than murderers...."

The translator paused, and another string of gibberish spewed from the speaker's mouth. Gallagher knew it was Yiddish, but he couldn't imagine how any people could produce such a godforsaken noise. How many times had he tried to take a statement from some cretin who couldn't even speak English? And the few who could were so proud to stick a sign in their store window, ENGLISH SPOKEN, like they were doing the Americans a favor. In his work, he'd seen it all—the idleness, the mental weakness, the filth, the anti-Christian and undemocratic ideas. No wonder the immigrants made such fertile ground for the European terrorists who wanted to import their anarchy to America.

He peered through the cigar smoke. It was so hot even the walls were sweating. Maybe two hundred men were packed into this basement coffeehouse on the Lower East Side, sitting at small round tables or leaning against the brick foundation. He recognized the usual types—students, cigar makers, mechanics, labor agitators, all dressed in torn trousers and dirty shirts with no collar. Gallagher had put on his oldest, most tattered vest and pants, but still he felt overdressed. There wasn't an American among them, he noted, just Jews, Russians, Germans, Austrians, Bohemians, Slavs, maybe an Italian or two. In their hands he counted more beer mugs than coffee cups.

The only light came from candles stuck into old bottles, scattered among the tabletops. Behind the long, dark bar hung a high mirror with a chipped frame and clouded glass. In front sat a bentwood chair, on whose seat stood the evening's speaker. Gallagher had seen the man at these meetings before. His name was Smolenski, and he published a newspaper. He was no more than thirty, with sandy-colored hair and beard. The face was gaunt, the frame skeletal. The cheap suit, no doubt his best, hung from him as though a good breeze would set it flapping. As he spoke, Smolenski pounded his fist into his palm. His eyes, blue and sunken, shone through his spectacles with an intensity Gallagher could only describe as hellish.

The young man waited while the translator continued in his own thick accent, "Go to the capitalists and shout for labor and bread. Go and get your bread. Go and get it from those who have too much. . . ." The interpreter was a fat, greasy man in his forties. Not exactly starving, from the look of him.

"All these buildings in the city, all this wealth, are what we made. But rather than lose a cent, the capitalists would see us starve. You have a right to the wealth you created. It is yours. Take it. If you cannot take it otherwise, then take it by force."

A murmur ran through the crowd. "Take it!" someone shouted. Gallagher had heard it all before—the ne'er-do-well's jealousy of the successful, the idler's hatred of the industrious, the criminal's contempt of the law-abiding. As the presidential campaign had heated up, there had been a spike in the anarchists' brazenness. They wouldn't be happy until they tore down everything decent and good in the country that had taken them in. Stealing Americans' jobs, insisting on their own babble, living in filth, degrading the country into something he couldn't even recognize.

Last year, when Captain O'Brien had offered him a place on the anti-terror squad, he'd welcomed the assignment. They'd had a hearty laugh over it, a good Irish Catholic to spy on the anarchists. But they didn't have much choice. There were no foreigners among the detectives, and it was hardly work they could trust to informers. But thanks to his Black Irish blood, Gallagher fit right in with the Jews and the rest of the rabble. True, he didn't speak any of their unpronounceable dialects, but they talked in so many different tongues themselves that there was almost always somebody to translate into English, the closest thing they had to a common language. Eventually, he got to know people. He saw things. He heard things.

Gallagher's eyes narrowed as he listened to what came next. "If policemen dare to stop us, knock them down. The police do not feel pain and hunger, do not know what starvation means. If we yell for bread, they arrest us. Let them arrest us. What use are the police anyway? Can they make jackets?"

"No!" the crowd yelled.

"Or pants or caps?"

"No!"

"What in hell do they do?"

"Nothing!"

"I'll tell you. They go to the Italian peanut stands and help themselves to peanuts."

Laughter rippled around the room.

The speaker was excited now, and the translator was having trouble keeping up. "Americans, don't think that the foreigners have come to rob you. Our interests are your interests. It is capital that has caused this suffering. Go up Fifth Avenue and shake up those fat millionaires. Fight for your rights. Don't listen to the priest and the rabbi. Don't listen to those little labor leaders who tell you to have patience and be quiet. Think of your starving wives and children first. Fight, I tell you. Fight!"

The coffeehouse erupted. "Fight! Fight! Fight!" Of course that would be one English word they all knew. The call echoed in the narrow space until Gallagher could feel it throbbing in his chest.

Finally, Smolenski climbed down, and the translator put up his hand for quiet. "Tonight I am happy to tell you we have a very special guest," he told the room. "You all know his work for the cause, you all know his bravery. Gentlemen, I give you Johann Most!"

The crowd began chanting, "Most! Most! Most!" as an imposing man stepped from a curtained room behind the bar.

Gallagher stretched to get a look. He had never seen Most, but he knew his story well enough. Exiled from his native Germany, imprisoned in England, he had immigrated to the United States more than a decade ago. All the while preaching his infernal gospel of "the propaganda of the deed." But what had brought the notorious anarchist out tonight?

Two men steadied him as he climbed onto the speaker's chair. At fifty, he still had a thick head of hair, streaked with gray. His beard was long and full, partially hiding his deformed jaw. From a childhood operation, they said.

Most was holding a glass of water in one hand. He raised the other, and the crowd stilled.

"Is anarchism desirable?" he began in English. "Of course it is. Who does not seek freedom? Every other solution to social injustice is but a half-measure and a patchwork. Private property increasingly exploits the poor," he went on, sounding more like a professor than a revolutionary. "The poor have less and less of the goods they produce. The government maintains this swindle, because the state is nothing more than the organized power of property. And so it only stands to reason that the unpropertied must destroy the state, eliminate private property, and establish ownership in common."

There was some applause from the back of the room. The speaker took a gulp of water.

"Is anarchism possible?" he continued. "Yes. The struggle for freedom is stronger than ever before, and we stand nearer to washing authoritarianism from the face of the earth. Fortunately, no country was ever more suited for anarchist agitation than present-day America. Just look around you. The ship is powered by stupidity, corruption, and prejudice. Good men have long been disgusted by government. They avoid voting, and so they are already anarchists, even if they don't know it yet."

Laughter.

"This country is now in the middle of an election campaign, but with capitalists vying against capitalists, will an election change anything?"

"No!" the crowd called.

"Of course not! Capitalists, police, press, clergy, the other hypocrites and philistines hate us with all their hearts, all their minds, all their souls. We make revolutionary propaganda because we know the privileged class will never be overturned peacefully."

He leaned forward, pointing a finger toward the low ceiling. "My friends, the time has come for action. It is time for the capitalists to die."

A hush fell over the room.

"What is the purpose of the anarchists' threats—an eye for an eye, a tooth for a tooth—if they are not followed up by action? At the first opportunity, the oppressors are to be dispatched to the other world. But are the capitalists and the police and the rest of the 'law-and-order' elite to be done away with in a dark corner so that no one knows what happened to them? Of course not. We have said it a hundred times: A single deed makes more propaganda than hundreds of speeches, thousands of articles, tens of thousands of pamphlets. The proletariat must be enlightened before it can be called into battle. The day is fast approaching when you will be called to action. Will you heed the call?"

The room answered with one voice. "Yes!"

"The future welfare of humanity lies in communism. It excludes all authority and servitude, and therefore equals anarchy. That is our goal. The path to that goal is social revolution. The route to revolution is action. Only energetic, relentless action will destroy class rule and establish a free society. Long live the social revolution!"

The crowd took up the cry. "Long live the social revolution! Long live the social revolution!"

Gallagher watched the shining, perspiring faces of the men around him. He was revolted by the message, of course. He had dedicated his life to protecting society, not to tearing it apart. And yet. Despite everything, he felt excited. Something in him had to admire the revolutionaries' passion. And the clarity of the idea, the logic behind it. If you believed in something with all your being, of course the end justified the means. In his own way, didn't he follow that same credo? So what if he had to plant some evidence to convict the guilty? So what if a prisoner had to be persuaded to confess? It was all in the name of justice, all for a greater good. All to protect the innocent, to save society from those who would destroy it. Desperate times called for desperate measures. And judging from the mob around him, the times had never been more desperate.

Just then a thin man pushed in front of him, so close that Gallagher could smell his body odor. He recognized him as the first speaker, Smolenski. In his hand was a stack of flimsy newspapers that he was hawking. As the man passed, Gallagher turned away, as though something across the room had suddenly attracted his attention.

Smolenski glanced at him, then continued working his way through the crowd. Following along behind, Gallagher saw, was a heavyset man with round features. Their eyes met. It was just for a second, hardly a flicker. But it was enough. The round-faced man made his way toward the back door. Gallagher followed.

❧

By the time Dutch reached Rose Street, the sun was already down. Not that the air seemed any the cooler for it. As he walked, he bit into a frankfurter heaped with sauerkraut. Sometimes that was the hardest part of roughing it, not the sleeping but the eating. Tonight, like every Monday, they'd be having pork and beans at the Newsboys Lodging House. It was his favorite, and there was no limit on seconds.

That morning, he'd woken up late, after sunrise. That was another thing about bumming, trying to get yourself up in time to get the early edition. He'd run down Rose Street and through the dank tunnel under the Brooklyn Bridge. In another few blocks he'd come to the back of the World Building, the gold-domed skyscraper Mr. Pulitzer had thrown up, like a challenge, right across the street from the offices of the *Tribune*. A couple of other boys were hurrying out, but most had already collected their stock and left. Dutch rushed into the delivery room, then stopped before a wooden counter, calculating. The hot wave and the presidential election had been good for sales. It was late in the morning, but the weather was clear. He decided to take a chance and invest in forty papers. He fished two dimes from his pocket and handed them to a man behind the counter, who gave him a brass token. He carried the token to another man standing beside bundles of newspapers, who took it and handed over the copies.

Dutch ran to the end of the block, past City Hall. He knew better than to try to sell his papers there; that beat belonged to older boys ready to pound him if he so much as breathed the word *World*. The clock on the Tribune Building said five to eight. Even later than he thought. He bought a banana from an Italian peddler, then, dodging men in their business suits, ran up Broadway to the corner of Pearl. He hoped he hadn't missed too many of his regular customers. He scanned the headlines, then began to cry in his high boy's voice: "Get your *World* here! Dozens more die of the heat! Get your *World* here! Only a penny! Get your *World*!"

Business was slow, and it was early afternoon before he sold out. He invested some of his proceeds in a crunchy mandelbrot from a bakery on Pearl Street, then went back to the World Building to pick up the evening edition. By seven they were sold, too, and he was headed toward Rose Street. Even after paying for his frankfurter, he still had more than seventy cents in his pocket. Tomorrow he'd go by the lodging house and put another dime in his bank account. From the start, he had resolved not to be like the other newsies, not to waste his money on shows and gambling and drinking. When he found his mother, he wanted to surprise her with how much he had saved for her.

He made his way down the alley and climbed the pile of crates that he was beginning to think of as his. He felt worn out. Slipping the embroidered handkerchief from his shirt, he stroked it against his cheek. In a moment he was asleep.

In his dream, he was sitting at his family's kitchen table. His father, just home from work, was seated at one end, wearing a white shirt with a stiff collar and a soft gray necktie. At the other end sat his mother. She had just taken off her apron, revealing her crisp shirtwaist and a big oval cameo pinned below her neck. Her blonde hair was hanging limp because of the cooking, and she hooked a loose strand behind her ear. Then she took a big wooden spoon, filled a dish, and set it before him. While he waited for his father to be served, he looked down on his plate: potato pancakes, red cabbage, and sauerbraten, all his favorites. His mouth watered. He had never been so hungry. Finally, his mother nodded. He picked up his fork and knife and cut a strip of the meat. But as he lifted it, he was shaken by a terrific *bang*. The kitchen door burst open, and a cold black cloud burst in, shrouding his parents and the table. The gust struck him with such force that he thought his chair would topple. Gripping the seat, he rode it like a wild pony, his hips bouncing on the wooden planks and his feet thrashing through the air. He held on like he'd never held on to anything in his life.

Dutch opened his eyes, breathing hard. It took him a second to remember he was back in the alley. He felt the stack of crates swaying beneath him. Holding tight, he braced for a tumble.

Then he heard a deep voice. "Goddamn it!"

Still groggy, he inched to the edge of the platform. Just below him a man was bent over a long, narrow bundle. At first it looked like a rolled-up rug. Then Dutch saw a pair of shoes sticking from one end. The heavyset man stood up, rested his hands on his hips, and stretched his back, like he wasn't used to this kind of work. As he did, he seemed to look straight into Dutch's face. Dutch stopped breathing. Maybe the stranger hadn't seen him in the dark. Then he heard a raspy voice yell, "Come here, you little son of a bitch!"

Dutch dove from the stack of crates. As he landed on all fours, he heard a clatter of wood behind him. At the end of the alley he turned onto the deserted sidewalk, then hesitated. The Newsboys Lodging House was just around the corner, but the door would be locked at this hour. He went the other way.

A couple of doors down he knew another alley. He darted in and crouched, trying to catch his breath. He heard footsteps approaching. They grew fainter, and he crept out just in time to see a dark figure disappear onto Duane Street.

He ran all the way to Pearl and crossed in front of City Hall. The Tribune clock said twenty after two. Dutch didn't see another soul. Throwing a final glance over his shoulder, he slowed to a walk, but his heart kept racing just the same. Behind the World Building, he slumped to the pavement and rested his forehead on his knees. Had he really seen what he thought he'd seen? Or had it been part of his dream? No, he was sure he'd seen a man lying in the dust, with the heavy one standing over him. And he'd never forget the deep voice echoing off the brick walls, "Come here, you little son of a bitch!" As he hunched in the dark, the scene played over and over in his mind, like looking into a Kinetoscope.

Eventually, he felt a cuff on the back of the head. He jumped to his feet but saw it was only Grady.

"Hey," Grady said, "you going to get your papers or what?"

Grady was thirteen and already had a growth of fine dark hair on his upper lip. He and Dutch weren't exactly friends, but Grady was all right. Once when Dutch had lost all his money, Grady had spotted him twenty cents to buy his stock. That was how the newsboys were, Grady said, the older ones looked out for the younger ones. But he was the only one who had ever looked out for Dutch. Grady was born in Ireland, he'd told him once, though he couldn't remember the Old Country. He'd been on his own since he was seven, after his folks died of a fever. He couldn't even remember what they looked like. He'd never

been to school, never learned to read the papers he sold. Once
Dutch had offered to teach him, but Grady had answered by
pounding him on the arm. Everything he knew he learned on
the street, he said, and that was good enough for him. But since
he couldn't read the headlines, he always needed help deciding
how many papers to get and what story to cry. When Dutch
was around, he would lend a hand. Grady didn't seem to hold it
against him that he spoke in proper English.

As they pushed toward the delivery room with the other
boys, Grady asked, "What happened to your cap?" It didn't
seem right to see a newsie without his cap.

"I lost it," Dutch answered. Then he had a sudden thought.
Sticking his hand in his pocket, he satisfied himself that he
hadn't also lost his money in the chase last night. The two boys
bought their papers, then crossed in front of City Hall. The
sun was just up over the East River, flashing off the World
Building's golden dome.

Grady asked, "You still staying in that alley behind Rose
Street?"

Dutch nodded.

Grady studied him. "What's the matter with you this morning? You look like you seen a ghost or something."

Dutch shrugged. Then he asked, "Hey, Grady, have you ever
seen a dead body?"

"A crape? Sure, lots of times."

"What do they look like?"

"Like somebody sleeping is all."

"Have you ever seen a killer?"

"Sure. They're ten for a penny down here. Why?"

"If you did, would you go to the police?"

"Cripes, no. You know what they say about cops. 'Their kind God don't want and the devil won't have.' Steer clear of those bastards."

Dutch pulled up short. He'd had another thought. Looking down, he saw that his shirt button was still undone. He slid his hand inside, though he already knew what he'd discover. As he ran up Pearl Street, Grady called after him, "Where you going? You bughouse or something?"

Dutch kept running until he turned the corner of Duane and Rose. The street was busy now, with delivery wagons and men on their way to work. He stood for a long minute, finding his breath and his courage. Then, as though treading on tacks, he inched into the alley. Halfway down its length, in place of the jumble from last night, he saw the crates stacked neatly against the wall again. There was no body on the ground. He followed the alley to its dead end. Nothing. Was it a dream after all? Or was the man on the ground only sleeping, like Grady said? He raked his hand through his thick blond hair. Well, that wasn't why he'd come back. But there was no sign of the handkerchief with the embroidered violet.

FOUR

Tuesday, August 11

RAFE UNBUTTONED HIS uniform coat and spread it over the back of his swivel chair. Then he took a seat and stretched his feet across his desk. He wouldn't have done either if Mr. Roosevelt or Minnie were in, but as it wasn't yet seven o'clock, he figured to have the office to himself for a while.

At quarter of five that morning he'd awakened to find sweat pooling in the hollow of his chest. It was too hot to go back to sleep. The sky had already begun to lighten, and he lay there for a while, watching the shifting shades of gray. At six o'clock he collected his clothes and stole into the kitchen. In another minute he was outside.

Allen Street was quiet, but on the Bowery the delivery wagons had begun to stir. A middle-aged man in evening clothes slunk out of a house across the street, threw a guilty glance over his shoulder, and hurried toward the elevated station. As Rafe crossed under the tracks, he saw that his usual newsboy was already there.

The boy seemed just as surprised to see him. "You're out early this morning, sir," he said as he handed Rafe his paper.

"So are you. What time do you start?"

"About now. You know, the early bird and all that."

"What's your name, son?"

The boy balked, then apparently decided the man was all right, even if he was a copper. "Grady," he said. But his look turned to disappointment on finding two pennies in his hand and not another nickel.

At headquarters, Rafe saw that Mr. Appleby's card was still on the commissioner's desk, where he had left it. He could only hope that the man's business wasn't as urgent as he'd claimed, or that the commissioner had gotten his telegram at the Union League Club.

Settling himself in his chair, he unfolded the *Sun*. The city had been even hotter yesterday than the day before, he read, with thermometers outside several Manhattan drugstores hitting ninety-seven degrees. And people seemed to be going literally mad with the heat. When someone in the Bronx had asked his friend if it was hot enough for him, the man had drawn a revolver and shot first the other, then himself. Yesterday alone, 179 people had been taken to the hospital with prostration. Fifty-four had died on account of the heat, making a toll of 112 since the start of the hot wave, a week ago yesterday. Rafe sighed. How many more would die today?

The *Sun*'s other lead story was about the election. The Democrat, William Jennings Bryan, had left Chicago after midnight on Monday, barnstorming through Indiana and Ohio, including McKinley's hometown of Canton, then made a speech last evening in Pittsburgh. Tomorrow night he would be here in New York, at Madison Square Garden, to officially accept his party's nomination. It was a gutsy move, Rafe had to admit, because New York was McKinley country. The force was taking no chances with Bryan's safety. Later today, the commissioners would meet with Chief Conlin to review his precautions for the event.

Rafe flipped the paper over and scanned the headlines beneath the fold. A short box in the center of the page attracted his eye.

PUBLISHER FOUND DEAD

MURDER SUSPECTED, SAY POLICE

What he read next caused him to sit up and drop his feet to the floor.

The body of William d'Alton Mann, publisher of the society magazine "Town Topics," was found early this morning in an alley off Rose Street.

The discovery was made by roundsman Horace Miller, who heard a disturbance in the area at approximately 2:15 a.m. Arriving on the scene, Officer Miller determined that Col. Mann was deceased. The preliminary investigation was conducted by detective sergeant Thomas Gallagher, of the 4th precinct. According to Sgt. Gallagher, the apparent cause of death was a blow to the head, and the presumed motive was robbery.

A native of Ohio, Mr. Mann served as colonel of the 7th Michigan Cavalry. After the war, he invented the boudoir railroad car and founded the Compagnie Internationale des Wagons-Lits. He assumed the editorship of "Town Topics" in 1891.

Rafe looked for a byline. *Jacob Riis, exclusive to the* Sun.

He stood up and went to one of the tall windows in the commissioner's office, but there was no movement yet in the news bureau across the street. After his activities last night, Riis would probably be in late today.

When Minnie arrived at seven forty-five, Rafe was still sitting in his shirtsleeves. She took one look at him and pulled up short on the threshold. "Good Lord, they've fired the commissioner!"

"What? No, no."

"Well, you look as though you've had some sort of shock."

"Have you seen this morning's *Sun*?"

She shook her head. "The boy wasn't there today."

Rafe handed the newspaper over his desk and pointed to the story. As he buttoned his coat, she read.

"Well," she said at the end. "So, Mr. Mann was a magazine publisher. Have you ever heard of *Town Topics*?"

"Vaguely. Can't say I've ever seen it."

"Funny to think he was just here," she said, with a glance toward Mr. Roosevelt's door. At police headquarters, murders and robberies were as common as cod. But the victims generally didn't have a run-in with the commissioner a few hours beforehand.

"What could Mr. Roosevelt have wanted with him?" Rafe asked as he took the paper back. Then more to himself, he added, "And what did he have to do with J. P. Morgan?"

Minnie gave him a puzzled look. As she unpinned her hat, he told her about the summons to Mr. Morgan's table on Sunday night, but she had no idea what to make of it, either.

The commissioner stalked in a little after eight o'clock, with a newspaper folded under his arm. To Rafe's question whether he had received the telegram at his club, he grunted in the affirmative.

Rafe followed him into his office. "Mr. Riis was also looking for you yesterday afternoon. He wanted to know if the two of you would be going out last night."

"Hmm? Is that right? Well, I had to see Appleby, didn't I?" Rafe was used to the commissioner's moods, but this morning he seemed particularly out of sorts.

As Mr. Roosevelt laid the newspaper on his desk, Rafe was surprised to see the familiar rays of the *Sun*'s nameplate. The commissioner was generally a *Tribune* man.

"You've seen the news then," Rafe said.

Mr. Roosevelt nodded. "Get me Gallagher's report."

As he came back into the anteroom, he saw Minnie watching him. "He wants to see the file," he whispered as he crossed toward the hallway. He didn't wait for a response.

He trotted down the central staircase to the first floor. The detectives' room was a wide, plain space, but Rafe never entered without a certain hesitancy, a jumble of intimidation and aspiration. Hanging from one wall was Thomas Byrnes's famed Rogues Gallery, an ornate wooden frame displaying hundreds of photos of the city's most notorious criminals, complete with physical descriptions, aliases, personal habits, and modus operandi. In the basement was another of Byrnes's innovations, the Mystery Chamber, a museum filled with photos, knives, pistols, clubs, and other mementos of his detectives' successes.

Glancing over at the long wooden counter, Rafe saw that he was in luck this morning. Mulcahy was on duty. That meant fewer questions, less grief.

"Sean, do you have that report on William d'Alton Mann?" Rafe asked. "Commissioner Roosevelt wants to take a look."

Mulcahy lifted a manila folder from a stack under the counter. The original would be at the precinct house, but a copy had been delivered here to headquarters, so recently that it hadn't been filed yet.

Rafe signed it out and started up the wide staircase. Then, on the landing between the second and third floors, he stopped. With studied nonchalance, he leaned against the wall and, oblivious to the steady traffic up and down the stairs, he opened the folder and began to read.

The details were as Jacob Riis had reported. Roundsman Horace Miller had heard a scuffle in the alley behind the Rhinelander Sugar Building, on the corner of Rose and Duane. Arriving a minute or so later, he'd found the body on the ground under a pile of overturned crates, as though there had been a struggle. Coroner Theodore K. Tuthill had been called to the scene and had confirmed that the cause of death had been a blow to the back of the head. The body had been taken to the city morgue at Bellevue Hospital, where it was awaiting autopsy. Death had apparently been recent, since there was no rigor mortis. Nor livor mortis, the posthumous bruising formed by pooling blood. The victim was wearing a navy-blue blazer, striped gray trousers, a bright-red vest and bow tie, and a pleated white shirt with gold cuff links. His wallet and watch were missing, supporting the presumption of robbery. Officers had canvassed residents of some tenements down the block, but no one would admit to hearing anything.

Rafe closed the file and made his way to the third floor, questions mounting with every step. Why would a robber have left behind a pair of gold cuff links? What would someone like Mann be doing in that neighborhood at that hour? How did Jacob Riis happen to be the only reporter in New York to hear about the murder in time to make the early edition? And why had Mr. Roosevelt known to buy a copy of the *Sun* this morning?

In the anteroom, Rafe could feel Minnie's gaze, but he avoided her eyes. In the inner office, he handed the file to the commissioner and turned to go.

"Well, what do you think?" Mr. Roosevelt asked.

"Sorry?"

"What do you think of Gallagher's report? Did Riis get everything straight?"

"Well, I—" Rafe began, but the severe expression on the commissioner's face told him there was no point making excuses. Finally, he said, "Well, there are a few things that seem strange. For one, the killer left a pair of gold cuff links that were probably worth more than anything in the wallet."

Mr. Roosevelt shrugged. "Maybe he overlooked them."

"That could be, but every man wears cuff links, and every thief worth his blackjack knows to look for them."

"Perhaps the killer was an amateur. Some desperate jack maddened by the heat. Or maybe he heard the roundsman coming before he could get them off."

"Maybe," Rafe allowed. "The other thing is, why would Mann have been on Rose Street at two in the morning? He lived in the Kenmore, up on West Fifty-seventh."

The commissioner crossed his arms. "There are plenty of diversions on the Lower East Side to attract a man of that ilk."

"But wouldn't he at least have gone home to change first? He was wearing the same clothes as yesterday morning, when he was here in the office."

Mr. Roosevelt handed back the unopened file. "If a man would put on a blazer and scarlet vest to meet with the commissioner of police, there's no telling what he would wear the rest of the day, or night for that matter."

And of course, that raised the most intriguing question of all—what was Colonel Mann doing in the commissioner's office, arguing behind closed doors, on the morning before he was killed? As Rafe reentered the anteroom, Minnie gave him a knowing nod. He realized she had heard every word.

❧

In an ivy-covered brownstone mansion at 219 Madison Avenue, on the corner of Thirty-sixth Street, J. P. Morgan was seated at his breakfast. The sun filtered through the twelve-foot stained-glass skylight, reflecting off the oak paneling and cranberry wallpaper, lending a rosy tint to the table linens and the stack of newspapers fanned crisply before him. He tapped a silver spoon against the tip of his four-minute egg, and as he dipped out the warm, sticky contents, he perused the morning's headlines.

As always, he began with the *Tribune*, which he'd trained his man to place on top. The headlines were what he would have predicted—the hot wave, the election campaign, the usual run of crimes great and small—nothing about him, his bank, his railroads or other corporations, and nothing likely to affect the markets one way or the other. He moved on to the *Times*, then to the *Sun*. Seeing nothing of special note under the nameplate, he turned the paper over, and his attention was attracted by a smallish box below the fold. As he read, he permitted himself the first smile of the day. He lit another cigar. Then, ringing for a servant, he ordered his carriage brought round.

⊰❦⊱

A little before noon, Minnie finally stopped her typewriting and whispered, "What is it, Rafe?"

He looked at her blankly, trying to pretend he didn't know what she was talking about.

"You've been staring at that same piece of paper for half an hour."

He let it fall to the desk. "I'm still thinking about Gallagher's report. There's something not right about it. I don't believe that Mann business was a simple robbery. But the commissioner didn't seem at all curious about it."

"That doesn't sound like Mr. Roosevelt."

"No," he said, "it doesn't." He thought for a second. "Has the commissioner seemed unusually short to you this morning?"

"Not so I noticed. Why?"

He didn't answer but went back to his paperwork.

A few minutes later, Minnie took a sidelong glance at the commissioner's open door, then leaned over her typewriter. "I imagine that solving a murder would be a real feather in an officer's cap."

He looked up at her. "I imagine."

"It might even be enough to get him on the list for the detective exam."

Rafe couldn't suppress a smile. Not for the first time, she had read his mind. And now he was reading hers. He knew that if things were different, she would be angling to get on the detective list herself. In that moment, he felt even more admiration for her than usual. If she could be the first female stenographer on the force, why not the first female detective? Somebody had to be. He looked into her blue eyes and found himself thinking, *If only her name were Katz or Kaplan, instead of Kelly.*

Minnie whispered, "Did the commissioner order you not to investigate?"

Rafe shook his head.

"As a rule, does he reward initiative and diligence?"

He nodded.

"Does he always stress the importance of doing what's right, even if it's inconvenient?"

He nodded again, but more slowly.

Q.E.D., declared her expression. She gave him a meaningful look, then went back to her typewriting.

Rafe studied her. He had been making the same argument to himself, but it was so much more convincing coming from her lips. He got up from his desk and knocked on

Mr. Roosevelt's doorframe. "If you don't need anything," he said, "I thought I'd go out for a while."

The commissioner looked up from a book he was examining. "Hmm? No, that's fine. Don't forget, at two thirty we have that meeting on the Bryan visit."

Rafe smiled at Minnie on the way out. Downstairs, as he stepped from the lobby into the midday sun, the pitiless heat brought him up short. On Mulberry Street, the light was shimmering off the pavement like a desert mirage. He stood in the doorway for another few seconds, then darted across the street to the newsmen's building. Inside the big front room, several reporters were sitting at battered desks, banging on typewriters, trying to make their afternoon deadlines.

"Has anybody seen Mr. Riis this morning?" he asked.

No one looked up.

"Does anybody know where Riis is?" he called.

Finally, a grizzled man in shirtsleeves gave him a glance. Rafe thought he might be the reporter for the *Times*. "Hasn't been in," he said. "Don't know where he is."

Rafe took a second before venturing outside again. Then, instead of retracing his steps, he turned south. He figured it was half a mile to Rose Street.

If he'd let his eyes travel up to the third floor of police headquarters, across the street, he might have noticed Theodore Roosevelt standing at the open window, watching him.

Despite the heat, Rafe made good time. By twelve thirty he'd reached the hulking brick mass of the Newsboys Lodging House. He stopped, took off his helmet, and mopped his forehead. Then he turned down Duane Street, where most of the block was taken up by the Rhinelander Sugar Company. Around the back, off Cherry Street, he found the alley. Along one wall was a neat stack of packing crates, presumably the ones whose collapse had alerted the roundsman last night. Not sure what he was looking for, he traced the alley to its end. The earth was ground to a fine powder on account of the dry weather, but he saw nothing out of the ordinary. When he reached the crates again, he bent over a jumble of footprints. Most were made by policemen's boots, he figured. He knelt on one knee, but if the murderer had left any trace, it, along with any impression from the body, had been destroyed by all the activity.

As he was about to stand again, he saw a spatter in the dirt. He poked it with his finger, then gingerly lifted it to his palm. In the noon sunlight it glowed a deep burgundy, nearly black. He inspected the ground more closely. Strange that a fatal fight hadn't produced more blood. He rubbed the speck between his thumb and forefinger. It crumbled and fell to the dust.

As he straightened up, he happened to glance at the stack of crates again. Inside one, a few feet off the ground, he noticed a small white object just catching the midday sun. At any other time of day, he never would have noticed it. Reaching through the crate's slats, he pulled out a woman's handkerchief, with a pale-blue violet embroidered in one corner. Now, that was odd. Was it just a coincidence, or a clue? He slipped it into his pants pocket.

As he returned to the head of the alley, he stooped over the earth. Among the muddle of footprints, he saw no more blood. But he did notice two narrow grooves in the dirt, about twelve inches apart. There had been no mention of them in Gallagher's report. Had the detective missed them in the dark? Rafe followed the tracks out to Rose Street, where they disappeared at the flagstone sidewalk. The furrows were too deep and too close together to have been made by a cart. Something had been dragged through the alley, and not long ago. Standing a few feet away, he set his own heel on the ground and pulled it through the dust. The indentation was identical.

But if the killer had knocked Mann unconscious in the street, why drag him into the alley? To gain more time to search the body? In that case, you'd think he would have found the cuff links. And how to account for the disturbance that alerted the roundsman? Had the victim come to and struggled? That seemed unlikely, considering Gallagher's report had mentioned only one blow to the head. It would be interesting to see what the coroner had to say about that. He wondered, could there have been a third person in the alley, someone else who had struggled with the killer?

He was still hunched over the drag marks when he was startled by a booming voice behind him. "Who the hell are you?"

Rafe turned and saw a tall, mustached man in a roundsman's uniform. "I'm Officer Raphael."

"What precinct?" It was given in the preemptory tone of a superior.

Rafe stood up. "From Commissioner Roosevelt's office. And you?"

The roundsman wavered. "Miller. From the Fourth."

"Horace Miller?"

"So what?"

"You found the body last night. I figured you'd be off duty long ago."

Miller snorted. "Me too, but I pulled a double shift on account of Bauer decided to get heat prostration."

Rafe took a step toward him. "I was wondering, when you found the victim—?"

The roundsman recovered his earlier pugnacity. "Oh, no you don't. Everything is in the report."

"But in the report—"

Miller leaned closer. "I said, it's all in the report."

"But there are a few—"

Miller reached to his waist and gripped his nightstick, two feet of solid locust wood. "You tell Commissioner Roosevelt I said that. Now you get out of my beat, and stay out unless you want to get prostrated yourself, you hear?"

They stood like that for a few seconds, nearly chest to chest in the dust and the heat. Finally, Rafe turned away. As he walked back toward Duane Street, he shook his head. Cops were notoriously territorial, but that seemed excessive even for one of New York's Finest. What was Miller afraid of? And why did he invoke Commissioner Roosevelt?

Dutch had spent a tense morning selling his papers, glancing over his shoulder every few minutes and startling at each crack of a carriage whip. And so, a little before noon, his stock sold out, he'd come to the Newsboys Lodging House. Hot wave or no, he decided he would sleep here tonight. Upstairs the industrial school was still in session, and the doors wouldn't open to lodgers until five thirty this afternoon. But in the meantime, maybe he'd skip the late edition and just sit here in the safety of the doorway, under the green awning of Uhlig & Co. Cloth House.

The clock on the building's corner read twelve thirty when Dutch noticed the dark, clean-shaven policeman come by. He studied the officer. His face was partly hidden by the helmet visor, but there was something familiar in the rounded cheeks, the close-set eyes, the prominent nose. Then the man took off the helmet to wipe his forehead. Dutch saw that it was Mr. Rafe, the kindly man who'd been with Mr. Roosevelt on Sunday night. So he'd been right—he was a cop. Dutch remembered Grady's command to steer clear of coppers, but Rafe was the only policeman who had ever showed him the slightest kindness. He had a sudden idea. Maybe there was something Officer Rafe could help him with. But he'd have to be careful not to let slip what he'd seen in the alley last night. It was bad enough to ask a cop for help, but Grady would kill him if he let himself get mixed up in some kind of investigation.

Rafe turned down Rose Street. Dutch followed at a distance, then stopped on the corner of Duane as Rafe went into the alley. Did the police already know what happened there? A while later Rafe came out and inspected something on the ground. Then another cop came up and they talked for a minute. Dutch thought maybe there was going to be a fight, but finally Rafe headed in his direction. As he grew closer, the boy saw Rafe's preoccupied look turn to one of recognition.

"What are you doing here, Dutch?"

Dutch shrugged. "The Newsboys Lodging House is just around the corner."

"Listen, stay away from that alley," Rafe told him.

"Why?" As though he needed another reason to do exactly that.

"Something happened there last night." Rafe seemed less friendly than on Sunday, Dutch noticed, like something was on his mind.

"What happened?"

Rafe hesitated. Then he said, "They found a body in there."

Dutch shuddered. So his first instinct had been right after all.

"Who was it?"

"Never mind. Just don't go in there, you hear me?"

Rafe began walking and Dutch fell in beside him. As they passed the lodging house, he felt his chance slipping away with every step. Finally, he blurted, "I need help."

Rafe didn't look at him. "Not now, son."

"Please," Dutch said.

Rafe stopped and considered the boy. Was this just some newsie swindle? But he saw desperation on his face, and more than a little fear.

"Please."

Finally, Rafe said, "Come with me."

Around the corner, on New Chambers Street, he stopped at a storefront he'd noticed on the way downtown. It had a green and white striped awning, and the gold lettering on the window read DELICATESSEN. He had to get some lunch anyway. What would it hurt to have it with the boy?

"Have you had anything to eat today?" he asked.

Dutch shrugged.

Rafe led him inside. Dutch couldn't remember the last time he'd been in a restaurant. On one side of the long, narrow space was a row of tables, where a few patrons were already seated. On the other side was a wooden counter with baskets of bagels and bialys and loaves of dark rye bread. In a glass case were platters heaped with corned beef and pastrami and bowls brimming with sauerkraut, pickles, and chopped liver. As delicious as everything looked, the smell was incredible.

They went to the counter and Rafe ordered two frankfurters.

Dutch asked for sauerkraut on his.

They headed to a table near the window. Rafe expected Dutch to attack the food, but the boy just sat there, staring up at him. Rafe took out his watch and glanced at the dial. "Dutch, I have to be back—"

Dutch asked, "Do you think that if you lose something somebody gave you, it means you'll never see them again?"

Rafe arched his dark eyebrows. What a question from a young boy. "That's hard to say. Who did it belong to?"

Dutch studied the white tile floor. Finally, he said, "My mother."

Rafe put his watch away. "She's gone?"

Dutch nodded.

"How long?"

"Since May fifth."

Just over three months. "What happened?"

Dutch took a deep breath. "We used to live up on York Avenue. Papa worked in a brewery up there. Not making beer. In the office. He was a bookkeeper."

"And then?"

"Times got bad. He lost his job."

Another victim of the brutal depression. "When was that?"

"Last summer. But for a long time he didn't tell Mama. He put his suit on and left the house every day, just like he was going to work." Dutch had squeezed his paper napkin into a ball, and now he began to spin it on the table as he talked. "But then we ran out of money, and Mama found out. He had a friend in New Orleans who said there were jobs down there. So he went, but there wasn't any job. We got letters from him once in a while, but they stopped. Then last fall we got a telegram from the police."

Rafe winced. "How did it happen?"

Dutch stilled the paper ball and looked up at him. "They found him in the Mississippi River."

"I'm sorry, son," Rafe told him. Then after a moment he asked, "What happened to your mother?"

"After Papa left, Mama started selling things. First her jewelry, then the furniture. After a while there wasn't anything left to sell, and Mr. Krauss said he was going to put us out. Then one day, I came home from school, and she was gone."

"She didn't leave a note?"

Dutch shook his head.

"You don't have any other family in New York?" Rafe asked.

"No. Mama and Papa came from Germany."

"That's why they call you Dutch."

"The newsboys started that after I told them where my folks were from." He picked up his frankfurter.

As he bit into it, Rafe took out a small notebook. "What's your mama's name?"

"Anna Maier." He spelled it for him.

Rafe set down the notebook and picked up his own hot dog. "At headquarters, I can see if she's turned up in any reports."

"What kind of reports?"

Rafe was going to tell him but thought better of it. "All kinds of reports. What does she look like?"

"She's tall."

"What color hair does she have?"

"Blond."

"What was she wearing the last time you saw her?"

Dutch thought. "A gray dress. I think it was the only one she had left."

Rafe wiped his mouth with his napkin. "Come by headquarters in a few days, and I'll let you know if I have something. But I have to warn you, there are lots of people missing in New York, and some never turn up, understand?"

Dutch nodded. "Do you live with your mother?"

"No, with my father and sisters and brother and nephew."

"Where's your mother?"

"She passed away five years ago."

Dutch was watching him, waiting for more.

"It was an accident. She went to visit my sister Sarah at her apartment on Henry Street. The building had one of those flat cellar doors in the sidewalk, but she didn't see that somebody had left it open, and she fell through and hit her head. They said she didn't suffer."

"Do you miss her?"

"Every day."

Dutch nodded. He finished his lunch in silence. Finally, he said, "They call you Rafe, but what's your real name?"

Rafe put his notebook back in his pocket. "Otto Raphael."

"Raphael." Dutch smiled. "Like the angel."

⚜

Even as he stepped down from the trolley, Rafe could sense the suffering. Straight ahead, defended by a high brick and iron fence, was the labyrinth of buildings belonging to Bellevue Hospital. Walking along the fence line, he left First Avenue and turned down Twenty-sixth Street, a shabby block known as Misery Lane, because happy people had no call to pass this way. Judging from the steady traffic this afternoon, misery was approaching an all-time high. Black ambulances rattled down the street, and anxious faces crowded the sidewalk in both directions. Bellevue, the city's public hospital, was where the victims of the hot wave were being brought in scores.

In the middle of the short block Rafe came to a gabled, brick and stone gatehouse. Beyond the wide central arch he could make out the hospital's mansard roof and iron verandas. Under the archway, two policemen were struggling to manage the crowd.

"In to the right, out to the left!" one was calling. "Administration straight ahead, morgue to the right, all the way to the end!"

Rafe followed the pessimists toward the morgue. The sidewalk led through a long quadrangle, then across a dying lawn. At the far end was a squarish, one-story building set off by itself. As the crowd shuffled in that direction, no one spoke. Torn between longing for information about their loved ones, Rafe imagined, and hoping there was no news. In the opposite direction a stream of people were leaving the morgue; from their expressions it seemed that most had learned the hard truth.

At a pier behind the building, across the street from a coal depot and lumberyard, a ferry was idling. A wagon was pulled up beside it, and four men were loading plain pine coffins onto the deck. They would be on their way to the potter's field on Hart Island, where bodies were taken if they hadn't been claimed in forty-eight hours. These days the gravediggers must be working around the clock.

Rafe followed the crowd through a wooden door and into a narrow vestibule with scuffed paint. The others continued straight ahead, but he stopped to speak to a sweating policeman near the entrance.

"Where can I find the director?" he asked.

"Captain White. In the viewing room. Thin. Mustache. Look for the lab coat. Good luck!"

Rafe wondered why luck would be necessary. He passed into a long, high-ceilinged room bathed in natural light from a clerestory. Reserved for times of catastrophe, the space was filled with low stone platforms. On the platforms lay row after row of bodies, covered with white sheets, with only their faces exposed. In the pinched aisle, relatives and friends were shuffling past, peering from shroud to shroud. Just then he heard a woman's cry; another loved one had been identified. The air was stifling, nearly unbreathable, filled with the overpowering odor of disinfectant meant to conceal something worse.

Near the wall stood a man in a white coat. He was thin, with a high forehead, dark hair and mustache, and the sunken eyes of someone who hadn't slept in days. Beside him was a young orderly. They were speaking to a middle-aged man, who was supporting a younger woman by the elbow. His daughter? They and the orderly moved off, and Rafe approached.

"Captain White, my name is Otto Raphael. I'm Commissioner Roosevelt's assistant at police headquarters. I'm here about Colonel Mann."

White turned on him. "Again?" he snapped. "I've already told you people, we'll get to him when we can! I have sixty bodies right now waiting for a cause of death! There's nowhere to even put them! We're stacking them in the hallways, for God's sake!" He paused, collecting himself. Then he pointed to a set of double doors. "Through there."

Beyond the doors Rafe found himself in a small, quiet room tiled in white. Running down the center were a dozen marble slabs set on iron bases. On each slab lay a figure draped in a white sheet. Here the faces were covered but the feet were not; hanging from each right big toe was a manila tag. At the far end, a short, round, balding man in a white coat was standing beside a body, writing in a notebook. He was working so quietly that it took Rafe a moment to notice him, and he was so intent that he didn't hear Rafe come in. Eventually, the man glanced up.

"Excuse me." Rafe's voice echoed off the tile. "I'm Officer Raphael. I'm trying to get some information on a William d'Alton Mann."

"Coroner Tuthill," he answered. He smiled as he pointed to the figure in front of him. "And this is your Mann, so to speak."

Under the sheet Rafe made out a rotund silhouette. "Have you finished?" he asked.

"Just." Dr. Tuthill lifted the sheet. Rafe looked at the face. It was yellow and waxen, hard to reconcile with the pugnacious dandy in the commissioner's office yesterday morning. The coroner turned the head to expose a purple gash behind the left ear. "There's your cause of death," he said cheerily. "Blow to the parietal bone."

Rafe studied the wound. "What can you tell me about it?"

"It was made with a blunt object, probably some kind of club."

"Was he hit hard? Is it possible somebody only meant to knock him unconscious?"

"The bone is crushed. It was a vicious blow, meant to kill."

"And there's only the one?"

He smiled again. "One was enough."

"Any defensive wounds?"

"No. Apparently took him by surprise."

Rafe asked, "Is it possible he was killed some other way, then hit over the head to make that look like the cause of death?"

Tuthill pursed his lips. "The autopsy turned up nothing else suspicious. Besides, if he'd already been dead there wouldn't have been so much bleeding."

"He lost a lot of blood?"

"A fair amount, yes. The force of the blow split the skin. There was quite a bit of blood on his clothes."

Rafe thanked him, but the doctor had already turned back to his notebook. Retracing his steps though the double doors, he located Captain White, standing off to the side, staring into space with an exhausted expression.

"Thanks for your help," he said.

The captain grunted in an approximation of an apology.

"By the way," Rafe asked, "who are 'you people'"?

White looked at him blankly.

"A few minutes ago, you said, 'I've already told you people I'll get to it when I can.' Who are 'you people'?"

"I'm sorry," White said. "You can see what it's like around here. But you're the second policeman to come by today asking about Mr. Mann. This morning a plainclothes officer came in."

"Really? Who would that have been?"

"His name was . . . It began with a *G*, I think."

"Gallagher. He's the detective on the case."

"Yes, that's it. He said Commissioner Roosevelt wanted the autopsy done right away, so the body could be released to the family as soon as possible."

That was odd, since the commissioner had shown no interest in either the family or the case when they'd discussed it that morning.

"He said Mann's daughter was anxious to reclaim the body. I guess they want to make sure it doesn't end up on Hart Island with the rest of them. Anyway, a son-in-law is supposed to claim it later today."

"Is it unusual for the police department to be so interested in when a body leaves the morgue?" Rafe asked.

"I suppose so. Maybe the commissioner is a friend of the family?" The young orderly appeared at the captain's side again. He spoke briefly in his ear, and the two made their way into the crowded center aisle.

Rafe left the morgue the way he'd come in, then passed through the hospital gate and into Misery Lane, thankful to be back among the living.

As he walked, he considered. Mann hadn't struggled with his killer. And judging from the lack of blood in the alleyway or on the sidewalk, he had died elsewhere. So who had caused the ruckus in the alley? Rafe felt a little tingle at the base of his neck: it was seeming less and less certain that Mann had been murdered by a common robber. And someone on the police force, maybe the commissioner, wanted the body out of the morgue as soon as possible.

As he strode up Twenty-sixth Street, he fumbled his watch out of his pocket. Five to two. With luck, he had just enough time to make it to the office before the start of the meeting on Bryan's visit. As long as the trolley horse didn't collapse on the way.

FIVE

GALLAGHER HAD JUST returned to the Fourth Precinct when he got word that Roosevelt wanted to see him in his office at one forty-five. It was nearly that now, but the detective took his time as he made the short walk up Mulberry Street to headquarters. When he got to the third floor, Captain O'Brien was already there, standing impatiently in front of Roosevelt's desk. The commissioner told Gallagher to come in and shut the door. As the detective turned to close it, he saw the female stenographer glance up from her typewriter with a curious expression. *Leave it to Roosevelt to hire a woman*, he thought.

Gallagher stood beside the captain, and Roosevelt thrust a piece of paper toward him. The cheap white stationery, with two creases across its width, was covered with oversized block letters traced with an exaggerated plainness, as though to conceal any connection to their author.

THEIR WILL BE TRUBLE AT BRYAN SPEECH.
THEY ARE GOIN TO SHOOT HIM.

"Here's the envelope," Roosevelt said, pushing it across the desk. It was the same inferior grade as the letter. COMISHONER ROSEVELT, it read on the back.

"I found it under my office door when I returned from lunch," Roosevelt said.

The captain and the commissioner were eyeing Gallagher expectantly. "No one saw anybody suspicious?" he asked.

"No," Roosevelt said. "My assistant and stenographer were also out." He exhaled sharply, as though what was coming next caused him pain. "I must admit I was skeptical yesterday morning, when you shared your concerns about anarchists in the department. But now . . ."

Gallagher tried to suppress a smirk. He liked to hear Roosevelt admit that he may have been wrong.

"Why would someone go directly to a commissioner with this?" Roosevelt asked him.

Gallagher shrugged. "To make sure it got noticed, I guess."

"Well, he has my attention," Roosevelt said. "Who could have written it? Surely not a police officer."

Gallagher shook his head. "Not with that spelling. Looks like a new immigrant to me. Maybe somebody overheard something in a café. Maybe a relative got wind of something. Maybe it's another anarchist who realizes that things are about to go too far."

Roosevelt leaned forward and peered over his pince-nez. Gallagher had never seen such a look on the commissioner's face. He decided it was fear and had to suppress another smile.

Roosevelt said, "I don't have to tell you what a disaster it would be if anything befell Mr. Bryan. It would throw the presidential campaign into chaos. It would cast dishonor on our city and on this department."

And you wouldn't come out so good yourself, Gallagher thought.

"You, among the entire anti-terror squad, have gotten closest to the anarchists," Roosevelt told him. "You're our best hope to stop this abomination." Was that disbelief Gallagher heard in his voice? He'd show the big man yet what he was capable of.

"The speech is less than thirty-six hours away," Roosevelt went on. "Of course, we will redouble our efforts at the event. What else can we do between now and then?"

Gallagher rubbed his thumb and forefinger over his black stubble, just to make him wait. "As a matter of fact, I have a meeting tonight with one of my sources," he said at last.

"Tonight?" Roosevelt asked. "Can't you make it any earlier?" His voice sounded even higher and thinner than usual.

Gallagher shook his head. "It doesn't work like that, Commissioner," he said, with exaggerated emphasis on the title. "I don't even know where the man lives. All I know is, he thinks the anarchists are overplaying their hand and he wants to tell me about it."

Roosevelt considered, then asked, "What time tonight?"

"Ten," Gallagher said.

"And you have no other leads to follow in the meantime?" O'Brien asked.

"Afraid not."

"All right," the captain told him. "Stick to your regular duties for the rest of the day, so as not to spook your man, and meet me and the commissioner first thing in the—"

"Tonight," Roosevelt cut in. "Here. What time?"

"I should be back by eleven," he told them.

Roosevelt gave a distracted nod, and Gallagher realized that he had been dismissed. He and O'Brien turned to go, but Roosevelt put his hand out. "Stay, Captain."

When Gallagher opened the office door, his eyes met those of the female stenographer, still tap-tap-tapping away on her machine.

~✸~

Rafe was sprinting upstairs as he heard the commissioner's clock chime two thirty. He rushed straight into the conference room next to Mr. Roosevelt's office, and panting and perspiring, took his seat at the long oak table. All the other places were already occupied. Dressed in his spotless blue uniform, Chief Conlin was about to review his plans for William Jennings Bryan's speech tomorrow night, for the benefit of commissioners Roosevelt, Andrews, and Grant. Apparently, Mr. Parker was boycotting, as he had most board meetings since Mr. Roosevelt had tried to have him removed for malfeasance and neglect of duty. Rafe's role at today's meeting would be to take notes, though he wasn't sure whether the commissioner wanted a simple aide de memoir or a detailed record that could be produced later if the need arose. Rafe took out his notebook and, with an effort of will, pulled his mind away from William d'Alton Mann and focused on the chief's words.

"The Democratic National Committee is adding temporary seating to Madison Square Garden," he said, "to raise the capacity to fifteen thousand."

15,000, Rafe wrote.

"Is that legal?" The question was from Frederick Grant, whose uncanny resemblance to his father, the late president, ought to have lent him a certain authority. But Mr. Roosevelt had never bothered to hide his low opinion of the son's intelligence. Without waiting for an answer, the commissioner asked, "How many men will you have on duty?"

"Two hundred," Conlin answered. The chief was known for his suave manner, but this afternoon he had adopted the weary tone of one forced to explain himself to those less qualified.

200, Rafe recorded.

"Is that all?" asked Mr. Andrews. The youngest of the commissioners, with a dashing mustache and the lean physique of a dedicated cyclist, he was another reformer and Mr. Roosevelt's only ally on the board. Yet his lack of experience, apparent even to Rafe, gave him only a limited effectiveness.

"Make it four hundred," Mr. Roosevelt said.

Chief Conlin's normally sallow complexion flushed, and his shaggy mustache began to twitch.

Mr. Roosevelt went on, "This will be without question the largest mass meeting in the city this year. And may I remind you, gentlemen, Mr. Bryan's enemies here are legion. We can afford to take no chances." He glanced around the table. Mr. Andrews was nodding.

Turning toward Captain O'Brien, the commissioner asked, "How many detectives will be on duty?"

"We've increased our number to fifty," the captain answered.

Mr. Roosevelt nodded with satisfaction. From the two men's expressions, Rafe suspected they'd discussed this ahead of time. But what had prompted the change? And why hadn't they brought Chief Conlin into their confidence?

Conlin ran his palm over his balding head. "But, Commissioner, the budget—"

Mr. Roosevelt cut him off. "Chief, may I remind you that it is the responsibility of the commissioners to allocate the five million dollars that the taxpayers entrust to us each year? The last thing we want is another Haymarket. Or, God help us, another Garfield." It had been ten years since the infamous bombing in Chicago, fifteen years since the president's assassination. "Since then the anarchists have only tightened their grip on Europe, and they are determined to export their terrorism to our shores. We can't be too careful. Especially now, when the hot wave has driven even peaceful men half mad."

Chief Conlin opened his mouth, then changed his mind. Rafe could see the fight melt out of him. "Very well," he said with an ostentatious bow of the head.

Rafe crossed out *200* and wrote *400*.

"If I may proceed?" the chief asked. "We will cordon off a square block around the Garden, beginning at five o'clock."

"Good," Mr. Roosevelt said.

"No one without a ticket will be permitted to enter the area."

"Excellent."

"The doors will open at seven, and Mr. Bryan is to begin speaking at eight."

Rafe wrote, *5:00–7:00–8:00*.

The chief went on. There would be ambulances standing by and a temporary infirmary set up in the basement, with surgeons in attendance. Nothing would be left to chance, he assured the commissioners. They had no cause to worry. But judging from the furrows in his brow, Mr. Roosevelt wasn't convinced.

Afterward, as they made their way back to the commissioner's office, Rafe thought Mr. Roosevelt might ask about his extended absence that afternoon, but he only said, "Rafe, write up your notes in a thorough memorandum." So there was his answer. If there was trouble at the speech, the commissioner wanted a detailed record of what the department had done to try to prevent it. "And let me see it before you file it," Mr. Roosevelt added. That was unusual. Rafe wondered, was it a measure of the matter's importance or some new lack of confidence in him? He couldn't shake the feeling that the commissioner had seemed curiously distant today, guarded, suspicious even. Did it have to do with the questions he'd raised about the Mann case? In any event, he knew this wasn't the time to tell him everything he'd learned this afternoon. Mr. Roosevelt stalked into his office, and Rafe went back to his desk to draft his memorandum. From across the anteroom, Minnie was watching him.

Later, he mouthed. Then he leaned in her direction. "Was Captain O'Brien here?"

"Yes," she said. "Right before the meeting." So Rafe was right, O'Brien and the commissioner had discussed the Bryan matter beforehand.

"With Detective Gallagher."

Rafe nodded, but uncertainly. Gallagher again? In ten months he had never seen Gallagher in the commissioner's office. Now he'd been there twice in two days, both times in the company of the chief of detectives.

Just then, Rafe and Minnie were startled by a cry from Mr. Roosevelt's office.

"Hi! Yi! Yi! Hey, Riis!"

Minnie gave a tolerant smile. The commissioner liked to summon his friend by leaning out the window and shouting across the street. Presently Jacob Riis bounded through the anteroom and into the inner office.

"Shut the door," Mr. Roosevelt told him.

The moment the latch had clicked, Minnie asked, "Well? Did you go to the alley?"

"Yes," he told her. "And to the morgue."

Her blue eyes widened in a most appealing way. "So that's why you were gone so long."

Rafe hoped it was admiration he heard in her voice. He wanted to draw out the story for her benefit, but Mr. Roosevelt's door might open at any time. "Despite what Gallagher's report said, Mann wasn't killed in the alley," he whispered. "He'd been brought there from somewhere else. His heels were dragged through the dust, and there was no blood to speak of."

She whistled, a bracingly unladylike sound. "You have to tell the commissioner."

He shook his head. "It's too soon. I need some idea of who or why." And he needed to understand why the commissioner seemed so uninterested in the case.

"Oh," he added, reaching into his pocket. "And I found this in the alley. A woman's handkerchief. It had fallen inside one of the crates. I never would have seen it, except the sun just happened to catch one corner." He held it up for her to see.

"That's strange," she said. "From the looks of it, it wasn't there very long. It's still clean and neatly folded."

Just then Mr. Roosevelt's door opened and Riis hurried out. Rafe pulled out his top desk drawer and laid the handkerchief inside. When he caught up to Riis, on the staircase, the Dane stopped and faced him, almost as if he were expected.

"I saw your piece this morning," Rafe began in a friendly way. "About William d'Alton Mann."

Riis nodded.

"Congratulations, another scoop. What luck you happened to be there, in the middle of the night and all."

"Half of all reporting is just luck," Riis said.

"But of course, if you put yourself in the right place, you improve the odds that luck will find you."

"Quite so," he said, starting downstairs again.

Rafe walked alongside him, dodging the other policemen on the steps. "I guess you were making the rounds at that hour alone, since the commissioner was occupied with Mr.—?"

"Appleby."

"Yes, Appleby. You've seen quite a few murder scenes in your time. I was wondering, did you find anything unusual about that one?"

Riis pushed his spectacles up the bridge of his nose. "No, not that I can say. I'm sure Detective Sergeant Gallagher has made a very thorough report."

"The fact that Mann was on Rose Street at that hour, dressed in his day clothes, that doesn't strike you as odd?"

Riis didn't look at him. "Not necessarily, no."

"Or the fact that the robber left a pair of gold cuff links behind?"

"You'd be surprised how often that happens."

"Or that there were heel marks down the alley, as though someone had been dragged?"

Riis shot him a look, and Rafe could tell he had caught the reporter off guard.

"We didn't see that last night," he said.

"'We'?" Rafe asked.

"Gallagher and Miller, I mean." He stopped at the landing. "Look, if you have questions about the Mann case, I suggest you take them up with the commissioner."

"Of course. I just thought that since you were there and he wasn't . . ."

But Riis had already started down the stairs again. Rafe watched him go. There was something about that familiar "we" that made him doubt it referred to just Riis, the detective, and the roundsman. What a shame that Mr. Roosevelt had just happened to be otherwise engaged on a night when the reporter had found a murder to write about. And how did Riis know that the commissioner had been busy with Mr. Appleby? Rafe had placed his own note to Mr. Roosevelt in a sealed envelope and hadn't mentioned the name to Riis. He supposed the commissioner could have mentioned it to him just now, but why would he have done that?

Rafe walked back upstairs distractedly, his eyes combing the treads as if for clues. That was the second time today that he'd been referred to the commissioner for more information about the Mann case. But not just yet, he decided.

With a bundle of the late edition tucked under his arm, Grady hurried past the Newsboys Lodging House and turned onto Rose Street. Earlier, around lunchtime, he'd spotted Dutch on the sidewalk with that copper who bought a paper from him every morning, the one who gave him a nickel that day. Seeing the cop and Dutch together, he'd ducked into a doorway. He'd been on the street long enough to have had more than a few scrapes with the police, and as a rule he tried not to attract their attention, not even from the friendly ones. He didn't know this copper's name, and that was fine with him. As he'd watched, Dutch and the cop had walked up the other side of the road, past the lodging house, and made the corner. He hadn't followed.

But later, he'd remembered Dutch's questions about killers and crapes and coppers, and he'd wondered what the kid was mixed up in. Just now, when he'd gone to pick up his afternoon stock, there'd been no sign of Dutch at the World Building. And he hadn't been on his beat at Broadway and Pearl. That left one place to check, the alley on Rose Street where he'd been bedding down. If he wasn't there, Grady would have to wonder if he got himself arrested, or worse.

Now Grady stood at the entrance to the alley and called Dutch's name. The only answer was his own voice echoing off the dusty bricks. He ventured a little way into the shadows and called again. Nothing. He turned to go, but a burly man was blocking his path. He recognized Gallagher, one of the worst cops he knew. Sometimes he thought the man would take a swipe at a newsboy just because he could. Grady stopped, and Gallagher started toward him.

Standing over him, he asked, "Grady, what brings you here on this warm day?"

"Good afternoon, Detective Gallagher," Grady said. "Nothing. Just looking for a place to sleep tonight is all."

Gallagher inched closer. "Did you sleep here last night?"

"No. Why?"

"Do you know who did?"

"Nobody I know. Why?"

Gallagher held up a gray newsboy's cap. Turning it over, he pointed to the initials inked on the inside band. "Who's 'D.M.'?" he asked.

Grady shrugged. "No idea."

Before he could see it coming, Gallagher grabbed him by the throat and pinned him against the brick wall. "You lying son of a bitch."

"No, I ain't!"

"You've done some stupid things in your short, miserable life, Grady. But this is the stupidest. It's one thing to snatch a wallet or two, but when you kill a man—"

Grady's eyes widened. "What are you talking about?"

"A man died here last night. And I come back today, and who do I find?"

"I told you, I was looking for a place to sleep."

"With your bundle of papers under your arm?"

"I was just passing by, and I saw the alley, and—"

Gallagher slapped him hard across the cheek. "Who's the cap belong to, Grady?"

"I told you—"

Gallagher slapped him again. "All right, then. Down to the station we go. Maybe you'll talk better down there."

"Hold on a minute," Grady said. "If it's a newsie's, they'll know at the lodging house—you know, on the corner." He felt the pressure ease just a little on his throat. "I bet they can tell you who belongs to it."

"I'm heading over there tonight," Gallagher told him, "but now I come here and find you." He leaned so close that Grady could see the flecks of dust in his razor stubble. "If you're playing with me, Grady, you'll regret it, you hear?"

"I ain't playing with you," he said. "They can help you out at the lodging house, I know they can."

Slowly, as though it was costing him money, Gallagher released his grip on the boy's throat. Grady watched him stalk up the alley. It was a mortal sin to squeal on another newsboy. But he hadn't really squealed, he told himself. He didn't say the cap belonged to Dutch. Dutch wouldn't be at the lodging house tonight anyway, with the heat and all. The next time Grady saw him, he'd warn him about Gallagher. He rubbed his cheek. He'd also give Dutch a good smack for not being square with him.

❧

Rafe stood on the corner of Fifty-seventh Street and Ninth Avenue, eyeing the front of the Kenmore Apartments. With its seven-story limestone facade and terra-cotta-and-iron trim, the building made an impression, substantial but understated.

A comfortable building for comfortable people. Rafe doubted many murder victims had called the Kenmore home.

He took out his handkerchief and wiped his forehead. The sun was down, but the thermometer hadn't budged. And he had to admit, it wasn't just the temperature that was making him sweat. On the long trolley ride uptown, he'd asked himself what he thought he was doing. He had never investigated so much as a lost dog before. What made him think he could solve a murder on his own? It was true, what Minnie had said about getting on the list for the detective exam. As usual, she had seen right through him and wasn't afraid to let him know it. Of course he wanted to make detective. Sometimes at night, when he couldn't sleep, he would lie in bed listening to his father and brother breathing, and he would think what a promotion would mean to the family—a bigger apartment, where they wouldn't have to sleep three to a room, far away from the filth and the crime of the Lower East Side. He would also think of the pride on Minnie's face when he told her the news.

And until very recently, he would imagine the commissioner's look of satisfaction as he presented him with the silver detective's badge. But over the past several hours, he'd become less sure about Mr. Roosevelt's approval. And he certainly knew better than to expect anything like that from his father. Even so, he imagined what it would feel like to carry a detective's badge in his pocket, and he knew the extra heft couldn't be measured in a few ounces of metal. He could sense himself on the verge of something, though he couldn't yet say what. The fact was, he couldn't not come to the Kenmore.

As Minnie had pointed out, Mr. Roosevelt hadn't forbidden him from looking into the murder. But why had the commissioner been acting so cold toward him? How would he react when he learned what Rafe was about to do? It was one thing to ask a few questions at the morgue; it was another to enter a murder victim's home under false pretenses. He gazed up again at the imposing facade of the Kenmore Apartments. Well, if he could run into a burning tenement in the middle of the night, he guessed he could do this. Crossing the street, he made for the building's entrance.

A liveried employee had the door open before Rafe reached the threshold. "Good evening, Officer." Then, leaning closer, he whispered, "I imagine you're here about the matter of last night. Such a shame. We've been expecting you."

Rafe tried to hide his surprise.

The doorman went to his desk and picked up a key. Rafe followed him through the lobby, past electric chandeliers, oak paneling, damask sofas. At the back they stepped into an elevator. The doorman closed the brass safety gate and pulled the lever, and the cab rocked into motion.

"Such a shame, such a shame," he was saying. "Such a friendly man. And very popular, you know."

"He had a lot of friends?" Rafe asked.

"Oh, yes. The very best people were always coming and going." He frowned. "But I thought the newspaper said it was a robbery. Why would you need to—?"

"We just have to be thorough," Rafe said. "You know."

"Of course." The elevator stopped on the sixth floor. At the end of the hallway, the doorman slipped his passkey into the lock, then stepped back. "There you are," he said. "I must return to my post, so just ring for the elevator when you're finished."

Rafe stepped inside. It was a big apartment, a rich man's apartment. In the foyer was a round table carved from some kind of dark, gleaming wood. In the living room, an antique sofa and chairs were arranged before a marble mantelpiece. On the walls were oil paintings of horses and hounds. No one had closed the windows or the curtains, and the last of the sunlight was reflecting off the polished parquet floor. He stood for a moment, taking in the unnatural stillness. *The stillness of the grave*, he thought.

On a low table near the sofa he spotted a silver cigarette box. Beside it was a copy of a magazine. *Town Topics* read the glossy, oversize cover, "The Journal of Society." Rafe picked it up and riffled the pages. It was a magazine for the upper crust, just as Riis's story had said, with articles on weddings, benefit galas, the racing meet at Saratoga, the sailings of New York's most prominent families. He laid it down.

In the bedroom were more antiques. Rafe went to the closet and opened the door. Hanging to one side were the evening clothes that Mann hadn't been wearing last night. On the far wall, under the window, was an elegant writing desk. Rafe walked that way. The top was vacant except for a green blotter and a silver pen set. He pulled out the narrow drawer and found several sharpened pencils. Reaching inside, he felt something smooth and flat. A small leather notebook. On the front, on a pasted paper label, was penned in a careful, angular script, *"Town Topics" Stock Purchases.*

It was a ledger. There were no headings, but the left-hand column was a list of dates, beginning on page one with September 5, 1891, and ending on page six with August 9, 1896—the day before Mann was murdered. Filling the right-hand column was a string of figures, most of which read *$2,500*. In the wider center column was a list of enigmatic words—*Golden*, *Capitol*, and *Steel*, among others. Rafe had heard that businessmen sometimes committed their telegrams and letters to code, and he guessed these must be code names for the individuals who had paid the amounts in the second column.

This year alone, Mann had supposedly sold shares worth nearly $50,000. Rafe whistled at the amount. He understood nothing more about stocks than he could glean from the business page of the *New York Sun*, but even he knew that a society magazine didn't need that much cash, or could be so attractive to investors. A more likely alternative began to take shape in his mind, and it had nothing to do with stock purchases. He took his pencil and notebook from his pocket, but as he thumbed through the pages of names, he realized he could never copy them all. Not if he were going to finish before the chatty doorman got curious and came to see what was taking so long. He slipped his own notebook back in his coat pocket, along with the leather ledger.

He glanced into the small, dark kitchen, then went to the outer hall and rang for the elevator.

As they rode down to the lobby, the doorman asked, "Nothing, right?"

"Not a thing," Rafe told him.

Walking east on Fifty-seventh Street, he noticed the brand-new building of the Young Men's Christian Association. But as he went, head down, pondering what he'd discovered and feeling overwhelmed by what he'd taken on, he neglected to notice another figure in the quiet, darkening street, following at a distance of half a block.

Rafe walked to Eighth Avenue and caught the southbound trolley. As the cable car jerked down the avenue, he asked himself, how did one conduct a murder investigation? Wasn't it just a matter of looking and listening and following where the evidence led, of forming theories and testing them until you teased out the truth? Wasn't it above all a matter of logic and determination? The idea was heartening, because Rafe was nothing if not logical and determined.

He took out the leather notebook and examined it in the streetcar's electric light. He started at the back, with the most recent entries. It appeared that Colonel Mann's final week had been a lucrative one. The last page read:

Aug. 4	Silverman	$2,500
Aug. 5	Canton	$2,500
Aug. 9	Corsair	$5,000
Aug. 9	Tulip	$5,000

The last two entries were written in pencil rather than ink. He guessed they were waiting for confirmation, when they would be rewritten in pen, like the others. He began paging through the rest of the list in reverse order. Canton had paid $2,500 every month since June. That made him the largest "stock purchaser" this year, at $7,500. Since January, there had also been payments from Central, Golden, Silverman, and Steel.

The trolley jogged onto Canal Street. At Broadway he transferred to a horse car, then, several blocks later, stepped down at the Bowery. The family apartment lay a little farther east, on Allen Street, but Rafe turned north. Seeing the new Y.M.C.A. on Fifty-seventh had given him an idea.

Between Prince and Spring, he came to the stalwart brick-and-granite facade of the Young Men's Institute. Rafe came here often, partly to escape the cramped apartment. But with its library, crowded schedule of concerts and lectures (including the one where he'd met Mr. Roosevelt), classes in everything from penmanship to first aid, and activities such as an orchestra and a debating club, the institute was a magnet for young men of the Lower East Side eager to improve themselves. Tonight the spacious lobby was strangely deserted. Of course, he realized. Everyone would be on the roof, playing chess under the electric lights or chatting over a cold beer.

The day's newspapers were kept on an oak writing table near the window. Standing over them, Rafe flipped through the stack until he found the late edition of the *Sun*. Then he pulled out a chair and began to examine the headlines. He hadn't been surprised that the first article about Mann's murder had been so brief, since it had been written in the dead of night and rushed onto the front page just before press time.

But he knew that Riis would have prepared a longer piece later in the day, with more facts about the victim's life, interviews with relatives and associates, maybe even some detail about the crime scene that had eluded Gallagher. He scanned page one, dominated by the stories about the hot wave and Bryan's talk. On pages two and three were continuations of those articles plus political notes from across the country. Four was devoted to sports, as usual. Page five was given over to short reports from around the city—progress on President Grant's tomb, the opening of a playground, various suicides and homicides—but nothing about William d'Alton Mann. And so it went until the final classified advertisement on page ten.

He turned to the front and went through every sheet again. Nothing. Now, that was strange for a reporter of Riis's caliber. He thumbed through the other papers but saw that in all of them Mann's murder had rated only a short article on an inside page. Body discovered . . . inventor of the boudoir car . . . publisher of *Town Topics*. None had hinted at anything beyond simple robbery.

He left the papers on the table and headed for the first-floor dressing room. Standing in front of his locker, he changed out of his sweaty uniform and pulled on black tights, a sleeveless striped shirt, a pair of high-topped shoes, and some well-worn boxing gloves. The gymnasium next door was also empty on this hot night. He passed by the rowing weights, Indian clubs, parallel bars, and climbing ropes until he reached the punching bag hanging in a corner. He shadowboxed for a few minutes to limber up. Then he attacked the heavy leather bag.

Jab, cross, jab, jab, cross.

The commissioner had been exaggerating the other night at dinner, when he'd called him a champion fighter, but Rafe knew his way around a boxing ring. Growing up on the Lower East Side, he had quickly learned the need to defend himself. He'd taken some boxing lessons and discovered he had a knack for it. Then he'd tested himself in some club fights, and he'd won more than he'd lost. He'd also discovered that he liked the discipline of training. Now that he was working for Mr. Roosevelt, he didn't get to the gym as often as he used to, but he still appreciated how some time at the punching bag helped him to think.

In his ride downtown, he'd thought about the ledger from every angle, but in the end he could think of only one reason why people would make large, secret contributions to a publisher: it looked like a textbook case of blackmail. If so, were the code names arbitrary, or did they have some meaning, some particular link to the victim? Considering the dozens of names involved, it may have been the latter, to help Mann keep track of where all the money was coming from. Among this year's contributors, could "Central" be a railroad magnate? Maybe "Steel" was a millionaire industrialist? Mann's little leather notebook could well be a who's who of New York society. The chatty doorman had mentioned how wealthy New Yorkers had found their way to Mann's apartment; maybe the visits weren't strictly social. Maybe one of the callers was a murderer, and maybe his name was hidden in the pages of the leather notebook.

Jab, cross, hook, cross.

In that case, the victims with the best motive might be those who had paid the most or those who had paid most recently. In this instance, the two categories were identical—the most recent victims had also been the most generous. He thought back over the final page. On August 9, Mann had penciled in $5,000 from "Corsair." The name was familiar, but he couldn't quite place it. He seemed to remember seeing it somewhere. In the *Sun*. An article about ... what? About a death in a family.

Jab, cross, jab, cross, hook.

Then he remembered. It was that story about J. P. Morgan's sister Sarah. She had passed away in Germany, and her body had come home aboard a steamship. And sailing out into New York Harbor to receive the casket had been Mr. Morgan himself, on his motor yacht, the *Corsair*. It was a strange word, *corsair*. Rafe had even looked it up in the office dictionary. And he'd smiled on discovering that the country's preeminent banker had christened his pleasure boat with a synonym for "pirate ship."

He considered Morgan's summons of Mr. Roosevelt to his table at the Union League Club, the hurried appointment with Mann the next morning, the argument in the commissioner's office. Rafe stilled the punching bag with his gloved hands. Why would William d'Alton Mann be blackmailing J. P. Morgan?

And who was his other most recent victim, "Tulip"? A woman, from the sound of it.

～✦～

"Damn you!" Blinks bent over the table and, with his one good eye, studied the twisting trail of dominoes. Snipe had just played his last tile, a double six.

"Shut it!" Jake whispered. "If Pop hears you, we'll be out on our bums!" Hanging not far away, on one of the white plaster walls of the Newsboys Lodging House, was a precisely lettered sign warning, BOYS WHO SWEAR OR CHEW TOBACCO CANNOT

SLEEP HERE, and the boarders knew from harsh experience that Pop Heig, the superintendent, stuck by a literal interpretation of the rules.

"That makes three cents you owe me!" Snipe said.

"Pipe down, dummy!" Boots told him. Dominoes, unlike the boys' preferred pastime, craps, was permitted in the lodging house, but gambling was not.

The boys were seated in the second-floor reading room. Soon they would be called upstairs for the night classes in subjects such as reading, writing, and singing. But eager to recoup his losses, Blinks turned the dominoes facedown, mixed them, and began to draw a new hand.

Hanging back as usual, Dutch was barely watching. His mind kept returning to the scene in the alley last night, and to his talk with Officer Rafe. He'd been hoping that Grady would pass by the lodging house that afternoon, but Dutch had seen no sign of him as he'd crouched on the front steps, waiting for the doors to open. He knew Grady would be fuming when he heard about the lunch with Rafe, but Dutch didn't care. He had to tell somebody what he'd seen in the alley, especially now that Rafe had confirmed his worst fears, that there had been a murder. The killer had looked Dutch dead in the face less than a foot away. But had the man seen him well enough in the dark to recognize him by daylight? After all, Dutch hadn't been able to make out the killer. *Don't worry*, he told himself, *Grady will know what to do.*

Well, at least the murderer didn't know his name. Still, there was no chance Dutch was going to sleep in the alley again or anywhere outdoors for a while. Heat or no, he'd be spending his nights in the safety of the lodging house, until Officer Rafe was able to track down his mother.

When the industrial classes had let out that afternoon and the doors had opened to lodgers, Dutch had been ready. Most of the boys wouldn't troop in until six or later, after they'd sold the evening edition. He'd never been in the lodging house before everyone else, and it was strange to wander through the empty, echoing spaces. He went up to the schoolroom on the third floor, where Pop Heig was stationed at a desk, behind a low iron grille. Dutch signed the register and paid eighteen cents—six cents for lodging, six for supper, and six for the next day's breakfast. So much for putting another dime in his savings account.

Pop reached behind him, took a locker key off the numbered board, and handed it across the desk. Dutch went to the washroom in the back of the building. That was another rule: all lodgers had to get cleaned up before supper. He hung his shirt on the hook above one of the sinks, filled the iron basin with hot water, and lathered his arms, hands, neck, and face. He dried himself on the towel tied to a ring on the wall, then went to the wide, low tubs across the room and gave his feet a good scrubbing. In the winter there might be three hundred boys jockeying for a place in the washroom. He knew it was a luxury to have the facilities to himself. What a waste he was too keyed up to enjoy it.

At supper, served at seven sharp, there were maybe fifty boys jostling in line. Sitting alone, as usual, Dutch helped himself to thirds on the corned beef and cabbage. Afterward he went downstairs to the reading room, where Blinks and Snipe were setting up their game. Now, as they were choosing their tiles for a final match, they heard Pop Heig's voice from the doorway.

"Dutch," he said, "come out here, please."

The other boys snickered, wondering what he'd done. As he shuffled to the hallway, Dutch prepared his defense, which would have to hinge on mistaken identity. But in the hall, he saw that Pop wasn't alone. Beside him was a heavyset man in a brown suit. He'd taken off his straw boater, revealing a head of curly black hair. The man had his back to Dutch, glancing down the stairs.

"Dutch," Pop said, "this gentleman would like a word with you."

As the stranger turned, Dutch saw that he was grasping a gray woolen cap. He recognized it instantly. Then was this the man from the alley last night? The man he'd seen dragging the body in from Rose Street? He decided not to wait and find out.

The stranger was blocking his path to the ground floor. Dutch ran the only other way he could, to the staircase leading to the third story. Taking the stairs two at a time, he could hear heavy footsteps behind him.

At the next landing, he stopped. The schoolroom was on his right, but its double row of desks would offer few hiding places. There was also the line of wooden lockers, but he was too big to climb inside, even if he'd had time. Beyond the schoolroom was the washroom. He ran for it.

To one side was the foot tub, and directly in front of him was the long line of washbasins. He thought about hiding in one of the water closets, but decided that was too obvious, and too hard to escape if he was cornered. He raced to the far wall and crouched under the soapstone slab supporting the basins. Stilling his breathing as best he could, he waited.

He saw a pair of brown shoes crossing the white tile floor. Walking now, not running, they hesitated, pointing this way and that. They went to the water closets, and each of the wooden doors slapped open in turn. Then the shoes reappeared at the sinks. Warily, in no apparent hurry, they moved closer. When they reached the last sink, they clicked to a halt.

Dutch stopped breathing. In another moment, a broad white face appeared under the rim of soapstone, like a full moon rising over a rooftop. A meaty hand jutted under the sink, but Dutch was too quick. Jerking to one side, he leapt to his feet. He was out the washroom door before the stranger could stand up.

He ran toward the down staircase. Pop Heig was blocking the hallway, watching him with an expression he had never seen on the superintendent before, not even when Smokes had stabbed Snoddy in the leg with a penknife.

"Dutch! Stop!" the superintendent called. "This instant!"

Dutch turned and ran up the staircase to the fourth floor. On either side of the hall were spacious dormitories, with more than a hundred bunk beds each. Like the rest of the lodging house, the rooms were deserted on this breathless night. At the back of one of the dorms were the dude rooms, where boys could pay four cents extra for a single cot with a white muslin privacy curtain. Dutch climbed into one of them. Standing on the white sheet, still breathing hard, he worked to keep the wire springs from squeaking.

There were footsteps outside, two sets this time. They grew fainter and disappeared across the hall. Dutch told himself this was his chance, but something kept his feet rooted where they were. Then the steps grew louder again, and louder still as they approached the dude rooms.

One by one he heard the soft rustle of curtains being pushed aside. Barely breathing now, he focused all his attention on the white fabric in front of him. The curtain parted, and the stranger's face appeared, sweaty and sneering.

The man reached for him, but Dutch was ready. He dodged to one side. The man caught his arm, and they tumbled to the floor. The stranger tried to maneuver his weight on top of him, but Dutch was faster.

He rolled away, and the man's momentum carried him too far to the side. Dutch sprang to his feet, but the man caught him by the ankle, and Dutch's chin slammed onto the wooden floor. He raised himself to all fours and kicked free. Springing to his feet, he sprinted to the dormitory door.

Standing in his path was Pop Heig, spreading himself wide to block the exit.

Without slowing, Dutch dove to the floorboards and slid headfirst between Pop's legs. He fled down the stairs. On the second floor, he saw the astonished faces of Boots, Snipe, Winks, and Jake in the doorway of the reading room. As he passed, they gave him a noisy cheer. One more flight and he was back on the street.

⌘

Later that night, Detective Sergeant Thomas Gallagher leaned his ample bulk against the brick wall behind him. It was well dark, but even through his tattered jacket, he could feel the day's heat radiating off the masonry. The auditorium door was wedged open to the alley, and he could hear the foreign voice droning inside. "An act of violence committed for the good of the country is no crime. . . ."

He still cursed himself for letting the goddamned newsboy get away. Well, now at least he had a name and a face to go with it. The urchin couldn't avoid him forever. He pushed the boy out of his mind. Taking out his watch, he held it up to the open door and tipped it until he caught enough light to read the dial: 10:10. This would be the one night the son of a bitch was late.

The first time they met, he'd been on the anti-terror squad for months and had nothing to show for it but the ravings of all the misfits who stood up at these godforsaken meetings. Then, three months ago, he'd been at yet another speech, in a saloon in Yorkville. After all the foreign poison had been spewed, he was standing at the bar, nursing a beer, just taking in the babble around him. As he drained his glass, he heard a German-accented voice say, in surprisingly good English, "They shouldn't have their election."

The voice was coming from Gallagher's right. He didn't turn but cocked his head in that direction.

The German went on, "I mean it. We should stop the election. It's all a fraud anyway. There's no truth to it. It's all crooked. One bullet would end the whole thing."

Gallagher stole a glance. Two men were leaning against the bar. The German was standing with his back to him. His companion, facing Gallagher, was a dark, nervous-looking man in a stained brown vest. The German was waiting for an answer, but his companion only studied the bar and rubbed his finger over a watery ring left by his beer mug. Not long after, the man gulped the rest of his drink and left.

Gallagher decided to take a chance. "Are you serious about what you said a minute ago?" he asked. "About the election?"

The German turned to face him. He was in his thirties, with thinning blond hair, round features, and heavy, sleepy eyelids. Gallagher's first thought was that he was a simpleton.

The round-faced man studied him. "What's it to you?"

Gallagher said, "I can help you."

And over the past three months, that's exactly what he'd pretended to do, everything from pumping him up with anti-McKinley, anti-silver hatred, to feeding him news stories about the presidential campaign, to pretending to listen to his half-baked screeds.

In that time Gallagher had learned more about the man than he wanted to know. About his father's rabble-rousing in Bavaria. About their escape to America, where they had landed without a dollar. How the whole family, adults and children alike, had earned pennies as cigar makers, living and working in a filthy one-room tenement, eating and sleeping surrounded by bundles of tobacco leaves. How he had finally found a decent job as a teamster, only to lose it in the financial crash. How the whole game was stacked against the workingman. How the government and the industrialists were in cahoots against the poor. How things had to change, by force if necessary.

Through it all, Gallagher had nodded and yessed him, but the whole time he'd been thinking, *What did you expect, a land of milk and honey? We didn't ask you to come here. If you don't like it, go back where you came from.*

He had no idea where things with the German were heading, but the man was the best connection he'd made in the better part of a year, and so he kept listening and nodding. Over
those three months, the man had never once asked why he was
taking such an interest. And so Gallagher had played him like
a North River shad, sometimes reeling him in and sometimes
letting him run. And now he had to play him only a little while
longer, until he pulled him into the boat for good.

He was taking out his watch again when he saw somebody
coming up the alley.

"Evening," the man said. Gallagher glared into his round
face. "You're late, Hofmann."

"Sorry," he said. "There was a little problem."

"What kind of problem?"

He waved him away. "It don't concern you."

"Everything concerns me," Gallagher told him.

"You care if my baby girl don't want to go to sleep?" Then
the man laughed.

Gallagher fought off the urge to punch him in his wide,
empty face. Instead he asked, "What have you heard about
tomorrow night, at the Garden?"

"Nothing. As far as anybody knows, nobody is planning a
thing. Not even a demonstration. Nobody will even admit to
going to hear Bryan. Mr. Most says it would be 'supporting the
effete capitalist system.'"

"I see," Gallagher said. After a moment he told him, "I have
to go." Roosevelt and Captain O'Brien would be waiting for
him at headquarters. He'd met his source, he would tell them,

but the man knew nothing about any attack. That meant they would load men into the Garden and hope for the best.

Gallagher looked him squarely in the eyes. "I'll see you soon."

"Oh, yes," Hofmann answered. Then his face split in an unearthly grin.

Gallagher stepped toward the open door to read the dial on his watch but nearly collided with a figure lounging there, ostensibly trying to escape the heat inside. Gallagher recognized him. Smolenski, the first speaker from last night, the half-starved Pole with the sandy beard and the stack of newspapers.

On seeing Gallagher, the man stood up straight, stuck out a paper, and said something unintelligible. Gallagher shook his head, and Smolenski took a step out the door and offered Hofmann a paper too. Hofmann waved him off, and the Pole turned back inside.

Gallagher watched him disappear into the crowd. Had he been eavesdropping? Last night, when the man was giving his speech in the coffee shop, he'd had a translator. But that didn't mean he didn't speak any English. Maybe he knew enough to make out what they were saying.

Just now he'd looked directly into both their faces. Was he wondering why the two of them were huddled in the alley, speaking in hushed voices while the rest of the crowd was pressed inside in the heat, listening to the speakers? Did he suspect that Gallagher was anything other than a fellow anarchist? Gallagher knew, from being on the other side, how things began to unravel. One loose end, and soon the whole skein came undone. He couldn't afford to take that chance. He turned and followed Smolenski into the crowd.

❧

Eammon Kavanaugh staggered out of the Wild Rose. He'd hoped it might be cooler outside than in, but there wasn't the hint of a breeze off the river. Dragging his uniform sleeve across his high forehead, he tried to collect himself. He hadn't meant to stay so late or drink so much, but lately he'd been doing that more and more.

Third Avenue was deserted at this hour. He turned under the El's arched iron girders and followed them north, his boots echoing over the paving blocks. In the distance came the rumble of the northbound train. He lurched down the block to the Ninth Street station, bought his ticket, and pulled himself up the stairs to the empty platform. Panting, he steadied himself against a steel post. The locomotive's searching headlight grew larger, and there was the shrill scream of metal on metal as the train braked. He took an uncertain step toward the edge of the platform.

As the train eased into the station, motorman George Webb spied a man slumped against the post in the center of the platform. *Great*, he thought, *another drunk.* They were a hazard of driving the late shift, along with the prostitutes and muggers. Then, as he watched, the man's ample midsection suddenly bowed out and he rushed toward the platform with enough force to snap his head backward. Webb slammed the brake lever, but it was too late. The man's arms and legs were windmilling, and he tumbled onto the tracks.

SIX

Wednesday, August 12

W HEN THE LIGHT seeping through the kitchen window finally grew bright enough for reading, Rafe cupped his hand over the glass globe and blew out the little oil lamp. He'd been dressed and sitting at the table for a good half hour, copying the notebook he'd found in William d'Alton Mann's apartment. Not that he had slept all that much beforehand.

Coming home from the Young Men's Institute last night, he'd found his family, along with most of their neighbors, out on the street. Nellie and little Harry were listlessly tossing a canvas ball, watched over by big Harry, while Sarah and his father slouched on the stoop, fanning themselves with pieces of cardboard.

"I can make a sandwich," Sarah offered, but Rafe said he'd picked up a pretzel on the way home.

"You were working all this time?" his father asked. Rafe didn't answer.

They sat in weary silence. The neighbors began drifting indoors, and when it was too late to do anything else, the Raphaels trooped up to the stifling apartment and lay down for bed. Big Harry was off in a matter of seconds, and it wasn't much longer before their father's breathing, blustering through the tiny bedroom, was also coming regular and shallow. But Rafe lay for a long while, the ideas ricocheting so wildly through his brain that he wondered why they didn't wake the whole household. No matter what direction he tried to steer his thoughts, he couldn't expunge the image of William Mann lying on his marble slab, or of all those other lifeless faces laid out in the viewing room. It was one thing to know that a man had been murdered or that hundreds of people had died of the heat; it was another to see the evidence firsthand. And he couldn't stop revisiting the dusty drag marks and the single drop of blood in the alley off Rose Street, or the unnatural stillness of Mann's apartment and the little leather notebook tucked in his desk drawer. Blackmailer or no, didn't Mann deserve to have his killer punished? Didn't he deserve justice?

But what would Mr. Roosevelt say? Before this morning, Rafe had never so much as taken a long lunch. Now, in a scant twelve hours, he had sneaked a look at a murder file, conducted unauthorized interviews, bluffed his way into a victim's apartment, and stolen a vital piece of evidence. What was wrong with him? Had he been overcome by blind ambition? Or was it the heat, like in all those stories in the newspaper?

The worst part was that he'd gone behind the commissioner's back. True, Mr. Roosevelt had been acting strangely of late, but before that he had always been square, even generous, with Rafe. Didn't the man deserve the same in return? When the commissioner heard the list of his offenses, Rafe wouldn't blame him if he fired him on the spot. Then what would the family do? He would be back in the meat market, and Sarah would be taking in piecework after all. They would never be free of the Lower East Side.

Whatever the consequences, Rafe knew he had to confess. But first he had to return the notebook to its rightful place. And before that he had to copy out the long list of names, so Mr. Roosevelt could see for himself. Not only "Corsair" but all the people who had reason to want Mann dead.

He finally drifted off, then awoke with a start. When it became clear he wouldn't be going back to sleep, he tugged on his clothes, went to the kitchen, pulled out a chair, and began to copy Mann's ledger onto a sheet of paper. He was on the last page when his father appeared in the bedroom door, his thinning hair standing up like straw and the gray stubble creeping across his chin. He grunted in Rafe's direction, slipped on the pants he was carrying, and went into the hallway, toward the water closet. Rafe hurried to finish before he got back.

"So what's that?" his father asked as he closed the kitchen door behind him.

"Nothing," Rafe said. "Something for work."

"Work, always work."

Rafe shut the notebook, folded the copy, and dropped them into the side pocket of his uniform coat. "You taught me that, Papa," he said. "To work, remember?" When there was no answer, Rafe went on, "I'll be out late again tonight. Bryan will be at the Garden, and the whole force is on alert."

His father grunted again. "The force, the force. That's all you ever think about. It was better before."

Rafe struggled to keep his voice down. "No, Papa, it wasn't better. Don't you remember? We couldn't make ends meet."

The elder Raphael's eyes narrowed. He wasn't used hearing that tone from his son.

Rafe softened. "Papa, I told you, we need this job."

His father stretched a calloused finger toward him. "No, Otto. You need this job. The butcher store ain't good enough for you no more. But if you think the goyim need you, think again. They don't want you, Otto. That's something else I thought I taught you—don't put yourself on the mercy of strangers."

"And what do you suppose you and Mama did when you brought us here from Poland?" Rafe shot back. "We didn't know a soul here. It was a whole country of strangers."

"You forget. You were only a little boy. But that was different. We had no choice. We were starving. They were murdering us. But here they don't want us neither. They don't remember. They think their parents all got off the boat with pressed suits and clean fingernails. They think they came from good Christian countries, not filthy places like Poland. That's what they call us, you know, 'filthy.' And they think we throw bombs and bring down their government. They think we're all anarchists and terrorists. Be careful with them, Otto. They're not your friends."

Rafe sighed. "This isn't Poland, Papa. There aren't any Cossacks in America."

"You think?" his father said. It wasn't a question.

❧

When Dutch awoke, his first thought was that he was back in the alley. Then it came to him. Last night, as he raced out of the lodging house and down Duane Street, his only goal was to escape. But when he saw he'd lost the man in the brown suit, he stopped running and considered where he was headed. He had directed his feet toward the World Building without thinking, so he continued in that direction. No one was on the loading dock at that hour, but the empty delivery wagons were pulled up in their usual place, waiting for the rooster edition to come off the presses.

He crawled under one of the chassis and tried to think. Was the man in the brown suit the killer from the alleyway? If not, where did he get his cap? Who told him to look in the Newsboys Lodging House? The questions circled and circled without end. In time, he passed out more than fell asleep.

Now he sat up in the dark. A heavy door slid open and boots clomped onto the wagon's floorboards above his head. There was a startling *thump* as the first bundle of papers tumbled onto the bed. Rolling to one side, Dutch propped his back against the building's wall. It wasn't long before sleepy-eyed newsboys began crowding in to pick up their early-morning stock. Dutch kept watch, and eventually he recognized Grady's lean features and greasy brown hair.

"Hey!" he called, pulling himself to his feet.

"What the hell—?" Grady said.

"I have to talk to you," Dutch whispered.

Grady pushed him up against the wall.

"Hey!"

The bigger boy gave him a cuff on the ear. "Didn't I tell you to stay away from coppers?"

Dutch flinched, expecting another shot. But Grady only said, "I saw you yesterday afternoon, talking to that tall cop."

"You mean Rafe? He stood me for a lunch. He's going to help me find my mama."

Grady gave him another poke. "The next thing I know, I got this bull slapping me around—"

"Rafe—?"

"No, you dope. This detective, Gallagher. You ain't been on the street too long, so you probably don't know him, but he's a real bastard. And he's smacking me and saying he's going to run me in—for murder, don't you know."

Dutch's eyes grew wide. Grady grabbed him by the collar and pulled him closer. "I went by the alley looking for you, on account of I didn't see you around and yesterday you was spouting all that stuff about crapes and everything. And Gallagher is there, and he's got your damn cap in his hand, and he wants to know who belongs to it."

"You told him, didn't you?"

Grady pulled himself up taller. "Course not."

"What does this Gallagher look like?" Dutch asked. "Is he kind of fat, with curly black hair?"

"That's him, all right. Did he find you?"

"Yeah, but he didn't catch me. I think he's the killer."

"He's a cop, dummy. What killer?"

Dutch shot him a suspicious look. "Hey, how did he know where to find me?"

Grady inspected his feet. Then he suddenly raised his head and asked, "Did you tell this Rafe that you were going to be at the boarding house?"

"I'm not sure. I might have, I guess."

"Well then, your friend Rafe must of told Gallagher. Them coppers stick together, you know."

Dutch furrowed his brow at the idea that Rafe could have done that.

Grady pushed up against him again. "Now what's this about a killer? Tell me what happened last night, or I'll give you a good one, hear?"

"All right. Ease up, will you?" Grady let go of his shirt, but he didn't back off. "Monday," Dutch began, "in the middle of the night, somebody came into the alley, dragging a body."

Grady whistled. "So that's why you were asking about crapes. Did you get a look at the killer?"

"No, it was too dark. He saw me, though, and chased me, but I got away."

"Did he see your face?"

"I don't think so. It happened so fast. I lost my mama's handkerchief and my cap, and I guess this detective Gallagher found them. Now he thinks I had something to do with it. What should I do?"

Grady saw the panicked look on his face. "Don't talk to Gallagher, whatever you do. He just wants somebody to pin the murder on. He don't care if it's you or me or somebody else. Stay away from him. I ain't going to tell you again."

There were tears in Dutch's eyes. "What will he do to me?" he asked.

Grady leaned closer and lowered his voice. "He'll drag you to headquarters and give you the third degree. You know, they got a room down in the basement where they grill you till you squeal. And stay away from this Rafe, too. I'm telling you, no matter what they say, cops ain't our friends." He gave Dutch a long look to make sure the point was taken. "Listen, I got to get my stock. It's getting late." He started toward the delivery room door. "Remember what I say. Just lay low. Next time, maybe you won't be so lucky."

After Grady left, Dutch slumped against the wall. Could it be true that Rafe had turned him in to Gallagher? Rafe had been kind to him. Could he really believe that Dutch had something to do with murder? It would mean taking a risk, but if all that was true, he decided, he needed to hear it from Rafe himself. And he needed to know if Rafe was going to help him find his mother or not.

He left the loading dock and began trotting west. The sun was up now, and the heat was already building. Then, as he passed through the park in front of City Hall, he pulled to a stop. After last night, this detective Gallagher knew what he looked like. What if he spotted him at headquarters? What if he arrested him or took him down to the basement and gave him the third degree, like Grady said? No, he decided, he had to find the truth. Besides, where else did he have to go, now that Rose Street and the Newsboys Lodging House were off limits?

At the corner, he headed north, toward Mulberry Street.

⚜

This time, Rafe didn't linger in front of the Kenmore up on West Fifty-seventh Street. Reaching the entrance, he strode into the tasteful lobby again, past the cut-glass chandeliers and damask sofas. He looked for the doorman but saw no one.

"Morning, Officer. You're back." The voice came through the open door of the elevator. Rafe was glad to see it was the same obliging fellow as last night. That should make matters simpler.

"I just need to check on a few things," he told him.

The doorman went to his desk and picked up his passkey. "Right this way, please."

As the paneled cab lurched into motion, Rafe asked, "Has anyone else been by the apartment?"

The doorman gave him a puzzled look, as if to ask, *Shouldn't you know that?*

Rafe caught the expression. "I don't mean police," he extemporized. "Mr. Mann's family, for instance?"

"No, only you."

As they rocked their way upward, a buzzer sounded and a bulb lit on the control panel. When the car stopped at the sixth floor, Rafe stepped aside to let the doorman lead the way. But he handed Rafe the key and said, "I have to get that call. Just lock up afterward and ring for me when you're done, would you be so kind?"

Rafe went to the end of the hallway. But as he turned the key, there was no satisfying *click*. The door was already unlocked.

Stepping inside the apartment, he saw from the foyer that the place was a shambles. Books had been swept from their shelves and thrown to the floor. Cushions had been pulled from the sofa and chairs. The hunting paintings had been ripped from the walls and heaped on the carpet. Rafe paused for a moment, taking in the chaos.

He picked his way through the detritus to the bedroom. The sheets had been stripped from the mattress, and the contents of the bedside tables had been dumped on top. The desk drawer had been pulled out and flung onto the writing surface. As Rafe stood in the doorway, trying to make sense of the debris, he became aware of the slightest rustle behind him, like the first warning of a summer downpour.

He had just started to turn in that direction when everything went black.

⁓⁂⁓

Rafe pushed himself upright and rubbed the back of his head. He could feel a painful knot rising. He examined his fingers but saw no blood. His helmet had been knocked to the floor; he figured it must have dampened the blow. His watch said seven twenty. He'd been unconscious for only a few minutes then.

Reaching into his coat, he felt his wallet and notebook still there. But the pocket's other contents, Mann's ledger and the copy he'd made to show Mr. Roosevelt, were gone.

He pulled himself up and sat on the edge of Mann's bed. In his months on the force, he reckoned this was the closest he'd come to a flesh-and-blood murderer. Even through the pain, the idea was strangely exhilarating. He wondered, had he been hit over the head with the same club that had killed Mann? If not for the helmet, would he also have wound up in the morgue at Bellevue? But if somebody were trying to scare him off the investigation, they didn't know him very well, he thought. The worst mistake an opponent could make when he was boxing competitively was to back him up against the ropes.

He pushed the idea from his mind. The doorman had said that no one else had been to the apartment, but someone must have crept up the stairway during one of his elevator runs. Someone who knew how to pick a lock, apparently.

Oh God, he suddenly thought, what would Mr. Roosevelt say when this mess was discovered and the doorman reported that an officer fitting Rafe's description had been the only one here? He forced himself to his feet. All the more reason to get down to headquarters and talk to the commissioner before anyone else did.

He pulled the apartment door shut behind him and, temples throbbing, stole down the five flights to the lobby. Peering from the stairwell, he satisfied himself that the doorman wasn't in view. He dropped the passkey on the desk and hurried out.

Half an hour later, Rafe was making his way from the trolley stop up Mulberry Street. His head was still pounding, and though it wasn't yet eight o'clock, the air was already so thick he could see it. His eyes were trained on the sidewalk as he rehearsed his speech to Mr. Roosevelt. Too bad he wouldn't have the copied-out list of blackmail victims to call into evidence. He would have to persuade the commissioner with his words alone.

As he made the turn onto the granite steps in front of headquarters, he caught a dingy streak out of the corner of his eye. He flinched, then saw it was only a child, darting toward him from across the street.

"Officer Rafe!"

"Dutch," he said curtly. "I don't have anything for you. I said it would be a few days before—"

"But—"

"No buts."

"*Please.*"

Rafe continued up the steps. "I don't have time for this now, Dutch," he called over his shoulder. "Come back in a few days."

The boy stood at the bottom of the stairs for a second, just in case Rafe changed his mind. What had he done to make him so angry? Even now was he telling Gallagher that his chief suspect was outside? Dutch wavered on the patch of flagstone, every nerve telling him to flee. Instead, he slunk across the street and crouched in the shadow of the press building's brownstone stoop. Rafe had to leave headquarters sometime, he figured. He just hoped that Gallagher didn't come out and find him first.

❧

From the third-floor landing, Rafe saw that the door to the commissioner's anteroom was open. He expected to find Minnie at her typewriter as he entered, but the cover was still pulled tight over the machine. The door to Mr. Roosevelt's office was ajar, and the commissioner's athletic frame was bent over his desk. He was in early this morning, maybe on account of Bryan's speech tonight. Perusing a newspaper, he didn't hear Rafe come in.

Rafe's pulse ticked up a notch. He would have less time to prepare his case than he'd thought. But better now, before the office got crowded and the commissioner became distracted.

"Good morning, sir," he called. "Do you have a minute?"

Without looking up, Mr. Roosevelt waved him inside. "Have you seen the paper? Yesterday was the hottest day of the year and the hottest August eleventh in the city's history. One hundred and thirteen people dead of the heat yesterday in New York alone. They say today may be the worst yet."

I've seen more than the newspaper, Rafe thought, *I've seen the toll firsthand.*

"And this man—what was his name?" He ran his finger down the column. "Eammon Kavanaugh. A fireman, no less. Last night he was hit by the Third Avenue El. It seems he'd been drinking, but the motorman insists he didn't slip onto the tracks, he jumped. He had some money problems, and he'd been acting strangely, but his family believes he was driven to it by the heat." He shook his head. "Turns out he was the brother-in-law of one of our detectives. Walsh, from the Fourth. Do you know him? He's taken leave for a few days. Get his address and send a bouquet to Mrs. Walsh and to the widow, would you? Charge it to my personal account."

Rafe didn't answer but reached behind him and closed the door. Mr. Roosevelt finally glanced up from the paper. As he took in his assistant's sweaty, disheveled uniform and pained expression, a change came over the commissioner's face, though Rafe couldn't be sure if it showed concern or irritation. "What in blazes happened to you?"

"Commissioner," he began in a rush, "I need to talk to you about William d'Alton Mann."

Mr. Roosevelt leaned back in his swivel chair. The morning light was flashing off his pince-nez.

"Sir, I don't believe this was a simple robbery," Rafe began.

"Oh, Rafe, not that again."

"Yesterday I went to the alley off Rose Street."

The commissioner's expression darkened.

"There were tracks in the dirt where Mann's body had been dragged from the street."

Mr. Roosevelt folded his arms across his wide chest. He didn't seem surprised by that bit of information, and Rafe suspected that Riis had already told the commissioner about their conversation in the stairwell. "Well, then, he must have been hit over the head on the sidewalk," Mr. Roosevelt said.

"No, sir. There was no blood either on the sidewalk or in the alley. According to the coroner—"

The commissioner's brow creased, and he leaned forward. "You spoke to Coroner Tuthill?"

"At the morgue."

Mr. Roosevelt stared at him in disbelief.

Rafe went on, "The coroner says it was a vicious wound, not meant to stun but to kill. It split the skin wide open. It bled a great deal. There was blood all over his clothes."

"So—?"

"So, the victim must have been moved after he was dead, after he had done his bleeding elsewhere. Either the blood had dried by then, or the killer took the trouble of wrapping the body before he dumped it. No robber would do that."

The commissioner looked as though he wanted to punch him. "But there was no blanket or any kind of wrap found in the alley."

"Exactly. The killer must have taken it with him. It was all planned out. And that's not all—"

Rafe was just coming to the hardest part, about Mann's apartment and the leather notebook, but the commissioner cut him off. "That's enough, Rafe."

"One more thing—"

Mr. Roosevelt slammed his palm on his desktop. "No, Rafe, no more. Not one more word. Leave the Mann case alone. That's an order, do you hear?"

Rafe knew there was no arguing with him when he was like this. His confession about Mann's apartment and the notebook would have to wait. As he turned to go, a stabbing pain shot through his skull. He put his hand to the back of his head and winced.

Out in the anteroom, Minnie was settling herself at her desk. "Morning, Rafe," she said. Then she looked up and saw the pain on his face, and her smile disappeared. "What's wrong?"

"I don't suppose you have any headache powder?" he asked.

"What's the matter?"

"I hit my head."

"Let me see." She motioned him around to the front of the desk, and he bent his head so she could get a look. As she parted his thick hair with her fingers, he caught the scent of lilac.

"That's a nasty one," she said. "We should get some ice on that."

"No time to go searching for ice," Rafe answered. "Not today. Bryan is already in town."

Reluctantly, she went back to her chair. "How did you do it?"

"I bumped it getting off the trolley car," he said. It was the first time he had ever lied to her, but he had decided that he couldn't let her be drawn into his mess.

She cocked her head. "I thought you walked to work."

"Not today. Too hot."

She nodded, but he wasn't sure she believed him. Taking a small manila envelope from her purse, she poured some powder in a glass and mixed it with water from the carafe on her desk. He drank it down as she went back to her chair.

"Oh," he asked after a minute, "did you pick up the *Sun* today? I missed my usual boy this morning," he added. At least that part was true.

She reached under her desk and handed him the newspaper. Spreading it out flat, he scanned every page, but there was nothing more about the Mann case. As he handed the paper back, he kept his eyes on his desk to avoid what he knew would be her inquisitive look. Then he busied himself opening the mail and pretending to read it. But the words' meaning eluded him. Even more than the fierce headache or the spreading fuzziness in his brain, he was derailed by his exchange with the commissioner.

Why was Mr. Roosevelt determined to ignore the facts of the Mann case? It couldn't be just distraction over the Bryan visit. As they heard yesterday, the department was ready, and in any event it would be Chief Conlin, not the commissioner, who would be responsible for carrying out the preparations. Rafe had attended enough disciplinary hearings to have a keen sense of when a fellow cop was covering something up. And that's exactly how the commissioner had been acting ever since the news of Mann's death. What was he hiding? Who was he protecting? Rafe didn't know which was worse, his feeling of guilt for not being square with Mr. Roosevelt or his aggravation from thinking that the commissioner wasn't being square with him.

As the morning dragged on, the throbbing in his head began to ease. But if anything, his resentment toward the commissioner only grew. Not that he could confide any of this to Minnie. Though he felt her eyes on him from time to time, he ignored her glances.

A little before noon, he remembered the flowers for Walsh's wife and Kavanaugh's widow. He went to a tall oak filing cabinet, pulled their files, copied the home addresses in his notebook, and stuck the book back in his pocket. At lunchtime he would order a couple of bouquets.

Just then Mr. Roosevelt appeared in his office doorway. "Rafe," he said, "You haven't forgotten we're sparring later, have you?"

Rafe looked up. True, he and the commissioner boxed every Wednesday afternoon, but he'd been assuming that between the heat and the Bryan speech they wouldn't be going today. As though reading his thoughts, Mr. Roosevelt said, "Everything is all set for tonight. The chief has got matters in hand. It'll be good for us to sweat the heat out." Then he turned back into his office.

Rafe finally allowed himself a look at Minnie. Leaning across her typewriter, she whispered, "The hot wave has finally driven him mad. And if you go with him, in your condition, you're just as crazy as he is."

Rafe couldn't disagree. But as always with Mr. Roosevelt, the suggestion had been a command, not an invitation.

⌘

Rafe and the commissioner tapped gloves, the boxer's traditional salutation before a bout. Although there wasn't a ring at the Young Men's Institute, they always came here for their sparring. For one thing, it was around the corner from headquarters, and for another, Mr. Roosevelt appreciated what he called the club's "salubrious moral tone." This afternoon the gym was deserted; apparently they were the only two men in the city mad enough to seek unnecessary exertion in this weather. By the time they arrived at the clubhouse, Rafe's uniform was sticking to his body, and as they left the locker room he could still feel the sweat running down his ribs beneath his sleeveless athletic shirt. He couldn't shake the feeling that the commissioner was hiding something by ordering him off the Mann case, and the heat and the headache had done nothing to improve his mood.

Rafe was thirteen years younger than the commissioner, with a good four inches on him in height and almost that in reach. When they sparred he would generally hang back, letting Mr. Roosevelt set the pace, attacking just enough to let him feel he'd had a fair fight. But this afternoon, Rafe wasn't so inclined.

He started with a few soft jabs, which the commissioner met easily. Rafe let him get off a jab-cross combination, then answered with a measured jab-jab-cross of his own. The commissioner gave a couple of defensive jabs. Then he let his hands drop, only a couple of inches but enough to let Rafe pivot and slip a hook to the jaw. He saw surprise flood the commissioner's face, followed by a toothy grin.

"Ha! Good one, Rafe!"

Roosevelt stepped forward and tried another jab-hook, which Rafe dodged effortlessly. He gave the commissioner a hard jab to the belly, followed by a hook to the temple. Roosevelt backed off, circling for a few seconds, collecting himself and looking for an opening. But Rafe kept his chin tucked and his eyes straight ahead, trained on the commissioner's chest.

Roosevelt came in with a jab-cross-hook. Normally Rafe would have let him land at least one of the blows, but today he stepped back, and the commissioner punched only air. Then while he was still off balance, Rafe gave him a couple more quick jabs to the body.

But the commissioner only grinned again. "That's it, Rafe," he said, as though he'd lost track of who was schooling whom.

Instead of mollifying Rafe, the patronizing tone only added to his exasperation. When Roosevelt came at him again, instead of dodging, Rafe stood his ground. He blocked the cross-hook, then when the commissioner let his head drift back, Rafe landed an uppercut squarely on the chin. Roosevelt staggered, and at first Rafe thought he might go down. But he recovered and gave the maddening grin again.

"Well done, Rafe! That's what my old Dutch grandfather used to call a real sockdolager!"

Rafe fell back, as though the commissioner had landed an uppercut of his own. His "old Dutch grandfather." Of course, that was it.

The Roosevelts were one of the oldest, most prominent Dutch families in the city. Everyone knew that. Especially a man who made it his business to track the peccadilloes of the moneyed class. That was why in his little leather notebook William d'Alton Mann had code-named Roosevelt *Tulip*, after the classic Dutch bloom. He must have smiled as he'd written that, an ironically feminine name for the doggedly masculine commissioner of police. And that must be why Mann and the commissioner had nearly come to blows in his office.

Mr. Roosevelt, like Mr. Morgan, had seemingly refused to pay, and Mann had left the amounts next to their names written in pencil, maybe hoping they'd come around in time. But what were they being blackmailed for? Maybe Mann had discovered some illicit business dealing on Mr. Morgan's part. As for Mr. Roosevelt, Rafe didn't have the slightest idea. He didn't appear the type for blackmailing.

As Rafe was still mulling the question, he was rocked by a hook to the side of the head. His earlier pain came rushing back, more powerful than ever.

"Rafe!" the commissioner was calling to him. "You let me get that in. Come on, give me a real fight, or I'll think you're mollycoddling me!"

Rafe felt his knees buckle, and then he was sitting on the floor. The commissioner knelt beside him, his grin now changed to a look of concern.

"Are you all right, Rafe? That's a first, me knocking you down!" Even through the muddle in his brain, Rafe could hear the note of satisfaction in his voice.

SEVEN

THE COMMISSIONER PUT his gloved hand around Rafe's shoulder and helped him to the locker room. While Rafe sat on a bench, rubbing his temples, Mr. Roosevelt showered and changed into his street clothes.

"Feeling any better?" he asked as he pulled up his suspenders. A fresh sheen of sweat had already begun to dot his forehead. "I guess that was a real wallop, eh?"

Rafe nodded without glancing up. Normally he would have shaken off the punch, but coming after the other blow to the head the shot had been doubly potent.

"Will you be all right to get back to headquarters on your own?" the commissioner asked.

Rafe gave him a confused look.

"I have a meeting out of the office this afternoon. It's not on the schedule. It's just come up." He gave him a big brother's pat on the shoulder. "Stay here as long as you need."

Rafe didn't know what to make of the sudden solicitousness. "The Garden—"

"Don't worry yourself about tonight. Chief Conlin has matters under control. I'm going out of curiosity, nothing more, to see what codswallop the Great Commoner has to sling. I'll see you in the morning."

He bustled out, leaving Rafe sitting with his head in his hands. Eventually the throbbing eased enough for him to think. Just a few days ago, he would have sided with Mr. Roosevelt over all his critics, would have trusted him implicitly no matter the weight of evidence against him. Now he didn't know what to think. It was a sickening sensation, as though the world were suddenly wrong side up. But he did know this—he wasn't going back to headquarters this afternoon, and he certainly wasn't going home.

Moving deliberately, trying to keep the headache bearable, he showered and dressed. He left the Young Men's Institute, and at the corner of the Bowery and Spring Street he boarded a cable car headed north, toward Madison Square.

❧

"Theodore, what a pleasant surprise." Mark Hanna extended his plump hand toward the commissioner, but his stiff expression suggested the opposite of his words.

"Likewise," Roosevelt replied through his forced smile.

After leaving Rafe at the Young Men's Institute, he had come directly to the Waldorf-Astoria. He'd considered inviting Morgan to join him, but in the end he'd decided it would be better to make this call alone. He passed purposely through the antiques-filled lobby. Then, retracing his and Morgan's steps from two days before, he took the elevator to the twelfth floor and strode down the carpeted hallway to Hanna's suite. This time Hanna answered the door himself.

"Come in, come in," he said. "I was just sitting down to lunch."

Roosevelt followed him to a polished mahogany dining table set for one. Resettling himself at the head, Hanna gestured to a chair on one side. He picked up his fork and knife and cut into a thick medallion of filet mignon. "How are plans for your western barnstorming coming?" he asked. "Have you and the campaign worked out your schedule yet?" His tone was offhand. They both knew that wasn't the reason for this visit.

"Nearly," the commissioner answered.

Hanna lifted a morsel of meat to his mouth and began to chew. "Good, good. I know you'll put your heart in it, Theodore. And come March, we won't forget your help." He cut into a scalloped potato. "It's not as though the police department has been easy, has it? Around the country they may applaud all these reforms, but here in New York it's a different matter. Yes, a fresh start in Washington might be just the thing. I hear you have your heart set on Navy."

Roosevelt sat up a little straighter and smoothed the front of his vest. "Well, it has been a lifelong interest, ever since my Harvard days, when I started writing my naval history of the War of 1812."

"Yes, yes, you've become quite an author, haven't you?" Hanna said. "How many books is it now? Three? Four?"

"Fifteen."

"Fifteen books. Well, that's splendid. It's always good to have something to fall back on. Like when the ranch went bust. Out in Montana, was it?"

"North Dakota." Roosevelt thought, *I've punched men in the face for less.* His smile was so tight his jaw was aching.

"That's right, North Dakota. Well, let's tend to the election first, shall we? Then we'll see about Navy. After all, if Bryan wins, there will be nothing to discuss. I'll be in Ohio, tending to my business, and you'll be, well . . ."

He didn't have to finish. He meant that Roosevelt would be unemployed, after being forced out as police commissioner.

Hanna bit into another slice of meat. "What about the precautions for Bryan's speech?" he asked.

"Things are well in hand," Roosevelt told him. "You needn't worry on that account."

"I certainly hope not, Theodore." Hanna gave him a level stare. "We do not want any trouble tonight, of all nights."

"No, of course not. Not to worry," Roosevelt said with a note of finality.

"By the way," Hanna asked, though they both knew there was no by-the-way about it, "how's the Mann investigation going?"

"That's why I came over this afternoon," Roosevelt said. Two days ago, Hanna had assured Roosevelt and Morgan that he would "take care" of the matter after hearing that Mann was threatening to blackmail prominent Republicans. Now Roosevelt wanted to ask exactly what form his attentions had taken. But instead he told him, "I have good news. The detective has filed his report."

"And?"

"He concluded that it was a robbery, pure and simple. No bearing on Morgan or any other Republicans."

Hanna took a sip of red wine. Roosevelt had the distinct impression this wasn't news to him. *My God*, he thought, *he even has spies at police headquarters. Who could it be?*

Hanna paused. "I hear a young officer has taken it on himself to look into the matter." He glared up at him. "Your assistant."

Under the table, Roosevelt began to rub his palms together. With a man like Hanna, the only thing worse than having to admit bad news was trying to deny it. "Well," he said, "there are a few loose ends. Some facts that don't quite fit."

Hanna was cutting another piece of meat but stopped mid-slice. "Theodore, are you the president of the board of police commissioners or not?"

"Not to worry," Roosevelt told him. "I've ordered an end to the investigation. It won't go anywhere."

Hanna leveled his knife in Roosevelt's direction. "It had better not."

"It won't. I personally guarantee it." He wanted to spit on the floor to get the taste of the words out of his mouth.

Hanna rested the cutlery on his plate and leaned closer. "Theodore, if you can't manage your own department—your own assistant—how can you expect to be considered for a position in the national government?"

Roosevelt studied the mahogany tabletop. He was afraid of what he might do if he looked the man in the eye.

After a moment Hanna said, "Whoever this curious officer is, maybe he's been mistaken in his choice of vocation. Maybe it turns out that policing isn't the career for him after all."

Roosevelt forced himself to glance up. Hanna was watching him, waiting for an answer.

The commissioner swallowed hard. Then he gave a slow nod.

❦

Minnie took the first, delectable slurp of lemon ice and let it run over her tongue. It was luxurious to the point of sin, and she couldn't care less that the vendor had doubled his price in the past week. It was so hot today that she hadn't had any lunch, and then she'd heard the tinkling bell and the Italian patter wafting through the commissioner's open window. She couldn't make out a word, but she'd understood perfectly. She'd grabbed her change purse and rushed downstairs like a child, hoping she wasn't too late.

Now, as she took another sip and started inside, she felt her long skirt catch on something. Turning, she saw a shoeless boy with no cap and unruly blond hair.

"Excuse me, ma'am," he said, releasing her skirt. "When is Officer Rafe coming back?" In answer to her puzzled look, he went on, "I saw him and Mr. Roosevelt go out a while ago." He hadn't dared go up to Rafe with the police commissioner there.

Minnie still didn't answer. She was wondering how the child even knew who Rafe and the commissioner were, never mind kept abreast of their comings and goings. Finally, she asked, "Who are you, son?"

"They call me Dutch," he said. His gaze drifted toward the lemon ice. "What's your name?"

"I'm Miss Minnie." She thought for a second. "Listen, Dutch." She reached into her purse and pulled out a nickel. "Run after that man and tell him you want a cone, then come back here. Hurry up, before he gets away."

Dutch hesitated, licking his lips. He threw an uneasy glance over his shoulder, then darted down the street. Soon he was back at her side, paper cone in hand.

"Come on," she said. "It's too hot to be standing out here in the sun. Don't your feet burn up on the hot sidewalk?"

"Naw," he said, "they're used to it."

She started up the steps, but he hung back, like a puppy straining at his leash. She guessed his previous experiences with the police department hadn't been entirely favorable. "Come on," she coaxed. "It's all right as long as you're with me." She stuck out her hand, and he finally took it.

She led him to a wooden bench just inside the front door. They sat without speaking, slurping their ices while Dutch cast wary glances at the people coming and going. After a minute she asked, "Do you know how hot it is today?"

He looked up and shrugged.

"It's so hot the devil went to Coney Island."

He gave her a lopsided smile. "Are you on the police?" he asked.

"I work in the office with Mr. Roosevelt and Officer Rafe, up on the third floor," she told him.

He nodded, as if that explained everything. "My papa worked in an office," he said. "He was a bookkeeper."

"Oh? Where is he now?"

He studied his lemon ice. "Gone."

"Where's your mama?"

"Gone." He looked up again. "But Mr. Rafe is going to help me find her."

"Really?" Strange he hadn't mentioned it. "Did he say how?"

The boy shrugged.

"Well, Officer Rafe and Commissioner Roosevelt had to go out for a while. I'm not sure when they'll be coming back. Want to wait with me?"

He considered the idea as he took his last gulp of lemon ice. Then, as if suddenly coming to his senses, he gave a shy shake of the head.

"It'll be all right."

He stood up and inched toward the door.

"It's all right, Dutch," she said, "I promise you. We can—"

But he was already gone. As she watched his sticky paper cone trace a slow circle over the granite floor, she wondered, *What on earth could have scared the child so?*

Rafe stepped down from the cable car at Fourth Avenue and Twenty-third Street and walked one block west to Madison Square. Once a genteel residential district—the commissioner had grown up a few blocks away, on Twentieth Street, and had played in this very park—the neighborhood had been commercialized, especially with theaters, and the well-off had moved to more fashionable addresses farther uptown. Two decades ago the Roosevelts had relocated to Fifty-seventh Street, just west of Fifth Avenue.

On its west side, along Fifth Avenue, the square was anchored by two celebrated monuments to affluence. The Fifth Avenue Hotel had long been considered the city's finest until a few years ago, when the Waldorf-Astoria had opened. On the opposite corner was located that temple of haute cuisine, Delmonico's, which Rafe had also never penetrated beyond the iron facade and the fussy lace curtains. On the square's east side rose the new Metropolitan Life Building. As he passed by the skyscraper this afternoon, Rafe saw oversized portraits of McKinley and his running mate, Garret Hobart, hanging from the white stone facade, and he remembered reading that the Republicans had leased space in the Metropolitan Life for their campaign headquarters.

On the park's northern corner rose the ornate colonnade, cupolas, and high tower of Madison Square Garden, open for only a few years now. This afternoon a string of wagons was pulled up in front, and workers in blue overalls were unloading the extra seats for this evening's speech. A few uniformed officers were scattered about, an advance guard of the hundreds who would be on duty tonight.

According to the slip of paper that Mr. Morgan had handed the commissioner at the Union League Club, Mann's business address was 17 Madison Avenue. In an unassuming block on the square Rafe found the building, a faded brownstone that had been a private residence before being converted to commercial space. He climbed the stoop and saw from the row of brass plaques beside the entrance that *Town Topics* occupied the ground floor. He pushed on the weathered French door and entered a narrow hall. To his right was another door, painted a bright shade of red.

The knob yielded, and Rafe found himself in a cluttered office similar to the newspaper bureau across the street from headquarters. In the air hung the stale odor of yesterday's cigarettes. Scattered about the room were a dozen battle-scarred desks, all unoccupied except for one with a lazy gray cat sprawled across the top. Where was everybody? Was Mann's funeral this afternoon? Spread over the floor was a worn red carpet, and on one wall was a larger-than-life oil portrait of Colonel Mann, complete with scarlet bow tie and vest, apparently his trademark. On the facing wall was a tall chalkboard with the heading IMMUNES written across the top, and below that a handwritten list of a dozen names, none of which meant anything to Rafe.

At the room's far end, away from the square, was an open door. Rafe peered inside. In one corner stood a huge rubber plant, its broad, waxy leaves pressed flat against the ceiling. But the room was dominated by a massive mahogany rolltop desk. Mann's private office then.

Rafe walked behind the desk, where a swivel chair was pushed back, as though its owner had just stepped out for lunch. The desktop was open, and the writing surface and cubbyholes were littered with papers—letters; penciled notes; long, narrow pages of type that Rafe assumed had something to do with the content of the magazine. He pulled on the top drawer; it yielded. Inside, among more scraps of paper and a sheaf of colored pencils, was a small silver revolver. Hardly standard issue for the publisher of a society journal. Seemingly Mann understood the risks he was running with his scheme. Rafe shut the drawer. Propped on a corner of the desktop was a photograph in a carved silver frame. He picked it up. A woman, pretty, much younger than Mann. A daughter?

"Anything of interest?"

He spun. Leaning against the doorway was a lanky, mustached man a few years older than Rafe. He was wearing a dark business suit and carrying a straw boater in his hand.

To his unspoken question, Rafe answered, "I'm Officer Raphael." He returned the photo to its place. "May I ask your name?"

"Harold Vynne," the man answered. The accent was English, the tone weary.

"Harold—?

"Vynne. Rhymes with *sin*." He flashed a mischievous smile. Apparently he enjoyed his little joke and used it often. Then he asked, "What took you so long?"

As Vynne came closer, Rafe saw that the suit was rumpled and the shirt collar smudged. The man's chin was shadowed with a dark stubble. From all appearances he hadn't been to bed last night.

He caught Rafe's look. "On Tuesday nights—well, Wednesday mornings—we read galleys and put the issue to bed. Who knows, this may be our last, but we got it out."

"You're the editor, then?"

"General editor, music critic, literary columnist." He pointed to the photo on Mann's desk. "And son-in-law."

Rafe asked him to spell his surname and he entered it in his notebook. "I'm sorry," he said. "It must have been a shock for your wife—?"

"Emma. Yes, they were very close."

"And for you. Have you been married long?"

"Less than a year, though I've worked here at the magazine practically since the beginning." Rafe could see Vynne calculating how much to add. "My father-in-law was not an easy man, Officer Raphael. But to go like this, it was a blow to the staff as well as the family."

"I'm sure. Is there a Mrs. Mann?"

"There were two Mrs. Manns, but I didn't know either. They've both been out of the picture for many years."

"Can you tell me, was Mr. Mann wealthy?"

Vynne raised his brows at the question. Rafe didn't care. Now that he'd started down this road, he wasn't about to let social niceties stand in his way.

"I've no idea," Vynne said. "He certainly acted as though he were."

"Is Mrs. Vynne an only child?"

"Yes."

"That explains why you went to Bellevue yesterday to claim the body."

Again he'd surprised Vynne.

"I was up there myself," Rafe explained. "The director, Captain White, said you were expected."

Vynne eyed him uncertainly.

"Did you ask to speed up the medical examination so the body could be released?"

Vynne gave him a confused look. "Rush the medical examination? I don't know what you're talking about."

"When is the funeral?" Rafe asked.

"Tomorrow morning. Saint George's."

Rafe made another note. "Why are you here in the office, today of all days?"

Vynne motioned to the disarray on Mann's desk. "I was just sorting out a few things."

Urgent things, Rafe imagined, to keep him up all night and away from his bereaved wife. "Where's everyone else?"

"It's always deserted on Wednesdays. The staff work on their articles on their own and come in only on Mondays and Tuesdays to finalize the issue. I just went out for a moment to get a bite to eat."

Rafe changed tacks. "Do you have any idea why your father-in-law might have been on Rose Street at two o'clock yesterday morning?"

"No."

"Do you believe he was the victim of a robbery?"

"Do you mind if we sit?" Vynne asked, moving toward a dusty leather sofa. Rafe sat heavily and massaged his aching forehead. Vynne pulled up a chair with a carved back and red velvet seat.

"On Monday nights we generally work late, putting the finishing touches on the copy and sending it off to the printer. This week we ended about 1 a.m., and the colonel left. I noticed that he'd forgotten his cane, and I went after him. As I opened the front door, I was surprised to see him get into a carriage. But it was gone before I could get down the steps."

Rafe listened for some sign of contrition, of missed opportunity, of if-only, but heard none. "He hadn't ordered a carriage?"

"No. He always walked home. He said the trip up Broadway helped to clear his mind."

"Even at that hour?"

"Yes. The colonel was fearless."

Rafe recalled the defiance on Mann's face as he'd stalked out of the commissioner's office. "What kind of carriage?" he asked.

"Nothing special. A brougham."

"Who was driving?"

"I'm afraid I couldn't say. I only saw him from behind."

"Young man? Old?"

Vynne shook his head. "I don't have the slightest idea. I barely got a glimpse."

Rafe leaned against the sofa's tufted leather back. "You're telling me the colonel got into a strange carriage an hour before his body was discovered, and you didn't think to mention it to the police?"

"You're the first member of the police who's come asking," Vynne countered.

"Detective Gallagher didn't speak to you?"

"Who's that? I never spoke to a Gallagher or to any other detective. Besides, there was nothing unusual in any of this. The colonel often conducted business at odd hours and in unusual places." He stopped, as though afraid he'd already said too much.

"We're aware of Mr. Mann's activities," Rafe said. "I imagine that's what you're trying to sort out here. And why you didn't rush to the police."

Vynne sat up straight in his chair. "I don't care for—"

Rafe raised his hand to stop him. "I've seen the notebook," he said evenly.

Vynne studied him, trying to decide if he was bluffing. "I don't know what you're talking about," he said at last.

Rafe leaned toward him and spoke in the same quiet tone. "Mr. Vynne, accessory to blackmail is a crime in New York State. So is destroying evidence. Now, why don't we start over, and I'll just ask you a few questions?"

Vynne considered, then nodded.

"Have you been to your father-in-law's apartment in the past two days?"

"Yes, Tuesday evening."

"What time?"

"About nine, I'd say." Not long after Rafe had been there.

"Do you have a key?"

"Yes. Well, Emma does. I borrowed hers."

"Why did you go?"

"Just to check on things."

Rafe gave him a skeptical look.

"I was hoping to find the notebook," he admitted, "but it was gone."

"Was that the only time you've been to the apartment since Mr. Mann's body was discovered?"

"Yes."

"You weren't there earlier today?"

"No," he answered with a little heat. "I said last Tuesday night was all."

Rafe studied his face. Did he seem like the kind of man who could hit a police officer over the head? "Has anyone else been up there?" he continued.

"Not to my knowledge."

Then they had no idea of the mess awaiting them, Rafe thought. "Do you have any clue where the notebook is now?"

"No."

Rafe wondered whether he should believe him. Presumably, as Mann's only child Mrs. Vynne was also his only heir. That might be motive enough to hasten his demise. But was this magazine editor capable of murder? Rafe had seen stranger things in his brief time on the force.

He asked, "These 'galleys' you were correcting last night, what are they exactly?"

"They're proofs of the new issue. We send the printer the manuscript by messenger on Monday night. He sets it into type and sends us galleys on Tuesday afternoon. We read the galleys, make alterations, and return them early Wednesday morning, so they can make the corrections and lay them out into pages. The magazine is printed and put in the mail on Thursday."

"Do you have a set of these galleys here?"

Vynne went to Mann's desk and picked up the narrow pages of type that Rafe had noticed. "This is a duplicate," he said as he set them on a low table in front of the sofa. "They don't have the corrections, but they'll give you an idea."

Rafe thumbed through them. "Where's—? You know what part I'm interested in."

Vynne leaned over the table and began flipping pages. Rafe smelled alcohol on his breath and wondered what form Vynne's lunch had taken.

"About halfway through," Vynne said. "Here." He pointed to a heading in exuberant cursive type: *Saunterings.*

Rafe examined the column. Then he turned the page and did the same for the next and the next, until he came to the start of a short story. He looked up at Vynne. "Is this all?"

"Yes."

Rafe asked, "Did your father-in-law ever mention the idea of publishing anything in this issue concerning J. P. Morgan or Theodore Roosevelt?"

"Nothing to me, certainly. I'd remember that."

"And nothing like that was added to the galleys last night?"

"No. I supervised the entire process."

Rafe nodded distractedly. If Mann had been intending to blackmail Mr. Morgan and the commissioner, why hadn't he made good on the threat? He'd had the opportunity, since the manuscript had been released to the printer before his death. Had he been planning to add his revelations later, if his victims failed to pay up? Had he decided not to tangle with the commissioner of police and the country's most powerful banker? Or had Morgan and Roosevelt decided to pay him off after all?

He turned to Vynne. "Did your father-in-law ever talk about who he got all his money from?"

Vynne took a deep breath. "Never. I knew he kept a note-book. He would refer to it on occasion. But I never saw it. Frankly, I didn't want to know about that side of the business."

Of course not. "In that case, how did you and the other staff members know who you could and couldn't write about?"

Vynne stood. "I'll show you." He led Rafe back to the outer office and pointed to the chalkboard with the heading IMMUNES. "If a name appeared on this list, that meant the individual was in good standing, immune from publication."

Rafe read through the names again. Mr. Morgan and the commissioner were not among them. "Is this a complete list?" he asked.

"Yes. The colonel always kept it himself. That's his handwriting. If a name wasn't on this list, it was, as he would tell us, 'open season.'"

"Where did he get his information?"

"Servants, mostly. Housekeepers, valets, coachmen. Employees not as content as their masters might imagine, or just in need of some extra cash. Maybe their son got arrested, or their daughter got sick."

"Did any of these informants come here to the office on the day Mr. Mann was killed?"

Vynne considered the question. "Well, yes, as a matter of fact."

"Who?"

"Someone we'd worked with in the past. But he was nervous, kept glancing toward the door."

"Who was it?"

"His name was Eamonn Kavanaugh."

Rafe tried not to show his surprise. Eammon Kavanaugh. Another of those men supposedly driven mad by the heat. Did Vynne know how Kavanaugh had met his end?

Vynne said, "The colonel showed him into his office and closed the door. When he came out, he was excited, said if the information panned out we would have to do some extensive rewriting in galleys."

"'Panned out'?"

"The colonel never approved anything for 'Saunterings' without at least two sources. He was very meticulous that way. As much as the Four Hundred may despise the column, no one has ever proved anything in it to be false. In this case, the colonel said that if we could get confirmation it would be the making of us, and *Town Topics* would finally get the national recognition we deserved."

Rafe leaned back against one of the desks. Was that why Mann had never published the threatened article about Mr. Roosevelt and J. P. Morgan, because he'd gotten even hotter information that same day? It would have to be something explosive, to push the police commissioner and the country's foremost banker from the magazine's pages. But Kavanaugh was a fireman, Rafe recalled. How could he have gotten hold of something so valuable to the publisher of *Town Topics*?

"You have no idea what it was?" Rafe asked.

"No. Whatever Kavanaugh said went with him and the colonel to their graves."

So Vynne did know about Kavanaugh's death. But he didn't seem shocked by it. Rafe asked, "You said you worked with him before. What other information had he given you?"

Vynne thought again. "It was last year. I don't remember exactly. Something about a police captain, I think."

Rafe wondered if it was a coincidence that Kavanaugh was brother-in-law to Jimmy Walsh, detective in the Fourth Precinct and dear friend of Thomas Gallagher. Or was Walsh feeding him information about crooked cops, then sharing the proceeds from Mann?

"Does the name James Walsh mean anything to you?" he asked.

Vynne shook his head.

"How much did your father-in-law pay for this kind of information?"

"I really couldn't say. I guess it would depend on how big a story it would make."

Rafe figured a story that made Mann want to rewrite an issue in galleys must be worth a lot. Was it worth killing over?

He turned to Vynne. "And the coincidence didn't strike you as odd? Someone comes and gives your publisher some information and the next night jumps in front of the Third Avenue El? Mr. Vynne, for a journalist, you're not very inquisitive, are you? But then again, you didn't want to get involved in Kavanaugh's death any more than in your father-in-law's."

At least Vynne had the decency to lower his eyes. "In the paper they said Kavanaugh jumped because of the heat."

"Right."

They stood quiet for a time. "So these names mean nothing to you?" Rafe asked, recalling some of the code names from the notebook. "Corsair. Tulip. Steel. Canton?"

Vynne shook his head after each one. "Well, of course, Canton is William McKinley's hometown in Ohio. It's been in the news lately, on account of the campaign."

"Of course," Rafe echoed, more to himself than to Vynne. Where the candidate had been conducting his "front porch campaign," meeting delegations, making speeches at his home instead of barnstorming across the country.

He asked, "Was your father-in-law a Republican?"

Vynne smiled thinly. "Hardly. He was a proud, life-long Democrat." Vynne was saying something else, but Rafe didn't hear. *My God*, he was thinking, *was Mann blackmailing McKinley? Is that who the commissioner has been protecting? Just how high does this thing go? And what in the name of God did it have to do with Eammon Kavanaugh and Jimmy Walsh?*

❧

Dutch was still crouched beside the newspaper bureau's brownstone stoop. After bolting down his lemon ice, he'd torn back to his hiding place, where he'd squatted for the rest of the afternoon, watching police headquarters across the street. He'd seen dozens of men, in uniform and not, pass through the heavy wood and glass doors, but Officer Rafe hadn't been among them.

As the shadows continued their steady creep across Mulberry Street, inching toward the building's limestone facade, Dutch was filled with a growing dread. For the past two nights he'd had no regular sleeping place, terrible nightmares, long hours awake and alone. And the days weren't much better, with no news-papers to sell, no steady meals, and the constant worry of who might be watching him—at first the killer but now this Detective Gallagher. And always there was the unbearable heat.

The deepening shadows had done nothing to lower the temperature, and even now Dutch could feel the heat pulsing off the pavement. He wiped his face with his shirttail. He had to think. Should he try to find Grady and ask him what to do? Should he stay here and hope Officer Rafe returned, so he could find out once and for all if he was a friend who could help him? Would he ever find his mother, or was he doomed to stay on the streets forever?

Around and around swirled his thoughts, until he felt dizzy from the effort. It was so hot. His head began to droop. He fought it for a time, but it was so much easier just to give in. At last his chin sunk onto his chest.

❧

One fifty-four East Eighty-fifth Street. Rafe compared the number on the building with what he'd copied in his notebook that morning, after Mr. Roosevelt had told him to order flowers for Walsh's and Kavanaugh's wives. He had never gotten around to it, but now, on his way to the El, he'd found a florist shop on Lexington and bought an armful of white gladiolas.

He examined the four-story brick building, which was set between similarly tidy rowhouses. The front door was freshly painted, and the windows looked recently washed. A pot of geraniums had been set on the stone stoop. Rafe climbed the steps and pushed on the door. In front of him was a narrow hallway and a staircase. To the right was another door with a neat, hand-lettered sign, slipped into a brass bracket: McGANN.

Up here, apparently, a family got a whole floor to themselves. He walked up the wooden stairs to the second story. PLUNKETT read the sign on that door. On the third floor, he found what he was searching for: WALSH.

He knocked. The door opened, and Jimmy Walsh's face appeared, looking even paler and more rodentlike than usual. On seeing Rafe, what little color it had seemed to drain away. Rafe took the opportunity to slip his foot between the door and the jamb.

Walsh said, "What the hell—?"

Knowing Jimmy's feelings about his kind, Rafe hadn't expected a warm Irish welcome. Still, he was surprised by the vehemence in Walsh's tone. He realized it was the sound of fear.

"Sorry to hear about your brother-in-law," Rafe went on. "Is Mrs. Walsh here? The commissioner asked me to bring some flowers."

Confused, Walsh glanced at the oversize bouquet. "She's with her sister-in-law," he said.

"That would be Mrs. Kavanaugh."

"What do you want?" Walsh asked. "You got some nerve—"

"Kavanaugh lived right around the corner, didn't he?" Rafe waited to be invited in, but Walsh was only giving him a beady stare. He went on, "What a shame. One day Kavanaugh goes to see his friend William d'Alton Mann, and the next thing you know, Mann is killed in a robbery and Kavanaugh ends up under the elevated."

At the sound of Mann's name, Walsh's bony Adam's apple began to bob. He stuck his head out the door and gave a nervous glance toward the stairwell.

"We can keep talking right here if you like," Rafe offered. "Or you can let me in."

Walsh gave him a hateful look but opened the door a little wider. Rafe brushed past him into a small foyer with a hall tree and a beveled mirror. Glancing into the parlor, he saw a neat sofa and a pair of matching chairs, all upholstered in brown horsehair and draped with lace antimacassars. He felt a wave of envy, tinged with suspicion. So this was what it was like to live on a detective's salary. Or did Walsh have some extracurricular income too?

Walsh closed the door but didn't ask him to sit.

Rafe towered over him. "You and I both know that Mann's death wasn't a robbery," he began. Walsh opened his mouth, but Rafe put up his hand. "Despite what your friend Gallagher says."

Walsh's Adam's apple began to work again.

"Not only that," Rafe said, "Kavanaugh went by Mann's office the day that Mann was killed."

"You're crazy!" Walsh said.

"There are witnesses," Rafe went on in a level tone. "Afterward, Mann seemed to think he was sitting on some pretty exciting news, started talking about remaking that week's issue."

"You're crazy!" Walsh said again, but this time his voice jumped half an octave.

"Were you close to your brother-in-law?" Rafe asked.

"Not especially."

"Did you ever talk to him, maybe about what was going on in the department?"

"Of course not!"

"Do you think he was unhappy? Was he the kind of man who would take his own life?"

Walsh had to struggle to keep his voice down. "How the hell would I know? I saw him at Thanksgiving and Christmas. What's it to you, anyway? This isn't any of your business. This isn't your case. What do you mean, coming up here and asking all kinds of questions, the day before we bury—?"

Rafe decided to take a wild shot. "Did he ever talk about politics?"

He saw the surprise on Walsh's face.

"What about the election? Was he a Republican or a Democrat?"

Walsh stared at him as though he'd lost his mind. But Rafe also thought he saw a glimmer of relief in his eye. "I tell you, I barely knew the man!"

"Did he know anybody working on the campaign?"

Walsh's face split in a smile that was more nearly a sneer. "Yeah," he said, "he and McKinley were like brothers. Old Bill didn't take a step without talking to Eammon." He gave his head a shake. "You're cracked."

For once Rafe was tempted to agree with Jimmy Walsh.

Just then the front door opened, and a petite woman came in, wearing a black armband over her white shirtwaist. Her eyes were red, and she was dabbing at them with a handkerchief. Seeing the visitor, she stopped.

Rafe took a step toward her and held out the gladiolas. "Mrs. Walsh. I'm Officer Raphael, from Commissioner Roosevelt's office. The commissioner asked me to come and express his condolences about your brother." He motioned toward Walsh.

"I was just telling Jimmy here what a shock it was to all of us at headquarters."

Mrs. Walsh's eyes brimmed as she took the flowers. "Thank you. It was so nice of you to come. Jimmy and Eammon were so close, you know. Best of friends, weren't you, Jimmy?"

Rafe gave Walsh a sidelong look. "So he was just telling me. Well, I know this is a difficult time. If you'll excuse me, I'll be going. Again, our condolences."

He made to leave, then turned back to Walsh. "Will you be at work later this week, Jimmy?"

"Friday."

Rafe nodded. "Good, we can have another talk then."

Mrs. Walsh opened the door for him. "Thank you, Officer," she said.

As the door closed behind him, he heard Walsh's voice. "Yeah, thanks."

Rafe made his way downstairs, struggling to piece together what he'd learned. Last year Kavanaugh sells Mann some information about a police captain. Information that could easily have come from Jimmy Walsh, his brother-in-law and, if you believed Walsh's wife, his best friend. Rafe had to admit, that seemed just the kind of thing Walsh would be involved in. Then earlier this week Kavanaugh goes to Mann again, apparently with something really hot. Within forty-eight hours both men are dead. So did this week's lead also come from Walsh? Was it also something about the department? What could it possibly have to do with William McKinley? Rafe wondered if he could have gotten something more solid out of Walsh if his wife hadn't come home.

What was Walsh so afraid of? Of ending up like Mann and Kavanaugh? Or of getting caught? He was clearly guilty of something, but what? Of abetting a blackmailer, or something worse? Was little Jimmy Walsh capable of murder? What reason would he have to kill either Mann or Kavanaugh, his partners in extortion? Was it a falling-out among thieves? Did Mann refuse to pay him? Could Kavanaugh have murdered Mann then jumped under the train out of remorse? Was he drinking so heavily that night to quiet a guilty conscience? Or did someone else send Kavanaugh to his everlasting reward—out of revenge, or to have one fewer partner to share the proceeds with, or to keep him from informing to the police? Who knew? But maybe Rafe wouldn't wait until Friday, when Walsh was back at work. Maybe he would pay him another visit tomorrow, after the funeral. In the meantime, there was someone else he needed to talk to.

⤋⤋⤋

It was a little after five o'clock when Rafe got to the news bureau. He had come despite his better judgment. He didn't trust Jacob Riis. He hadn't ever since he'd read his well-meaning but misinformed essays about the Jews and other immigrants, and he felt even less confidence in him after their conversation in the stairwell at headquarters, when Riis had been evasive about the commissioner's whereabouts on Monday night.

But it wasn't just his doubts about the reporter's trustworthiness that made Rafe uncomfortable with this visit. It was the risk. Not abstract, anonymous danger but the intensely personal kind, the kind that could end a budding career. After Mr. Roosevelt had ordered him to halt his rogue investigation, Rafe had questioned both Harold Vynne and Jimmy Walsh. And now he was about to inch out even further on that creaky limb and interview Jacob Riis, one of Mr. Roosevelt's closest friends. How could he expect that wouldn't get back to the commissioner?

But strangely, the deeper he got into the investigation, the freer he felt. He could only be fired once, after all. Having already crossed that threshold, what did he have to worry about going further? In any event, he couldn't stop himself now. He'd resolved to get to the bottom of Mann's death even when it had looked like an isolated murder, the kind that happened hundreds of times a year in New York. Now that the commissioner seemed to be stalling the investigation, now that a detective was acting guilty, now that Harold Vynne was suggesting it might reach all the way to Republican headquarters, he was more resolute than ever. But he had to act fast, before the commissioner put an end to his prying once and for all. And he had questions that only Jacob Riis could answer.

He pressed against the news bureau's weather-beaten door. In the big front room, many of the desks were vacant, the reporters having already filed their stories for the afternoon editions. Those who were left were lounging in their shirtsleeves, thumbing through the papers or bantering across the crowded space, filling time and waiting for some news to happen. In the back corner, the nightly poker game was already in progress.

Rafe was relieved to see Jacob Riis at his desk near the front door, writing in a notebook. Another heartfelt treatise on the plight of the city's immigrants? He stood over the desk until Riis finally squinted up through his wire spectacles.

"I need to talk to you," Rafe said.

Riis set down his pencil, reluctant but seemingly not hostile. "Come to my private office," he said. Maybe he had some things he wanted to talk over with Rafe as well.

He led Rafe up a rickety staircase whose treads complained under every step. At the top they passed what must have been bedrooms when this had been a private house, but today their scuffed doors were shut tight. They walked to the end of the hallway then climbed another set of stairs until they came to a single door. Passing through, they stepped onto the building's metal roof, which was shimmering in the late afternoon heat. Did Riis bring him up here for privacy, Rafe wondered, or to guarantee that the interview would be a short one? He followed Riis to the front of the building, where a waist-high brick parapet overlooked police headquarters, across the street. On the third floor, Rafe saw the familiar corner window marking Mr. Roosevelt's office.

Riis turned to him. "You just caught me. In a few minutes I'm heading over to the Garden to hear Bryan. Are you going? It'll be interesting to see if he can fire them up the way he did in Chicago. Although I don't know how he can top that 'Cross of Gold' business."

Rafe was surprised by the friendly tone. He hadn't known what to expect after their confrontation in the stairwell yesterday morning. In answer to the question, he shook his head. He'd thought about going to hear the speech until the commissioner had disinvited him. What had he said? *Don't bother going to the Garden tonight. I'll see you in the morning.* Besides, Rafe had other things on his mind now.

The sun was beating on his back, and he could feel the steady drip of perspiration beneath his woolen uniform. "You know," he began, "I was surprised that you never published a follow-up story about William Mann. No interviews with colleagues or family members, no description of the murder scene, nothing about the police investigation. Here you have the great luck to happen on a fresh murder—of a prominent citizen, no less, the publisher of a society magazine. And except for that one rushed report, you do nothing with it. Isn't that why the editors boxed that first piece on the front page, to tease readers, so they'd want to pick up a later edition, hoping for more details? Your competitors weren't so lucky. But you were there, you spoke to Gallagher and the roundsman, Miller. You could have made a real story of it. But—nothing. Doesn't that seem a little strange for the *Sun*'s star police reporter?"

Riis shrugged. "Mann's employees and family wouldn't talk to the press. Gallagher and Miller had nothing more to say. Until the murderer is caught, there is no story."

Rafe wasn't persuaded. "Or maybe someone spoke to you in the meantime." He inclined his head toward police headquarters. "Maybe someone was with you that night in the alley off Rose Street. Someone you've been spending all your evenings with lately. Someone who suggested that this particular story wasn't worth your time."

Riis watched him noncommittally. Finally, he said, "Theodore and I did go down to the Lower East Side on Monday, same as every other night for the past week. We happened to be near Rose Street when we heard Roundsman Miller's whistle. We got there less than a minute after he did. Miller ran to a call box, and Gallagher arrived not long afterward."

Rafe thought about Gallagher's skimpy report and then Miller's irate silence when he ran into him in the alley the following day. "Did the commissioner order them not to pursue the case?"

Riis thought for a moment. "I don't know. He spoke to them, but I didn't ask what he said. What's all this to you, anyway?"

Rafe pressed on. "And what reason did he give when he asked you not to follow the story?"

Riis hesitated. "He said it was in the nature of a personal favor."

So that was it. That was all it took for a powerful man to subvert the free press. A favor from a friend.

"He didn't say anything—?" Rafe began then thought better of it. He'd been assuming that Riis knew of Mann's activities, but now he wasn't so sure. Maybe that brief article on the front page of the *Sun* contained everything he had on the case. Was that why Riis was speaking to him now, to try to find out more himself?

Riis finished the question: "About the blackmail?"

So Riis did know something. But how much? How could Rafe give him enough to keep him talking without saying too much himself? "He was blackmailing J. P. Morgan," he offered. He figured if Riis knew about the blackmail, he had to know about Morgan's part in it.

"About his infidelities," Riis said.

So that, not illicit business dealings, was what Morgan had
to hide. He decided to risk a new tack. "What about William
McKinley?" he asked. "Can you think of anything he might
want to keep quiet, anything that could hurt him in November?"

Riis seemed taken aback by the question. "Mann couldn't
have been blackmailing McKinley. He's as clean as a new-mown
field. Like many people, he got into some financial straits in
ninety-three, back in Ohio, during the crash. Guaranteed some
loans for the wrong person, found himself owing more than a
hundred thousand dollars. For a time it looked as though he
might have to resign as governor, but Mark Hanna and some
other rich friends came to his rescue, and he was reelected
handily. That's it. There's nothing else even remotely scandalous.
The man has been a pious Methodist all his life. He's as straight
a pine as you're likely to find in politics. Before the convention,
he even forbade Hanna from making some patronage deals to
seal the nomination."

"What about Hanna?" Rafe asked. "Does he have anything
to hide? He made his money in coal, didn't he?"

"Coal and iron." Riis shook his head. "Doubtful. He's an
operator, like any politician, but he's been plotting this campaign for four years, working on it full time since last year. He's
too smart to do anything that could jeopardize the election—or
his own career. He's obviously angling for some office to repay
him for his pains."

So Riis knew about "Corsair," but apparently he knew
nothing about "Canton." What about "Tulip"? Sweat was
streaming down both men's faces, and Rafe could feel he was
coming to the end of Riis's patience. He would have to give him

something else. He just had to hope that Riis liked, or feared, the commissioner enough that he would honor his promise to him not to write another article about William d'Alton Mann.

"Mann tried to blackmail Mr. Roosevelt too," Rafe said.

But this time Riis wasn't surprised. "So Theodore mentioned. He had the nerve try it in police headquarters the day he died. It was about Theodore's brother, Elliott."

It was Rafe's turn to be caught unawares. "The alcoholic."

"The second anniversary of his death is coming up." Riis smiled. "You know Theodore. When Mann threatened to publish a—how did he put it?—'a tender tribute to Elliott's most untimely and tragic passing,' Theodore threw him across his desk."

Of course. The decline of his much-loved younger brother had been a nightmare for the commissioner, only heightened by the terrible shame—the drinking, the carrying on with married women, the illegitimate son, the sanatoriums and suicide attempts—all leading, heartbreakingly but also mercifully, to his passing at age thirty-four. Even the reputable newspapers had feasted on the story. God knows what the swindler Mann would have done with it. And Rafe could only imagine the effect such an article would have on Elliott's widow and children, not to mention the commissioner's wife, Edith, who lived in dread of any scandal involving her husband. And it certainly wouldn't have helped the commissioner's career at this delicate juncture. No, Mr. Roosevelt couldn't afford to have Mann dredge all that up again.

Riis didn't know everything, but he knew enough. And now Rafe had told him more than he'd ever confided to the commissioner. He thought about asking Riis not to mention their conversation to Mr. Roosevelt, but how could he expect him to withhold such a secret from one of his closest friends? What would Mr. Roosevelt do when he found out what Rafe had learned—not only that Mann wasn't killed in a robbery but that he'd been blackmailing the rich and powerful, including the commissioner, who had tried to cover up the publisher's crimes? He gave a rueful smile. Maybe his father would get his wish; maybe he'd have his son back beside him in the meat market after all.

"You believe that McKinley's campaign is somehow involved in this?" Riis asked. "Does it have something to do with Ferris Appleby?"

"Appleby?" Rafe answered. "How did you know that? I never told you he'd come looking for Mr. Roosevelt. And the note I gave you, to give to the commissioner, was in a sealed envelope."

"I was with Theodore when he opened it," Riis said. "At the bar of the Union League Club. Then he went to have a chat with Appleby."

"Who is this Appleby? What does he want, and why was it so urgent?"

"I don't have the slightest idea. He works for the Republican National Committee, I believe. Theodore didn't say, and you know he's not a man you can press."

Then Rafe thought of one more question, something that had been bothering him for the past three days. "Tell me," he said, "why did the commissioner invite me to go with you and him to the Lower East Side last Sunday night? It's the only time he's ever done that."

"He said you were a bully fellow, that you'd be good company, that's all."

Rafe nodded. "Thanks for all the information," he said, though he wasn't sure how much of it to believe. He turned away and hurried across the metal rooftop, back toward the stairs. It was time to have a talk with Ferris Appleby. And he thought he knew where to find him.

EIGHT

DUTCH AWOKE WITH a start. He tried to remember where he was, then saw police headquarters across the street. The shadows had climbed halfway up the front wall. It was getting late. He wondered how much time had passed.

Sitting up on his heels, he watched the comings and goings across the street. Several policemen entered and several left, but there was no sign of Officer Rafe. Maybe he'd already gone home for the day.

Dutch cursed himself for being so careless. Then he gnawed on a ragged fingernail, wondering what to do next. Before he could come up with a plan, he heard a door slam. Stretching up and peering over the top of the stoop, he saw a man leaving the news bureau and trotting down the stairs.

"Mr. Riis!"

The reporter startled. "What the—?"

Dutch rushed his words, before the man could get away. "What time is it, please, sir?"

Mr. Riis gave him an annoyed look but stopped anyway. "Who are you, boy? What are you doing down there?"

"I'm Dutch, Officer Rafe's friend. I saw you two together the other night, on Roosevelt Street. I need to talk to him. Do you know where he is?"

Mr. Riis gave an impatient shake of the head as he took out his watch. "It's five thirty. Rafe left here fifteen minutes ago."

Dutch wanted to slap himself. "Where is he?"

"I don't have the slightest idea." Then the reporter was gone.

Finally, Dutch stood up. He looked first one way then the other, before racing across the street. He darted up the tall front steps of headquarters and stole into the cool lobby. He glanced at the bench where he and Miss Minnie had eaten their lemon ice, as though expecting to find her still sitting there. She'd said that Rafe worked up on the third floor. Dutch made a line for the wide central staircase.

He'd covered only a couple of steps when he felt a rough hand on his collar. Spinning, he found a burly man looming over him. He wasn't wearing a uniform, and he had curly black hair. The detective they called Gallagher, the one Grady had warned him about, the one who had found his cap in the alley and chased him through the Newsboys Lodging House.

Dutch squirmed, but Gallagher only tightened his grip. The boy saw that he was smiling. Not a friendly smile like Rafe's, but a cruel, wicked smile.

"Well, well," Gallagher snarled. "I see we got us a tadpole on the line." He lifted Dutch by his collar until the boy's feet came off the floor and he was kicking air. Gallagher pressed his round, red face into Dutch's. "I'll show you what we do with boys like you," he hissed.

Just then a pair of uniformed officers came down the steps. "Help!" Dutch called. "Help me!"

But they only chuckled. "Gallagher's got himself a real dangerous one this time," one of them said.

"A regular felon," said the other, and they both laughed as they strolled toward the front door.

Gallagher dragged Dutch toward the staircase, and the boy thought maybe he'd be hauled in front of Commissioner Roosevelt. But instead of heading up, they turned down toward the basement.

"Rafe, help me!" he yelled. "Rafe!"

Gallagher thought, *How the hell does the street kid know Raphael?* Then Dutch kicked harder, and Gallagher twisted his shirt collar until the boy thought he would choke. His bare heels banged on every tread, and at the bottom Gallagher dragged him down a narrow corridor. An open doorway flashed by, then they stopped before one that was closed. Peering up at the wall, Dutch read a wooden plaque with carved gold letters: *Mystery Chamber.*

Gallagher threw the door open and pitched Dutch inside. The boy slid across the smooth stone floor, until his head banged against a wooden display case. The detective lumbered in behind him, slammed the door and, taking a heavy key ring from his pocket, picked through it until he found the one he was looking for. He slipped it in the door's lock and twisted. *Click.*

The room had a musty smell, and it was dark except for the dingy light filtering through the tiny windows. Dutch saw several more display cases running the length of the room. Hanging from the rough plaster walls were more glass-fronted cabinets, brimming with menacing objects—knives, handcuffs, nightsticks, pistols of all sizes and shapes. Dutch gave a shiver. So this was the torture chamber that Grady had warned him about.

Gallagher put his hands on his knees and bent over him. "This is where we put the bad boys. Boys that don't want to cooperate. Boys that need to think over what they've done." His words echoed off the arched brick ceiling. "You got away from me at the lodging house, but I promise you won't be getting away from me here."

He put his hands on his hips and stretched his back. "All I want to do is ask you a few questions. That's not so bad, is it? About Monday night. About what you saw in that alley off Rose Street." He took a rumpled gray cap out of his pants pocket. Dutch reached out to grab it, but Gallagher snatched it back with a snort. "Not so fast, boy. You see, I know you were in the alley that night. Now tell me, what did you see?"

Gallagher didn't care who committed the murder, Grady had said; he just wanted somebody to hang it on, even if it was a lowly newsboy. Dutch opened his mouth, but he couldn't produce a sound. He could feel the hope seep out of him, like air out of a balloon. He pressed his lips tight, but he couldn't hold back the sobs. His shoulders rocked, and he felt hot tears slip down his cheeks. He rubbed his eyes with his shirtsleeve.

"Poor boy." He heard the sarcasm in Gallagher's voice. Then the detective went on, with an even harder edge, "Look here. You think I'm stupid? You can't take me in with your crocodile tears. You're going to stay here till you talk, understand?"

Dutch ventured a look at him. "I—I didn't see anything," he got out. He saw Gallagher's meaty palm coming down on him, but he wasn't fast enough. It landed on his temple, and he felt a *crack* as his head snapped back against the wooden case again.

Gallagher was standing over him now, his hand raised. "Is that how you want it?" Dutch closed his eyes, but the blow didn't come. "I'll tell you what," the detective said. "I got to go do something, see. You think things over while I'm gone. Don't even think about touching anything in here, and don't think about making any noise, either, or you'll know what real trouble is." Dutch didn't dare to open his eyes, but he could feel hot breath on his cheek. "And when I come back, you be ready to tell me everything you saw that night. Everything, got it? And if you don't ..."

He heard heavy footsteps moving off. Squinting, he saw Gallagher take the keys from his pocket and fiddle with the lock. Then the detective stepped into the hallway and slammed the door behind him.

※

By the time Rafe got to Madison Square, there was already a buzz around the Garden. Cops huddled under the arcade, while mounted officers stood on the corners and patrolmen set up the wooden sawhorses that would control tonight's crowd. Down the block, Rafe strode to the Metropolitan Life Building, where the Republican campaign had its headquarters, and entered under the larger-than-life portrait of William McKinley that hung from the gleaming white facade.

Just inside the front door, he pulled up short. He'd heard of the Marble Court, of course, a lobby so sumptuous it had become a tourist attraction, reproduced on countless picture postcards. But he had never seen anything like it. He walked across the polished white floor. Straight ahead was a monumental staircase carved entirely of the same material. The second story was encircled with white marble columns and balustrades, and the third was surmounted by white marble arches and vaults. Rafe stood gaping, trying to take in the sheer extravagance of the place. Then, as his gaze drifted toward the first floor, he was doubly astonished: Striding down the great staircase was Theodore Roosevelt.

Rushing across the marble floor, Rafe flattened himself into a recess under the stairway. In another moment, when the commissioner's back came into view, he saw that Mr. Roosevelt wasn't alone. He was talking to a middle-aged man in a black frock coat. As the man inclined his head toward Mr. Roosevelt, Rafe got a look. Ferris Appleby of the Republican National Committee, the man Rafe had come here to see.

The pair crossed the lobby, apparently unimpressed by the opulence around them, and passed into the street. Rafe followed as far as the tall bronze door. They paused on the sidewalk and shook hands. Then Mr. Roosevelt turned south—toward police headquarters?—and Appleby strolled north, in the direction of the Garden.

Rafe eased outside and stood in the doorway until the commissioner rounded the corner toward Fourth Avenue. He trailed Appleby past the sooty steeple of the Presbyterian church, then turned east onto Twenty-sixth Street. The block had already been sealed. Appleby stopped at the police barricade and fished a ticket out of his pocket. The officer let him pass. Rafe sidled past the guard and shadowed Appleby from across the street.

A few paces down from the corner, on the street's south side, Appleby ducked into a building with plate glass windows and black-painted trim. Squinting through a window, Rafe saw him standing at a bar, one foot propped on the brass rail that snaked along the floor. Rafe entered the saloon. The place was like thousands of other bars in New York—tin ceiling, mirrored backbar, tall wooden stools—except for one thing: but for the barman, it was deserted. As Rafe sidled up he heard Appleby order a beer.

"It'll have to be a short one," the barman said. "The police have sealed the block, on account of Bryan being at the Garden, and we're getting ready to close."

Appleby glanced at the wall clock. While he waited for his drink, he helped himself to a pickled egg from a glass bowl. Lost in his thoughts, he paid no attention to Rafe, even when he took off his helmet and set it on the bar. The barman reappeared, and Rafe ordered a root beer for himself. At the sound of his voice, Appleby turned. He seemed surprised to see a policeman. Rafe could see that he didn't remember him.

"I know," Rafe said conspiratorially, "it's against regulations for me to even be in here, but it's so damned hot." They stood side by side for another minute, then Rafe said, "Mr. Appleby. I thought it was you. I'm sorry I didn't recognize you at first."

Appleby stared at him in confusion.

Rafe stuck out his hand. "Otto Raphael. Commissioner Roosevelt's assistant. We met the other afternoon at headquarters."

Appleby took Rafe's hand but still seemed at a loss.

"I made sure the commissioner got your message," he said.

At last Appleby placed him. "Oh, yes, thank you. In fact, I just this minute left the commissioner."

"He said he was coming to see you," Rafe lied. It was amazing how easily the lies were coming these days. "I'm on my way to the Garden myself. As you can imagine, there's a lot to do before tonight. But first, something against the heat, eh?"

Appleby picked up his own mug. "Too bad yours isn't a little stronger."

Rafe smiled back. "The price of duty." He took a long swallow of the sweet, foamy liquid and returned the glass to the bar. Without glancing at Appleby, he said, "That Mann business came as quite a shock, eh?"

Out of the corner of his eye he could see Appleby give him a searching look. "I should say," the other finally agreed.

"A shame to see a man cut down like that," Rafe said. Deciding to take a chance, he turned and met Appleby's gaze. "I wonder, were Mann's activities widely known at Republican headquarters?"

Appleby gave a knowing smile. Rafe could see that he was the kind of man who liked to know things, and to impress others with his knowledge. Though the bar was empty, Appleby inclined his head and whispered, "Well, the candidate wasn't aware, if that's what you mean."

"No, I wouldn't imagine."

"He would never have let us—well, you know."

"Of course not," Rafe extemporized. "He's much too straight for that."

Appleby smirked. "But Mr. Hanna, well, he's a little more liberal-minded. And he's never pressed for cash, which helps, of course."

So that's where the money to pay Mann had come from, the same coal and iron fortune that was helping to fund McKinley's campaign. Was Appleby always so indiscreet? Rafe wondered. And was the beer in his hand the first of the afternoon?

"Of course," Appleby went on, "if he'd gotten wind, Mr. McKinley would have booted that jackass Kellogg clear off the national committee."

"Yes, of course," Rafe murmured. The name meant nothing to him. No, wait, that was one of the people on Mann's list of immunes. He asked, "Where is Kellogg from again?"

"He's a state senator from Ohio. Represents McKinley's district." Appleby leaned closer again. "Between us, I think Mr. Hanna should have forced him out. A man who would behave like that. And with four children."

"He's from Canton," Rafe said.

"That's right."

So the "Canton" in Mann's ledger wasn't the candidate, just another well-connected man with something to hide.

Appleby took a gulp of beer. "At least Mr. Hanna should have made him pay to clean up his own mess. But he claimed not to have the means. Well, I can tell you this, after the election he's going to have to come up with the money himself or his secret is going to come out anyway."

"Not necessarily," Rafe corrected. He glanced from side to side. "Now that Mann ..."

"Oh. Yes, I suppose so," Appleby said.

Rafe gave a quiet sigh. After all his efforts, after all the leads he'd chased, after risking his job, he seemed no closer to discovering Mann's murderer. And tomorrow, or maybe even later tonight, when the commissioner was no longer preoccupied with Bryan's speech, Jacob Riis would tell him of Rafe's ongoing insubordination. The best way to rescue his career was to find the killer in the few hours left to him. But how, when he was back to where he'd started? Mann must have been murdered because of his blackmailing scheme, but the killer was anybody's guess.

He realized that Appleby was speaking. "I imagine the Bryan business is keeping you occupied at headquarters."

Something in the man's tone suggested more than small talk. "By the time of the speech, we'll have more than four hundred men posted here," Rafe offered.

"Yes, so Mr. Roosevelt said. I hope it's enough."

"It was the commissioner's idea to double the detail. There'll be quite a crowd, but that should do it."

"It's not the size of the crowd I'm thinking of," Appleby said. "It's the other business."

Rafe tried to nod knowingly.

"You can imagine our concern," Appleby whispered. "And now it seems we were right to worry. If, God forbid, anything like that did happen, who knows? The outpouring of sympathy for Bryan and the Democrats would be enormous—maybe even enough to alter the course of the election."

It dawned on Rafe that Appleby's urgent message to the commissioner the other afternoon might have had nothing to do with the Mann murder after all. Consumed as he was with the case, he may have jumped to the wrong conclusion.

He leaned closer. "That's why the commissioner visited Mr. Hanna just now," he guessed, "to give him a personal report." A report on what he could only guess.

"Yes," Appleby said. "He wanted to make sure we knew about the arrest."

"Of course." *What arrest?*

"The commissioner has been quite obliging," Appleby said with a smug expression. "Word is he's hoping for something at Navy. He's offered to do some stumping out west." That was news to Rafe.

"Apparently the man confessed, after a little persuasion from your detective, if you know what I mean."

"Which detective?"

"He didn't say. But how do we know the Pole doesn't have friends? If you ask me, the Democrats should cancel the speech. But of course Bryan won't hear of it. Called it 'a Republican ploy to steal my thunder.'"

Rafe tried to make sense of it all. A plot concerning the speech tonight. The arrest of a Pole. Appleby's belief that coconspirators might still at large. No wonder Mr. Roosevelt had been adamant about putting on so many extra patrolmen. He must have known about the plot before the meeting yesterday afternoon. But why hadn't he reported the threat to the group? From Conlin's skeptical reaction, Rafe was sure the chief knew nothing about a possible attack. Not for the first time, Rafe was afraid he was in over his head. *Logic and perseverance*, he reminded himself.

The barman pointed to the clock, and Appleby downed the rest of his beer.

Rafe bid him a friendly goodbye as they left, and Appleby headed toward the Garden's main entrance. Rafe retraced his steps to Madison Square Park, where the ticket holders' line already stretched down the block.

He crossed the street and entered the square. The park, being outside the police cordon, was packed. As he pushed through the throng, his brain lurched in a dozen different directions. Why would a terrorist action be planned for Bryan's speech? Bryan was the hero of the working class. Why not McKinley, champion of the rich? It must be a matter of opportunity, he realized. To the anarchists, one candidate was pretty much the same as another. With McKinley holed up at his home in Canton, he wasn't presenting an opening. But here, in Madison Square Garden, at the biggest public meeting of the year, Bryan offered an irresistible target.

And what form was the violence meant to take? An assassination, like with President Garfield? A bombing, like at the Haymarket? The anarchists didn't much care, as long as it terrorized the city, and the nation. Rafe recalled his father's words: "They think we're all anarchists and terrorists." And now, as if to prove them right, here apparently was a terror attack planned by a Polish immigrant, maybe more. If that didn't bring the

American Cossacks down on them—the innocent as much as the guilty—nothing would.

Was that why the commissioner had been acting cold toward him? he suddenly wondered. With the anarchists planning an attack, did Mr. Roosevelt doubt Rafe's loyalty? Despite everything, beneath it all was the commissioner just as anti-immigrant as the rest of the department? Rafe shook off the question.

He looked at his watch. Six fifteen. Forty-five minutes before the doors would open to ticket holders. There were already more than four hundred cops here, but since they presumably knew nothing of any plot, they'd be more concerned with spotting drunks than terrorists. For that matter, what could he hope to accomplish here himself? No, he had a better idea. Forgetting the heat, forgetting his throbbing head, he sprinted out of the park and headed east, toward Fourth Avenue.

There were no cabs, and finally Rafe jumped onto a trolley. As he stood in the packed rush-hour car, he thought about the Pole who was being held at headquarters. The man had confessed, according to Appleby, "after a little persuasion from your detective." The commissioner hadn't mentioned which detective, but Rafe had a hunch. Gallagher was on the anti-terror squad. Was that why he'd been strutting in and out of Mr. Roosevelt's office over the past couple of days, because he'd uncovered an attack planned for the Garden tonight? The more Rafe thought about it, the more sense it made. And it would be just like Gallagher to beat a confession out of a suspect.

But wasn't it odd that Gallagher was also the officer investigating Mann's murder? Were there no other detectives in the Fourth Precinct? Or was there some connection between the cases? Vynne had said that Mann's informers were servants who spied on the wealthy. Could one of his spies have gotten wind of an anarchist plot, maybe from a fellow servant? Was that the spectacular story Mann was planning to break in the next edition of *Town Topics*? Was that why he was killed, not because of his blackmailing?

Conlin probably knew nothing about the plot because the commissioner didn't trust his own chief enough to take him into his confidence. Maybe Mr. Roosevelt was afraid that word would leak and cause a public panic. Or reflect badly on the department. That wouldn't do if the commissioner were hoping for an appointment in a McKinley administration.

The streetcar jolted to a stop, and Rafe was thrown against the woman standing ahead of him. Glancing out the front window, he saw that a draft horse had gone down on its knees, stranding a movers' van across the tracks. As Rafe watched, the teamster jumped from the wagon and raised his whip. He brought it down hard on the horse's back, but the beast barely managed to raise its head from the pavement. The driver lifted his hand again, and Rafe looked away. It was clear the horse wouldn't be getting up, no matter how much the man flogged it.

Rafe peered out the trolley's side window to get his bearings. To his right was the plain brick pediment of the Mercantile Library. They were in Astor Place. Maybe half a mile from headquarters. He pushed his way to the door, jumped down to the pavement, and began to run like someone's life depended on it.

∼∗∞

Dutch heard the lock click shut. He made himself count to thirty, then ran to the door. He jiggled the knob, though he knew it was pointless. He raised a fist over his head but stopped before bringing it down on the door's varnished oak. What good would banging do? Or yelling? There was no one but other policemen.

He leaned his back against the door and looked about the dim room. Other than the display cases with their shining weapons locked inside, there was no furniture, no stray tools, nothing at all. On the opposite wall was a line of narrow windows, arched in brick. Across each one, inside the glass, was a row of thick black bars. Dutch moved toward them.

That's when he saw a pair of bare feet dangle into view, stretching to find the ground. They looked as though they hadn't seen water in a month. As Dutch watched, scabby shins followed, then some dusty knickerbockers. The feet caught the earth, and in another second a face bent toward the glass then, startled, jumped back out of view. But Dutch had gotten enough of a look.

Grady reappeared. Apparently, he'd recognized Dutch, because he was shaking his head as if to say, *I told you, this is what happens when you get mixed up with coppers.*

"What are you doing?" Dutch called through the dirty glass. And how did he manage to get back here, away from the street?

Grady pointed to him.

"You were looking for me?" Dutch asked.

Grady glanced from side to side, then decided to risk speaking. Bending close to the glass, he said, "I saw you run across the street."

"How did you know I was down in the basement?"

Grady pointed to his eye, then to Dutch.

"You saw that, too?" He must have followed him as far as the front door. That took guts, especially after Grady's run-in with Gallagher in the alley. It occurred to Dutch that maybe Grady was a better friend than he'd given him credit for.

Grady knelt and gazed beyond Dutch, taking in as much of the room as he could through the tiny window. He pointed to one of the glass cases hanging on the wall. Dutch turned and saw a row of nightsticks on display. He looked toward Grady and shrugged.

Grady pantomimed putting his elbow through the glass case, grabbing one of the weapons, and swinging it down on an invisible target. Then he cocked his head and closed his eyes, as though unconscious.

"He'll kill me," Dutch said.

Grady opened his palm and made a sweeping gesture toward the room.

Dutch followed his hand, taking in any number of potential instruments of torture, all neatly arrayed in their glass cases, just waiting for Gallagher to come back. He turned to Grady.

The older boy was nodding sagely. "Do it," he mouthed.

By the time Rafe reached Mulberry Street, he looked as though he'd been caught in a cloudburst. His uniform was soaked through, and sweat was flowing down his forehead and into his eyes. After jumping from the trolley, he'd pulled off his helmet and tugged open the top two buttons of his uniform coat, but that had accomplished nothing except to add to his wild appearance. As he sprinted down the Bowery, pressing one hand against his throbbing temple, shoppers flattened themselves against the storefronts and mothers hugged their children to their skirts.

It was six forty-five when he reached headquarters. The Garden would be opening in a quarter hour. He ran through the lobby and down the stairs, past the telegraph office and the shut door of the Mystery Chamber. A little farther down, the hallway jogged to the right; at the end was another door, leading to the building's few holding cells. Since prisoners were generally booked in the arresting officer's precinct house, these cells didn't see much use. But this afternoon a young patrolman named Schneider was stationed at the entrance. There must be a prisoner. "Gallagher isn't in there, is he?" Rafe asked.

Schneider took in the soaking uniform, the wild look in his eye. "What the hell happened to you?" he asked. "Gallagher hasn't been by in hours. Why?"

"I need to talk to the Pole," he said.

Schneider turned out his lower lip and shook his head. "Orders are, nobody talks to the prisoner."

"Whose orders?"

"Gallagher's. I don't know what the poor bastard did, but it must have been really something."

Rafe moved a step closer. "Well, I just left Commissioner Roosevelt, and my orders are to have a word with the prisoner. I need to see if I can get anything out of him before it's too late."

He could see Schneider considering it. "What did he do?"

Rafe pursed his lips to show he wasn't at liberty to say.

"Well," Schneider said, "you know what a son of a bitch Gallagher can be."

Rafe made another step toward the door. "If you don't take my word for it, go upstairs and ask for yourself," he bluffed. "Mr. Roosevelt is up there now. Tell him how you wouldn't open the door for me, even on his orders. You'll be retirement age before he lets you on the street again."

Schneider winced. Rafe knew he'd been cited for sleeping on duty a couple of months ago, and he'd had the rotten luck to be caught by the commissioner himself, on one of his midnight rambles with Jacob Riis. That's how he'd been pulled back to headquarters and assigned this pitiful duty.

"All right, all right," Schneider said. He took a ring of oversize keys from his pocket and held one up for Rafe.

Rafe took the ring and slipped the key into the lock. The door clicked open. Beyond was a short, dim hallway. To the left were three small cells, with iron bars running from floor to ceiling. The only light entered though a few narrow windows, arched and barred and set high in the outside wall. The first two cells were empty except for a wire cot with a thin mattress rolled up on top.

Rafe stopped in front of the last cell. In the dim light it took him a second to understand what he was seeing. The cot had been pushed against the outside wall, under the window. On the floor beside it, a figure was slumped with his feet stretched out in front of him and his back propped against the bricks. His head was sagging forward, onto his chest. There was no movement, no sound. Rafe couldn't tell if the man was breathing or not.

He fumbled with the keys until he found the one that opened the cell door. Kneeling beside him, he lifted the man's head and examined his face. The prisoner let out a low groan.

He was about his own age, Rafe saw, with fair hair and a thin beard. His face was bruised, and one eye was swollen shut. That must be the "persuasion" Appleby had been talking about. Wrapped around his neck was a worn brown leather belt, folded through the buckle to form a slip knot. On its free end was a ragged tear. Overhead, a short length of the belt was looped around an iron bar in the cell window. Apparently, the worn leather had given way under the man's weight.

Rafe gave him a shake, and he groaned again. Then, with tremendous effort, he opened his good eye. On seeing Rafe's uniform, he drew back. He squinted around the cell, as if trying to recollect where he was and what had happened to him.

"Bistu oukey?" Rafe asked. Are you okay?

The prisoner's sunken eye opened a little wider on hearing his native Yiddish. He struggled to focus on Rafe's face.

Rafe pulled the belt away from the man's neck. The skin beneath was red and broken. "Mayn nomen iz Otto Raphael," he told him. "Vos iz dayn nomen?"

The man glowered at him, as if to say, *What's that to you?*

"Vos iz dayn nomen?" Rafe repeated.

The man watched him. Finally, he said, "Abram Smolenski."

Rafe kept talking in Yiddish, hoping to help the prisoner come around. "I was born in the village of Krasnopol, in the province of Podlaskie, under the Russians. My family came here when I was a boy, after the pogroms started. What about you, where are you from?"

The prisoner pushed him away. "What does it matter where I'm from?" he rasped. "What concern is it of yours? They just sent you here because you speak Yiddish."

"What did you do?" Rafe asked.

He drew himself up. "If I wouldn't talk to your thug, even after he did this—" he touched his swollen eye—"why do you think I would talk to you? You, an immigrant yourself, you should be ashamed—"

"But you did talk," Rafe said. "To the detective, Gallagher."

"I have nothing to hide," Smolenski fired back. "I have committed no crime, except to ask for food for the hungry, houses for the homeless, jobs for the unemployed. Good jobs, not ones that will maim and kill workers, not jobs that steal the childhood from the little ones who work in the mines and factories. And this is my reward." He pointed to the iron bars. "This is your great American capitalism, your justice."

Rafe sat back on his heels. "Tell me what happened."

Smolenski sighed. "You know what happened. This morning, your thug comes to my office and arrests me, I don't even know for what. My only crime is to edit a newspaper that seeks to tell the truth."

"What newspaper?" Rafe asked.

The Pole glanced around the cell and gave a bitter smile. "It's called *Frayheyt*," he said. *Freedom.*

"Gallagher brought you down here, and you made a confession."

"Confession to what? I have nothing to hide."

"What did you tell the detective about the terror plot?"

"Terror plot, terror plot! What terror plot? You people see terror plots everywhere. What is wrong with you?"

But Appleby said the Pole had confessed. "You admitted the crime. You signed a confession."

"Why would I sign? The thug wrote something out in English, but I refused. I tell you, I have done nothing."

Rafe had a sudden thought. "Do you speak English?" he asked.

Smolenski shook his head. "Only a little."

"If you're innocent, why did you do this to yourself?"

The man let out a sour laugh. "You think I did this? You're a bigger fool than I thought, Officer Raphael."

"Gallagher did?" Rafe asked.

"He hit me with his nightstick—here," he said, feeling the top of his head. Rafe could see a good-sized lump and dried blood matting his sandy hair. "And the next thing I know, you're bending over me."

Why would Gallagher stage his suicide? To save the nuisance of a trial? Was Gallagher capable of murder?

"You had no plan to go to Madison Square Garden tonight?" Rafe asked.

"For what?"

"Do you know somebody named William d'Alton Mann?"

"More questions!" the Pole shouted. "Always more questions! I don't know him!"

Rafe studied the prisoner. Was he really ready to take the word of a suspect over one of the department's own detectives? If the man didn't admit to knowing anything about the plot, if he said he hadn't signed anything, what kind of confession did Gallagher have?

Then he understood. Damn Gallagher. Inside every immigrant he saw a terrorist. Now he'd arrested an innocent man and concocted a phony confession. But if the only evidence of the supposed plot came from Gallagher, how could they be sure there was a plot at all? Maybe Gallagher had fabricated that, too, to crush the hated immigrants. On the other hand, if there really was a plot, then the actual perpetrator was still free. Someone who even now could be making his way toward Madison Square Garden. And that was a risk Rafe couldn't afford to take.

"A dank," he told the prisoner. Thank you. He knew it wasn't enough, but there would be time for more later. He sprinted through the door at the end of the hallway and threw the heavy keys into Schneider's lap. The patrolman yelled a curse after him, but Rafe was already halfway up the corridor. He called, "Look after the prisoner! Get a doctor, right away!"

As he ran, he kept his helmet in his hand but rebuttoned his tunic. By the time he got to the third floor, his breathing was ragged and his face was running with fresh sweat.

Minnie, working late, was bent over her typewriter. On seeing him, her eyes widened and her fingers stilled above the keyboard. "What happened to you?"

"Is the commissioner in?" he asked. He knew it was a long shot, but he had to try.

"No, he hasn't been back all afternoon. What's the matter?"
He stole a look into Mr. Roosevelt's office.

"I said he hasn't been here. He must be on his way to
Madison Square Garden by now. What's going on?"

Rafe rubbed his eyes. His head was pounding so badly it
nearly drowned out her voice.

"Rafe!" Minnie had stood up from her desk and was coming
toward him.

He gazed into her face. He couldn't involve her in this
insanity. It was one thing if he lost his own job, but he wasn't
about to jeopardize hers.

Standing in front of him now, she took his clammy wrists
in her hands. "Rafe, let me help you."

He pulled away. Then he ran out the door and down the
staircase. He didn't look back.

NINE

BEFORE GRADY KNEW what was happening, it was already too late.

He'd been urging Dutch to break into one of the glass cases and find a weapon he could use to escape from his basement prison. Now through the narrow arched window he saw Dutch startle, then sprint across the room toward the door. The instant it swung open, he bolted out, but someone on the other side tried to slam it again, pinning him between the door and the jamb.

Grady could make out Gallagher's red face in the hallway. As the detective pressed his weight against the door, he stuck out a hand to grab Dutch by the neck. Dutch threw his head back, and when Gallagher snatched only air, he tipped forward and sank his teeth into the heel of Gallagher's hand. The detective's face screwed up in pain, and he pulled away, cracking the door open a little wider. Dutch disappeared into the hallway. In another instant, Gallagher was after him.

Suddenly, Grady was alone at the window. Straightening up, he took a good look around. He was in a narrow, paved courtyard, with the walls of police headquarters rising on all four sides. To get out, he had to retrace his steps. He had come here by darting through the unguarded front door and down a hallway, then lowering himself through an open window six or seven feet to the ground. Apparently, no one had seen him—*Some cops*, he thought—but what with all the windows looking down onto the yard, he figured it was only a matter of time.

He took a running start and made a jump for the window-sill. His fingers caught it but slipped, and he fell back to the ground. Then he paced off a dozen feet, turned, and began to run again. When he reached the wall, he found a foothold on the brick arch above the basement window. Pushing off, he got high enough to thrust his arms through the open sash and catch the sill. He heaved himself over and fell inside.

He glanced from one end of the hallway to the other, then ran to the lobby and out the front door. He had expected to see Dutch's skinny legs tearing up the street, ahead of the pursuing Gallagher. But in one direction the sidewalk was empty, and in the other were only a couple of men strolling, taking their time on account of the heat. Grady made his way down the steps, determined to find his friend before Gallagher did.

❧

As Dutch cleared the doorjamb, he started running, past the telegraph room and up the main staircase to the deserted lobby.

His first thought was to race straight to the third story and find Officer Rafe. Then he had another idea. He flung himself onto the floor and rolled under the wooden bench where he and Miss Minnie had eaten their lemon ice.

Flattening his back against the wall, he watched the lobby and struggled to quiet his breathing. In a second, he saw Gallagher coming up from the basement. The copper stopped, breathing hard, then threw a look up the empty staircase and cocked his head for a listen. Then he dashed out the front door.

Dutch counted to ten and scrambled from under the bench. He ran back toward the stairway and began to take the steps two at a time, but before he had made the first landing, he could hear heavy footsteps behind him. Turning, he saw Gallagher barreling in his direction. "Come here, you little son of a bitch!"

The crude words and the rasping voice struck something deep, but Dutch had no time to try and place why. As fast as he could, he reached the second story. One more floor to Rafe's office. Glancing over his shoulder, he could see that he was increasing his lead over Gallagher. But as he made the turn onto the next flight, he nearly ran into two older men in business suits standing together in the wide hallway.

"Stop him!" Gallagher yelled from below. Dutch was gone before they could react.

From the third-floor landing, he spied Gallagher a good way below. He had no idea where on this floor Rafe's office might be, so he ran into the first doorway he saw. In front of him, sitting at a desk, was Miss Minnie.

"Where's . . . Rafe?" he managed, out of breath.

She seemed even more startled than he was. "Dutch—?"

"Please," he huffed. "I need to . . . talk to Rafe."

She saw the terror on his face. "Rafe's not here," she told him.

"Where?"

"Madison Square Garden."

Dutch heard the footsteps on the landing. He hesitated, then decided that, however much Miss Minnie might want to, she wouldn't be able to protect him from Gallagher. Without another word, he tore through the office door and into the hallway.

Minnie rushed after the boy and saw him reach the stairway just as Gallagher was staggering to the top. He dodged past the detective, taking him by surprise. What the poor child had done, Minnie couldn't imagine, but as Gallagher turned to pursue him, she heard herself whisper, "Run, Dutch!" Then she grabbed her purse and made for the stairs.

※

Grady lingered at the bottom of the tall granite steps. Normally, he wouldn't have stood so long in front of a police station, but he'd been stuck here trying to figure out what to do. Some copper had left one of those new police bicycles leaning against the lamppost, and Grady ran a finger idly over its chromium handlebars. When he heard the slap of bare feet on stone, he turned to find Dutch sprinting past him down the front steps.

"Run!" Dutch yelled as he flew past.

Grady's first impulse was to do just that, but he made himself hold his ground. He was thinking of the whack on the side of the head that Gallagher had given him in the alley the other day, and all the whacks New York's Finest had given him over the years. As Gallagher came running out the door, the boy extended his foot. Just a few inches, but enough. The detective lurched forward, flailing his arms and catching Grady around the shoulders. As they tumbled, he came down hard on Grady's leg. There was a *crack*, then the worst pain Grady had ever felt. He thought, *So that's what it's like to break a bone.*

Gallagher pushed himself partway up and pounded his fist on Grady's bad leg, making him scream in pain. He called again after Dutch, "Come here, you little son of a bitch!"

Dutch had turned at the sound of Grady's scream. Now, again, the words struck a chord, not just in their raspy timbre but the exact phrase. With a force that nearly stopped him dead, he realized why. It was the same voice, and those were the same words he had heard in the alley off Rose Street, as he'd leaped from the pile of crates and run for his life. The detective hadn't just gone to the alley later to investigate the murder. It was Gallagher who had chased him that night, Gallagher he'd seen bending over the body. Did that mean that Gallagher was the killer? He put his head down and, pumping his arms, ran for his life.

As Dutch raced up Mott Street, he had no thought but to get to Madison Square Garden. He'd heard of the place. It was the building with the naked gold lady on top. Some kind of theater. He'd even seen it from a distance one time when he was out with his mother. But he'd never been there, and he had only a hazy idea of where it was. Probably near Madison Square, wherever that was. Well, Broadway led to just about everywhere. If he went up Broadway, he couldn't go too far wrong.

Mulberry dead-ended half a block north of police head-quarters, just past a big stone church. Dutch turned to the left onto Bleecker. The street was run-down, like all the streets around here, and tonight it was deserted, with little traffic and few pedestrians. As he ran down the empty sidewalk, he dared to look behind him. Gallagher had recovered from his fall. Out on the open street, he was hitting his stride, closing the distance between them.

At the end of the next block, two big banks anchored the corner of Broadway. He turned north. Broadway couldn't have been more different from Bleecker, with hotels and stores and office towers lining the avenue as far as he could see. Some of the buildings must have been a dozen stories or more, looming over the pedestrians below. The sidewalk was teeming, mostly with men in business suits and couples in evening dress. It was too crowded to run without bumping into people. Besides, he doubted he could run all the way to Madison Square Garden, not in this heat. He slowed to a brisk walk, trying to catch his breath and disappear into the crowd. Fortunately, nobody was more invisible than a New York City newsboy.

⁂

By the time Minnie reached Grady, he was sitting with his back propped against the granite steps. His legs were stretched out in front of him, and he was holding his left shin with both hands. "Where did that boy go that just ran by here?" she asked.

Grady shook his head. That's when she noticed a tear slipping down his dusty cheek. "What happened to you?" she asked.

"It's busted," he told her.

She knelt beside him. "Let me take a look at that." From the swelling she tended to agree with his diagnosis.

He gave her a weak smile. "But I slowed the bast—I mean, the copper—down all right."

"You're a friend of Dutch's," she said.

"Yeah, I guess you could say that."

"Where did he go?" she asked him again.

He gave her a suspicious look.

"It's all right," she said. "I work with the police."

He turned away. Clearly, that wasn't the way to win his trust. She tried again. "I'm Dutch's friend, too. I can help him."

He turned toward her. "How do you know Dutch?"

Minnie thought for a second. If Dutch knew Rafe, maybe this boy did, too. "I work with Officer Rafe," she said.

Grady looked her in the eyes. "Rafe's okay, for a copper," he admitted. Finally, he told her, "Gallagher's after Dutch. They went up there."

Minnie glanced in that direction, but they had already made the corner. "What did Dutch do?" she asked.

"It ain't what he did, it's what he saw, more like. I wouldn't want to be in his shoes when Gallagher catches him."

"What did he see?"

Grady only shook his head. She would get nothing more from him. She went inside to the telephone switchboard, and a few minutes later a surgeon arrived from the Tenth Precinct, just down the block. While he examined the boy, Minnie considered her options. Dutch was no doubt headed toward Madison Square Garden, but with police stationed everywhere, he would never get inside.

Why was he so desperate to find Rafe? And why was he so terrified of Detective Gallagher? What Gallagher wanted with him, she didn't know, but she felt a deep urge to protect the boy. And she ought to let Rafe know something was wrong, that Dutch needed him. How could she get to the Garden in time?

That was when she saw the gleaming police bike leaning against the lamppost.

❧

Gallagher turned the corner onto Broadway and spotted the capless blond head bobbing through the crowd. He was relieved to see that the boy had slowed to a fast walk. The detective slowed, too. He knew there was no way he could outrun the urchin, especially in this infernal heat.

He'd like to kill the little bastard. It was humiliating, really, the trouble he'd caused. All because he'd been somewhere he shouldn't have been and seen something he shouldn't have. Just like a newsboy. They were all thieves and snoops at heart. Most weren't even American. And now, tonight, when he should already be inside Madison Square Garden, here he was out on the street having to corral the little son of a bitch.

Well, there was nothing for it. At least he was heading in the right direction. He took out his watch. Seven thirty. There was still time. He'd deal with the newsboy first, then he could concentrate on the real business of the evening. He picked up his pace.

❧

The sidewalk clock standing in front of some fancy hotel read seven thirty as Dutch raced by. The sun was down, and the roadway was already in shadow. Soon the electric streetlamps would be switching on. He swiveled again but couldn't pick out Gallagher in the crowd behind him. It seemed the detective had given up running, too. But did he still have him in his sights? Was he gaining on him? Every stride, he reminded himself, was one step closer to Madison Square Garden and to Rafe. But would Rafe be able to protect him? Would he even believe him when Dutch told him what Gallagher had done?

North of Astor Place he passed a row of department stores, their cast-iron facades and wide plate glass windows filled with every geegaw money could buy. At Tenth Street, Broadway took a jog to the left, and a carved stone steeple rose directly in front of him. To one side of the church was a peaceful garden, with pink roses climbing over an iron trellis. It looked like the kind of place where nothing bad could happen to you. As he hurried by, the church's thick wooden door opened, and a lady stepped out wearing a black flowered hat and a pair of spotless white gloves. He hadn't been in a church for months, and he was tempted to run inside. Then he asked himself what Grady would do and kept moving.

"Hey, lady!" he called. "Which way to Madison Square Garden?"

She startled, then turned a thin, kind face in his direction. "Straight up Broadway," she said with a perplexed expression.

Across the street was another department store. JAMES McCREERY & Co., according to the sign above the entrance. The tall arched windows and the tan awning seemed familiar. He was sure he'd been there once with his mother. "Just to look," he remembered her saying. Even when his father was working, they could never have afforded anything at McCreery's.

How much farther could it be to Madison Square Garden? He glanced behind him again. This time, sandwiched between two men in straw boaters, not twenty feet away, he saw Gallagher's bloated face. He was huffing and covered with sweat, and his eyes locked on Dutch with a hatred that made him shudder.

Without thinking, Dutch leaped off the curb and into the street. Broadway was wide here, with two trolley tracks running down the center, and crowded with every kind of vehicle. He dashed between a black hansom and a lumbering beer wagon, only to find himself in the path of a northbound streetcar. The driver pulled on his bell but didn't slow. Dutch hopped to the side just in time, and as the trolley passed he grabbed the brass handrail to pull himself onto the car's back step. He felt a wrenching pain in his shoulder, then his hand slipped and he was pitched headlong toward the pavement.

Recovering his balance, he dodged traffic and made for the opposite curb, toward the storybook windows of McCreery's. A middle-aged shopper loaded down with packages was emerging just as he reached the entrance. Dutch ducked, but his head grazed her elbow, and her arms flailed in a shower of bags and boxes. He grabbed hold of the open door and ran inside.

The store was just as he remembered. The high ceiling was hung with huge electric chandeliers. Along each of the outside walls, under a row of tall windows, a line of sleek wooden cabinets were fitted with drawers and doors of all different sizes. In front of the cabinets were wooden counters, where well-dressed ladies sat on swivel stools while salesmen unfolded bolts of colorful fabrics. A quiet hum filled the room, echoing off the ceiling and the tile floor, almost like the drone of praying voices. McCreery's seemed like another place where nothing bad could happen to you.

He avoided the wide center aisle, with its tall fluted columns, and made for a narrow archway off the showroom. He crouched inside, his eyes trained on the store entrance. A few seconds later he saw Gallagher rush in. He spoke to a trim man who had hurried to the front door, drawn by the ruckus with the lady and her packages. Dutch guessed he was the manager, or maybe the store detective. Gallagher showed his badge, and the two talked briefly. Then they fanned out, the manager moving toward the far side of the store and Gallagher taking the near.

Gallagher peered down the center aisle, then, seeing nothing suspicious, started in Dutch's direction. Looking behind him, Dutch saw an oversized cardboard box. He pulled off the top. As he was climbing inside, a face appeared around the corner of the cabinet. The boy was a couple of years younger than Dutch, dressed in a dark blue suit with a bleached white collar and a floppy blue tie. Dutch thought he was the cleanest boy he had ever seen. His eyes met Dutch's, then traveled down to his stained shirt and worn knickerbockers and bare feet. It was too late to make a run for it. Dutch put a finger to his lips, drew the cardboard top over him, and curled up in the darkness, trying to still his breathing.

In a moment, he heard Gallagher's husky voice ask, "Sonny, have you seen a boy come this way?"

There was a pause. Then Dutch heard a high voice answer, "No, sir."

Dutch counted to twenty before he cracked open the lid. Gallagher was nowhere in sight. Dutch gave the clean boy a wink as he crept by, and the boy flashed him a wide grin.

He crept to the end of the counter and stood just high enough to peer over the top. Gallagher was about a quarter of the way down the center aisle now, talking to one of the salesmen. Dutch straightened up and, against his every instinct, forced himself to move deliberately, trying not to attract attention. McCreery's was one place in New York where a newsboy definitely was not invisible.

Just then a man called, "Stop!" Turning, Dutch saw the store manager pointing at him. Gallagher had heard him too and was running up the center aisle. Dutch sprinted to the front door, threw it open, and spilled back onto the sidewalk.

As he ran across Twelfth Street, Gallagher was close behind him. The sidewalks were just as crowded here, but Dutch knew that even a brisk walk was no longer an option. He raced up Broadway, knocking into pedestrians, running up their heels, leaving a string of shouts and curses in his wake. More hotels and theaters flashed by, but Dutch barely took them in. He came to the broad expanse of Fourteenth Street, stretching before him like the Red Sea before the Israelites. Beyond beckoned the leafy canopy of Union Square. On the near corner, a potbellied traffic cop was standing in his sweat-stained uniform, trying to exercise some control over the chaotic intersection.

Dutch heard Gallagher's voice. "Officer, stop that boy!"

The patrolman fixed his eyes on Dutch then took a step toward him, but Dutch spun away easily. The man put a small brass cylinder to his lips, and as Dutch waded into traffic he heard the shrill call of a police whistle. He dodged and weaved his way into the park, darting directly in the path of a police cyclist in a peaked cap and blue double-breasted uniform. The wheelman reached across his handlebars but missed. While he spun his bicycle around, Dutch began running up the park's wide center path.

Dutch knew Union Square. For several nights he had slept under a bench here, until a patrolman had run him off with a swat of his nightstick. Just inside the park's entrance, the central path split off to the east and west. In between lay a broad grassy oval, dotted with trees and ringed with wooden benches. Dutch hurdled a bench, startling a young couple, and raced over the grass. By now the wheelman was peddling up the western path, eyeing the boy like a circling tiger.

Taking the more direct route, Dutch reached the end of the oval before the cyclist did. Just beyond, several winding pathways converged on a round drinking fountain. In the center stood a bronze sculpture of a woman with an infant in her arms and another child standing beside her. Dutch had often wondered about the statue but had finally decided that she must be a mother protecting her babies.

He skirted the fountain, keeping it between him and the policeman, then dodged onto another swath of grass. The wheelman circled the monument and came up to the east, but again the boy got there first and darted across the cinder path.

He had reached Seventeenth Street, the square's northern boundary. Ahead of him was a small brick building shaped like a fat cross. He leapt the low picket fence and crawled into the bushes growing along the foundation, hugging the ground and fighting to catch his breath, all the while watching for the cyclist. Then the copper stopped, one foot planted on either side of the bike's center bar. He peered this way and that, but he looked hot and tired, and Dutch could see his heart wasn't in it. Eventually, the man made a lazy circle around the building, then drifted back into Union Square.

Dutch counted to sixty. Then he stood and wiped his forearm across his brow to mop the sweat. He brushed the dirt and twigs off his clothes as best he could. Not seeing the wheelman or Gallagher or any other cop, he dodged across the street. He turned west, and in half a block, as he knew he would, he came to Broadway again. The sidewalk was even more crowded here, mostly with men in dark suits and straw hats. Everyone was walking north with a deliberate stride, as though they were all headed to the same destination.

Dutch fell in step. He looked behind him from time to time but saw no sign of Gallagher. He turned to a man beside him. On the man's lapel was a celluloid pin with a picture of a crucifix and the slogan, No cross of gold, no crown of thorns.

"Hey, mister," Dutch said. "How far is it to Madison Square Garden?"

The man laughed. "Just follow the crowd, sonny. You're not far. A young Bryanite, are you? Good for you!"

Dutch had seen enough headlines in the newspapers he sold to know that William Jennings Bryan was running against William McKinley for president. But since he hadn't been able to peddle his papers for the past couple of days, he hadn't known that Bryan was coming to New York.

He kept moving. Every so often he threw a look over his shoulder, but he saw no sign of Gallagher. In another few blocks, Broadway grew even wider as it merged with Fifth Avenue. On the corner of Twenty-third was the biggest and fanciest hotel Dutch had ever seen, its entrance flanked by thick columns holding up a simple stone pediment. FIFTH AVENUE HOTEL, said the letters carved above the door. Parked outside was a handsome landau with the top down and red, white, and blue bunting hanging from the sides. Hundreds of men were gathered around the carriage, spilling from the sidewalk into the street. Some were holding signs that said FREE SILVER and CROSS OF GOLD and YOU TELL 'EM, BILLY! As he swept by in the throng, Dutch heard a man asking, "Tickets for tonight? Anybody have extra tickets for tonight?" It hadn't occurred to Dutch that he'd need a ticket.

To his right was a large park with winding paths and towering trees. He remembered being here with his mother, too. The trees had shone red and gold in the sharp autumn sun, and the two of them had sat on a bench and eaten sandwiches they'd brought from home. Now, on the square's northeast corner, atop her tall, square tower, Dutch spied the landmark he'd been searching for—the golden lady who floated above Madison

Square Garden, with a hunter's bow in her hand and a bit of fabric flowing from her bare shoulder.

The throng surged across the roadway and into the park, but tonight the trees offered no relief from the stifling heat. At the park's northern end the crowd came to an abrupt stop. Ducking under and around the swarm, Dutch pushed his way to the corner of Madison and Twenty-sixth. Across the street was the Garden's main entrance, hidden under a long row of pointed stone arches that reached all the way out to the curb. Behind an uneven line of wooden sawhorses, policemen were inspecting tickets before allowing anyone through. Excited voices echoed off the tall buildings. With all the pushing and shoving, Dutch thought a riot might break out at any minute.

He huddled against a building and tried to think. He supposed he could explain to the patrolmen that he needed to see Officer Rafe, but considering his experience with New York's Finest, he quickly rejected that idea. Well, he'd been dodging policemen all afternoon; maybe he could do it here too, just duck under a sawhorse and lose himself in the crowd. Not likely, he saw, since cops were stationed every few feet down the length of the barricade.

From behind came the sound of horses' hooves. Turning, he saw a black vehicle creeping down Twenty-sixth Street, parting the crowd as it went. As it pulled even with him, Dutch saw a red cross painted on the side. Below that, large gold letters read AMBULANCE and BELLEVUE HOSPITAL. Between the tailgate and the cabin was a flat, open bed with an arched roof and low wooden side panels. Seeing his chance, Dutch pushed his way to the curb, climbed onto the vehicle's low metal step, and lifted himself over the back. Flattened against the tailgate on the ambulance floor, he held his breath and waited for a shout from the crowd or the driver or the police, but there was only the *clop-clop* of the animal's hooves and the buzz of thousands of people.

As he'd climbed inside, Dutch hadn't dared to look behind. If he had, he might have noticed a dark, burly man in a cheap suit, emerging from Madison Square just in time to watch a small, shoeless boy disappear into the back of an ambulance. Gallagher rubbed his sleeve across his red, sweaty face, then pressed through the crowd toward the police barricade.

TEN

WHEN THE AMBULANCE stopped its halting progress, Dutch figured they'd reached the police line. He pressed himself even tighter against the tailgate.

"You got to be on Twenty-seventh!" he heard a deep voice yell. The driver must not have been able to hear above the crowd, because the same man shouted again, "Twenty-seventh! The Twenty-seventh Street door!" Then Dutch heard the scraping of sawhorses and felt the ambulance veer to the left.

Madison Avenue was even more packed than Twenty-sixth Street, and for long moments the vehicle scarcely moved at all. Every so often, Dutch poked his head over the side rail and searched the Garden's high stone walls for just one unguarded opening. There was a row of plain square windows, but every one of them was shut tight. Toward the far corner a loading ramp led up to a pair of heavy wooden doors. They were open, but two policemen were stationed outside.

The ambulance made the corner then rocked to a stop. Peeking over the rail again, Dutch saw a cop talking to the driver. His heart jumped: were they going to search the back? Then he saw a line of patrolmen stretching down the street behind him, away from the Garden. Farther down the block, half a dozen carriages were coming his way. The one in front was a fancy open landau with bunting down the sides. The same carriage he'd seen in front of the Fifth Avenue Hotel.

As it drew nearer, Dutch could make out four men seated inside. One was tipping his hat and waving as a cry went up from the crowd, "Hurrah for Bryan!" So that was the famous William Jennings Bryan. Dutch was surprised at how young he seemed, and how handsome, with his broad shoulders and dark hair and open, friendly face. He looked like the sort of person you could tell your troubles to. As the carriage rumbled past, Dutch would have sworn the great man stared him in the eye and smiled.

After another minute, the policeman stepped to the curb, and the ambulance continued down Twenty-seventh Street. On this side of the Garden was a back entrance, covered by a stone portico. That must be where Bryan was headed, too. Between there and the near corner was another row of big square windows. The first was closed, but electric light was spilling through the second. Dutch studied the sidewalk. It was crowded, but all heads were turned down the block, toward Bryan. He lowered himself over the tailgate and slipped into the dark street.

Staying low, he worked his way toward the black iron fence surrounding this side of the building. He was behind the crowd now. Stepping onto a crossbar, about two feet off the ground, he gripped the fence's top rail and hiked himself up, until he was straddling the top. Then he swung himself across and dropped silently to the ground.

No one seemed to have noticed him. Creeping to the open window, he looked inside. It was some kind of workroom. In the center was a wide table, and along two walls were shelves filled with cans of paint. Against another wall were stacked huge rectangles of wood and canvas. The one on top was painted with red, white, and blue swirls, like an American flag. He lifted a leg over the windowsill and rolled inside.

The place smelled like turpentine. That must be why the window was open, to air it out. To the left was an open door, giving onto a bare, cramped hallway. He crept there on his hands and knees and peered down its length. At the far end was another corridor, where a crowd was standing with their backs to him. He tiptoed in that direction. Just then a cheer went up. "Good luck, Billy!" someone called. "We're with you!" cried another. Dutch couldn't see Bryan's head, but he could track the man's progress by the ripple he made through the crowd. Flattening himself against the wall, Dutch eased up some dimly lighted steps. At the top was an archway. Beyond, a huge space yawned before him. He moved closer and looked inside.

Below, above, all around him, stretched the monstrous cavern of Madison Square Garden. It was the most amazing place he'd ever seen. Thousands of people, some sitting, some standing, were pressed together on the enormous floor. Above them rose three galleries filled with seats, stretching in an unbroken oval all the way to the smoky ceiling and the skylights, open tonight on account of the heat. But what impressed Dutch as much as anything was the spectacle of the thousands of electric lights shining down from the metal arches that supported the roof.

Skylights or no, the place was stifling. All over the auditorium men had taken off their jackets, creating a sea of white shirtsleeves. Everywhere was the steady flutter of palm-leaf fans. Not far to Dutch's left, a dais had been built, jutting out into the arena. The platform was draped with bunting, and on either side hung two enormous portraits. The one on the left he recognized as William Jennings Bryan, but he couldn't guess who the man with the mustache might be. Some other politician, he figured. Between and above the pictures were crammed more flags and shields and bunting. On the stage, a few important-looking men had already taken their seats.

Over the drone of the crowd, he heard someone shout, "Three cheers for Bryan!" Music suddenly filled the hall, and turning, he saw a brass band pumping away in one of the galleries. More men in black frock coats trooped onto the dais. Then Bryan appeared. The crowd erupted, and Dutch had to put his hands over his ears. The candidate waved and bowed but then took a seat while some other man with a long white beard approached the speaker's table. The music stopped, and the man called out, "The meeting will please come to order! Let us have order!"

Dutch gazed around the huge arena. How could he possibly find Rafe in this chaos, even assuming his friend was inside the hall and not out on the street somewhere? True, he'd be wearing his police uniform, but there must be hundreds of policemen here. How could he get close to any of them without being thrown out? He scanned the crowd, shaking his head.

❧

Rafe had found Roosevelt on the far side of the hall, directly across from the dais. After leaving Minnie, he had sprinted to Broadway and hailed a hansom, thinking to save time. But before they reached Union Square, traffic toward the Garden came to a crawl. He jumped from the cab and began running. At Madison Square he shoved his way through the crowd until he reached the Garden's main entrance, where the police command post was located.

The other officers took in his disheveled uniform and his wild expression and must have decided that either he was mad or his mission must be as urgent as he claimed. Yes, a sergeant told him, the commissioner had already arrived. He'd left word that he would be at the back of Section F, in the center of the second level.

Rafe ran toward the staircase. Most of the ticket holders were in their seats, and he dodged only a few latecomers as he charged up the steps. At the top, he spotted Roosevelt standing alone in the aisle at the rear of the section, craning his thick neck toward the crowd below. Rafe could see why he'd chosen the spot: it gave him a clear view of the speaker's platform and the audience.

Roosevelt noticed him coming. "What in blazes happened to you?" he asked. "I thought I told you to take it easy for the rest of the day."

"I have to speak to you," Rafe blurted. "I know about Smolenski, the Pole."

Rafe saw the surprise flicker across Roosevelt's features, followed closely by doubt.

"I just talked to him," Rafe said.

The commissioner eyed him, then answered in a strained but level tone, "You shouldn't have done that, Rafe."

"The man is innocent," Rafe went on. "He doesn't know anything about a plot against Bryan."

"Come here," Roosevelt ordered, leading him toward the back of the aisle, away from the audience. "What do you mean?" he hissed, his voice no less vehement for being muted. "He signed the confession."

"No, he didn't," Rafe countered. "He doesn't even speak English. Gallagher signed the confession." He waited, but Roosevelt turned and surveyed the crowd, curiously unmoved by the news.

"And Gallagher tried to stage the Pole's suicide," Rafe added.

Roosevelt swung back toward him. "What are you talking about?" He was struggling to keep his voice down.

Rafe answered in a rush: "Gallagher knocked him over the head and hung him with his own belt, to make it look as though he'd killed himself. I found him unconscious on the floor of his cell. If the belt hadn't snapped, he'd be dead."

Roosevelt brought his hands to his hips. "And why would Gallagher do that?" But Rafe noticed he didn't deny that Gallagher was capable of such a thing.

"I don't know why," Rafe said. "But I do know he arrested the wrong man. That means the real plotter could still be at large." He gestured toward the fifteen thousand people packed into the Garden. "He might be here right now—"

Roosevelt eyed the dais, where a few dignitaries had started seating themselves amid the bunting.

"I think it has something to do with Mann's murder," Rafe told him.

Even in the dim light of the arena he could see the commissioner's jaw muscles begin to work. "Oh, Rafe, not that again. Not now. Not here."

But Rafe wouldn't be put off. All the heat and pain and doubt and frustration of the week distilled into this moment, and he fired back, "Yes, now. Here." He had never spoken to the commissioner that way, and he could see that Roosevelt was as surprised as he was.

"Not so loud," the commissioner ordered, with a worried glance toward the audience.

"We both know that Mann wasn't killed by a common robber," Rafe went on in a lower but still urgent tone. "I can't tell you how, but I believe the two cases are connected. Gallagher is the link."

Roosevelt glowered. "I ordered you to stop—"

But Rafe was beyond caring. "I know about Morgan and Elliott and all the rest. All your rich, powerful friends who were being blackmailed by William d'Alton Mann. All the reasons you weren't in a hurry to find Mann's murderer."

Roosevelt's eyes pinched into dark slits, and for a second Rafe thought he would be on the receiving end of another uppercut, even more punishing than the one he'd gotten in the gym that afternoon. Still he said: "You, a police commissioner, willing to let a murderer go free."

Roosevelt wavered, then blew out a heavy sigh. "No, Rafe. Not 'go free.' I would never violate my oath and let a murderer go free. But sometimes justice deferred is superior to justice rushed."

Then Rafe understood. What would it hurt if Mann's killer, and his blackmailing, were exposed after November 3, when William McKinley would be safely on the way to the White House and Theodore Roosevelt would be headed to the Navy Department?

The realization didn't diminish his anger. "And Mann isn't even the worst part," he went on. He pointed toward the crowd, murmuring in their seats. "This is the worst part. If there is going to be a terror attack, did you really think you could prevent it by keeping it secret?"

Rafe could see the commissioner struggling to control himself. Why wasn't Roosevelt the brawler punching back? Was it because they were here in the Garden? Then he realized: he had struck him in his most vulnerable spot—his moral superiority. "I couldn't bring the whole department into it," Roosevelt finally said in a guilty tone. "There are some things—"

Rafe pressed the attack. "But that didn't stop you from confiding in your Republican friends, and even in the Democratic National Committee."

"Obviously," Roosevelt went on in the same defensive voice, "I had to inform the Democrats so they could decide whether to go ahead with the speech."

A pair of men hurried by, looking for their seats. Roosevelt waited for them to pass, then said, "But I didn't have to tell the Republicans. Hanna's spies told him about the threat not long after I found out."

Rafe wasn't surprised that Hanna had spies in the department. "So that was why Ferris Appleby was so desperate to find you that day."

"Hanna wanted to make sure I was taking the proper precautions." He sighed. "Look, Rafe, it's been a hard week. Tonight let's just focus on the matter at hand, shall we? We can talk this through later, back at the office."

The words rang with the same condescension Roosevelt had shown him in the boxing ring that afternoon, when he'd forgotten who was schooling whom. Rafe responded the same way he had then, by punching harder. "It always comes down to politics, doesn't it? You didn't tell Chief Conlin, even though—"

"You know what Conlin's like," Roosevelt countered. "If he knew, the whole city would know. But Captain O'Brien is aware. In fact, he was the one who reported the threat."

True, at the meeting about Bryan's visit O'Brien didn't seem surprised by the order to put on extra men. "Do the rest of the detectives know?" Rafe asked.

"Just O'Brien and Gallagher."

And that was your plan? Just pack four hundred cops into the Garden and hope for the best?"

Roosevelt drew himself up. "I assure you," he sputtered, "my only intention was to prevent an attack by, by a gang of terrorists."

"'A *gang* of terrorists'?"

"Of course. Who organizes something like this on his own?"

"You let the speech go ahead even though there could be more plotters at large?" No wonder he hadn't been disturbed by the news about Smolenski's phony confession.

"And what should I have done?"

"Stop the speech, as soon as you got word of a possible attack."

Roosevelt shook his head. "Bryan refused to call it off. How would that look, if a Republican police commissioner cited some unproven plot to cancel the Democrats' biggest meeting of the year, during a presidential campaign? The press would crucify me."

Even as the two faced off, more officials were trooping onto the stage.

"You could at least have warned the public," Rafe parried.

"Warn them of what exactly? We don't even know if there will be violence, or what form it would take. A shooting? A bomb? What kind of announcement could we make that wouldn't just spread panic? Besides, how do you warn the public without warning the plotters?"

"At least no lives would be in danger. It was your duty."

Roosevelt leaned toward him. *"Don't tell me my duty."* Roosevelt's voice was so cool it chilled Rafe. "Even if an attack were prevented tonight, the terrorists would still be out there, waiting their chance. And next time we would probably have no warning at all. No, better to set the trap now and see if they walk into it."

Rafe nodded but not in agreement. Of course that would be Roosevelt's approach. The same maverick impulse that drove him to prowl the streets in the middle of the night, hunting for derelict cops. He had to do everything his way.

Three cheers rang out for Bryan, and from across the arena a brass band started up with "Dad's Old Silver Dollar Is Good Enough for Me." Then the music quieted, and Senator Jones, chairman of the Democratic National Committee, began to speak. "The meeting will please come to order!" he announced in his Arkansas twang. "Let us have order!"

Rafe looked out over the throng. "All right. Your trap is set. Now what?"

⁂

The metal plaque on the wall said she was in Section B, so Minnie figured Section F must be to the right, toward the center of the Garden. As she hurried in that direction, three cheers broke out for Mr. Bryan, and a brass band began to play.

Traffic had been heavy up Broadway, and the going had been slow as she'd steered her pirated bicycle close to the sidewalk, trying to avoid hitting pedestrians on one side and being run down by hansoms on the other. She still couldn't say what had gotten into her to commandeer a police bike, except that Dutch needed help. Madison Square had been mobbed, so she'd turned onto Fifth, then taken advantage of the police cordon to ride over Twenty-seventh Street to the Garden's back entrance. A couple of times officers had blocked her way and she'd had to show her police credentials. On reading her name, the patrolmen had looked up and down her perspiring figure, as if to say, *So you're the commissioner's lady stenographer.* But they'd let her through.

Once inside, she had to explain herself all over again. The guard at the Twenty-seventh Street door told her that Mr. Bryan had just gone in, and he directed her to the command post on the other side of the building. A sergeant there told her she should be able to find both Rafe and the commissioner upstairs, in Section F.

At the top of the steps, she made a sweeping turn to the right. Ahead, she saw Rafe and Mr. Roosevelt standing in the wide aisle, looking out over the crowd. But there was no sign of Dutch or Detective Gallagher. Rafe and the commissioner were deep in conversation, and as she drew nearer she was taken aback to hear that it wasn't entirely cordial.

⁓❦⁓

Cheers broke out for Bryan, but the figure standing on the ramp overlooking the swarming floor of Madison Square Garden wasn't taking in the spectacle. Instead, Gallagher's gaze was fixed on the back of an ordinary newsboy. He had seen the urchin climb into the ambulance, and he'd watched him jump the fence and slip through the open window. The detective had walked calmly to the Garden's Twenty-seventh Street entrance and, flashing his badge, had slipped in just ahead of the candidate. Then he'd seen the newsboy creep up the stairs to the auditorium.

On the long pursuit up Broadway, Gallagher had figured at first that the boy was simply trying to get away from him. He'd just missed him in the department store and then lost him at Union Square. He'd been standing on the corner of Broadway and Seventeenth when he saw him cross the street and fall in with the crowd. Then he realized his great good luck: the brat had been heading toward Madison Square Garden all along. Gallagher was puzzled by that until he realized the stenographer must have told him the Jew would be there. He and the boy seemed to have struck up some sort of friendship. Was the newsie just planning to squeal about the little episode in the Mystery Chamber, or had he recognized him from the alley after all? It didn't matter, because whatever the little son of a bitch knew wasn't going any further.

Music started, and the candidate entered to applause. Gallagher watched him bowing and waving to the crowd. There was no question that Bryan would make a fine president. One who had the common people, not just the swells, at heart. But more than that, Bryan understood what was happening to America. How places like Poland and Russia were sending their scum to pollute the country he loved. They were taking away jobs, driving down the wages of God-fearing Americans, and turning the United States into a mongrel nation he didn't even recognize anymore.

The real solution, of course, was just to turn the ships around. But the Republicans needed the cheap labor for their mills and factories and mines. That was why their platform called for the status quo on immigration—just admit all the simpletons who land at our doorstep, then grant citizenship to the broods they whelp here. At least the Democrats were willing to keep out the worst of the worst, to—how did they put it in their platform?—"prevent the importation of foreign pauper labor." It wasn't enough, but it was a start. And so, a few weeks ago, when he'd read in the paper that Bryan was coming to the Garden, he recognized a once-in-a-lifetime chance when he saw it. It was all so perfect, he sometimes wondered: was it preordained, like some kind of divine summons?

A plan had begun to form in his mind. If an immigrant was accused of trying to assassinate Bryan, the plot would backfire, of course. The people's sympathy would swing to the Democrat, and he would be elected. The government would be forced to take action, not only against new immigrants but against the ones who were already here. More important, the real Americans would finally decide they'd had enough and teach the foreign scum what America was all about. If a few skulls were cracked, so what? If a few tenements burned in the process, good riddance. There were enough honest, God-fearing patriots out there to do it. All they needed was a spark. And that would come tonight.

He tucked his elbow to his ribs and felt the comforting bulk of two pistols. Not only his own .38-caliber revolver but also a .45 that Jimmy Walsh had found in a gun shop downtown. He'd thought about concealing that one somewhere in the Garden, but in the end he'd decided that was too risky. And so he'd kept it in his locker at the Fourth Precinct, planning to fetch it late this afternoon. He locked the newsboy in the Mystery Chamber while he ran down the block to retrieve it, but then when he came back, the little bastard managed to get away from him. Well, no matter, he told himself now. There was still time for everything. He let his eyes travel from the stage up to the third gallery, almost to the roof, where a red velvet curtain was hanging limply. Yes, that was the place.

The music died as abruptly as it had begun, and Senator Jones smoothed his long white beard and began his introduction. "The meeting will please come to order!" he called. "Let us have order!" Gallagher figured, judging from Chicago, that Bryan would talk for at least an hour. That should be enough time. But first he needed to take care of the goddamned newsboy. Without that, it was all for nothing. He inched up the ramp, toward the auditorium.

⚜

As the man with the long white beard began to speak, Dutch studied the sea of faces, still puzzling over how to find Rafe. Then, somewhere down the aisle, a movement caught his attention. Turning, he saw a familiar figure hulking toward him. Gallagher. Dutch began running the only way open to him, down the steps to the Garden's wide oval floor.

At the bottom of the long flight of stairs, he turned to his right but then stopped short. A policeman was standing not twenty feet in front of him. He spun and ran the other way. The next opening was about forty feet ahead, directly under the speaker's platform. As he got closer to the dais, he could hear laughter rippling through the auditorium. *What could that man be saying that's so funny?* he wondered. He pushed apart the forest of bunting hanging from the platform and darted inside.

From underneath, he saw that the dais had been built over another set of stairs. He ran up the steps, then, as he drew nearer to the platform's wooden floor, he dropped to his hands and knees and began to crawl. He was so close to the planks that he could hear the shuffling of feet and the scraping of chair legs. At the top was a wide crack of light. He poked out his head. Bryan was speaking now. As Dutch wriggled out and scurried toward the back of the gallery, he heard the candidate's voice echo through the hall: "We do not underestimate the forces arrayed against us."

Dutch glanced over his shoulder but couldn't find Gallagher. Then, as he swiveled toward the front, he saw that the detective was ahead of him again. Instead of following under the dais he must have run up the other staircase. Their eyes met, and even from this distance Dutch could see the menace and resolve. The boy swung in the other direction. He was moving away from the dais now, toward the narrow end of the Garden's oval. On his right was another stairway, leading back toward the crowded floor. He ran past it, toward a section of box seats. From the speaker's stand, Bryan intoned, "But when the laws undertake to make the rich richer and the potent more powerful . . ."

By the time Dutch reached the end of the long aisle, Gallagher had gained on him. The only direction left was up. The boy leaped onto an armrest, startling a man in a gray suit. In front of him was a red velvet curtain tied with a gold sash. Dutch grabbed it, but as the curtain took his weight, he heard a tear. The curtain sheared partway off its rod, sending him swinging over the seats below. There was a gasp from the crowd. Digging in with his hands and bare feet, he managed to shinny up the fabric. Then, as the curtain reached the end of its arc and made its backward swing, he clutched the box's brass rail and spilled inside. The crowd cheered.

These box seats were full of shirtsleeved men scribbling in notebooks, too preoccupied to take much notice of him. All but one. As Dutch raced by, the man grabbed him by the arm. Dutch recognized him. "Sorry, Mr. Riis," he said, just before he dug his teeth into the reporter's wrist. As the boy dodged past the other chairs, Bryan proclaimed, "The commandment 'Thou shalt not steal' must be applied to the great as well as to the small, to the strong as well as the weak."

At the rear of the box hung another red velvet curtain. Pushing through it, Dutch found himself in a hallway. He started down a staircase, but after only a few paces he heard footsteps below, and Gallagher's red face reappeared around the turn of the stairs. Dutch wheeled then darted back up the way he had come.

One level higher up was another box, filled with men in evening clothes and ladies in fancy gowns. Below, Dutch could still hear Gallagher's footsteps echoing in the stairwell. He ran up another flight and found himself at the top of the Garden, just below the light-studded roof. Even this high up the seats were full. Bryan seemed small and far away, but his voice carried. "Honest money cannot be expected at the hands of those who deal dishonestly with the American people."

Dutch stopped to catch his breath. Coming toward him were two policemen. Neither was Rafe, and both were slapping their nightsticks on their palms. To his right, another set of stairs led to an open door. He ran through and slammed it behind him.

At the top of the stairs, he reached the roof café, deserted tonight. To one side rose the tall tower with the famous gold lady on top. Occupying two other corners were the Garden's pointed cupolas. Between them, running along the outer wall, was a double row of slender stone columns. Overhead stretched metal arches hung with electric lamps, all dark.

Below, Gallagher saw the rooftop door slam shut. He paused in front of it, panting and wiping his face with the sleeve of his jacket. Then he pushed the dead bolt home. *That should hold the little bastard for a while.* He turned back downstairs, toward the alcove with the red velvet curtain.

~❦~

In their perch on the second level, Rafe and the commissioner were standing in tense silence when they heard laughter rising from the crowd. Turning toward the dais, they saw the source: a ragged boy was about to dive under the speaker's platform. The mop of blond hair looked familiar, and crazy though it seemed, Rafe would have sworn it was Dutch. There was no doubt as to who was chasing him: Detective Sergeant Thomas Gallagher. Rafe turned to the commissioner, but he appeared just as confused as Rafe.

They were startled by a woman's voice behind them. "It's Dutch, all right," she said. Minnie's hair had fallen to her shoulders, and her shirtwaist was damp with perspiration. "He came running up to the office. He was frantic to find you, Rafe. I told him you were here. Gallagher must have chased him all the way."

Rafe blinked at her. "What does Gallagher want with him?"

Minnie shook her head. "Nothing good."

"How did he get in the Garden?" asked the commissioner.

She shrugged. "He's a newsboy, isn't he?"

As the candidate droned on, the three of them, like the rest of the audience, were absorbed in the chase unfolding on the other side of the auditorium. A minute later, when Dutch grabbed the curtain and dangled over the crowd, Rafe took off in that direction.

The commissioner called something after him, but his words hung in the air as Rafe raced out of view.

❧

Gallagher had chosen the spot with care: from the small alcove overlooking the auditorium there was a clear line of sight to the dais, and it was right next to the stairway to the roof. He glanced down the corridor. Apparently, the two uniforms had lost interest in the newsboy and had gone back to their posts. Gallagher pushed aside the heavy curtain.

Standing against the wall was the anarchist Hofmann, his round face white and gleaming with sweat. The detective huffed out a sigh of relief. Like most immigrants, the man wasn't very bright, and Gallagher had been afraid he wouldn't be able to find the alcove, even with the map he'd drawn him.

On seeing Gallagher, Hofmann closed his eyes and let out a deep sigh, though it wasn't clear if it was in relief or resignation. "Did you bring it?" he asked.

Gallagher pulled the .45 from his suitcoat pocket. Hofmann's eyes grew bigger. Gallagher handed it to him grip-first. Hofmann took the gun and cradled it like a baby.

"You're sure you've used one of these things before?" Gallagher asked.

"In the old country. My papa and I shot at targets."

Gallagher hoped he was telling the truth. At first, he hadn't cared if the German even knew how to pull the trigger, because he wasn't planning to give him the chance. He'd figured that stopping a would-be assassin should be enough to waken Americans to the immigrant threat, so he'd planned to interrupt Hofmann before he'd even gotten off a round.

But over long nights nursing a beer and listening to the anarchists' blathering, his idea had evolved. Gunshots ringing out in the vast, crowded confines of Madison Square Garden would be so much more dramatic, so much more effective for his purpose. He had smiled at the realization: it would be his own "propaganda of the deed." When he'd floated the plan to Hofmann, a couple of weeks ago, the half-wit had seized on it with the zeal of the true believer. But of course, the odds of Hofmann, or anybody, hitting a man with a pistol from this distance were slim, and the odds of killing him minuscule. But the German would get his shot. If some other "dignitary" on the dais were wounded, all the better.

Hofmann swung open the revolver's cylinder and gave it a spin, inspecting the six brass cartridges inside. Then he snapped it closed and peered down the barrel toward the floor. "Bryan is far away," he said. "It's not an easy shot." Maybe the man knew something about guns after all. Gallagher suddenly found himself hoping Hofmann wasn't too experienced.

"Give me ten minutes," the detective told him. That should be plenty of time to dispense with the newsboy.

Hofmann gave him a tense look, then nodded uncertainly.

"Afterward—" Gallagher prompted him.

"We meet on the roof," Hofmann said stiffly, as though rehearsing lines from a play. "To escape."

"Just up those stairs," Gallagher said, pointing through the curtain.

He stepped out of the alcove, but the German followed him. "You will be there, yes?"

"I'll be waiting," Gallagher told him. As he started up the stairs, he suppressed a smile at the man's naivete. What could ever make him hope he would survive this night?

He'd be damned if he'd let some uniform make the arrest of a lifetime. No matter how many cops Roosevelt packed into the Garden, Gallagher alone would know where to find the would-be assassin. In his mind he'd already written the head-line: N.Y.P.D. Detective Slays Bryan Shooter. After that, his career would be made. Not even Czar Theodore, as the press was calling him, would have the nerve to get rid of him. Who knew, maybe one day he would take Captain O'Brien's place as chief of detectives. Or what was to stop him from becoming superintendent of the whole force? He smiled. And of course, a foreigner trying to shoot a presidential candidate wasn't likely to do the goddamned immigrants any good, either.

Rafe halted at the top of the Garden's wide central staircase. He had run to the building's far side then vaulted the steps two at a time. As he gained the upper level, he saw Gallagher about fifty feet away, coming down from the roof. Maybe Dutch had managed to get away after all.

Gallagher glanced in his direction, and Rafe flattened himself against a pillar. He peered around it just in time to see the detective disappear behind a red curtain. That was odd. Although Rafe longed to run to the roof and see if Dutch was safe, he lingered there, watching. After a minute, Gallagher emerged, and Rafe was surprised to see a second man step out. Rafe didn't recognize him. Was he another detective? No, the fear on his face was the mark of an amateur. Then Rafe saw the pistol dangling from his hand. The two men exchanged words, their heads pressed close together. Gallagher clapped him on the shoulder in an encouraging way. Then the other man disappeared again, and Gallagher climbed the stairs to the roof and closed the door behind him.

Rafe crept toward the velvet curtain. He stopped outside and slowly drew it back.

Inside the alcove, the stranger was standing with his back to him, gazing out over the auditorium. Intent on his purpose, he didn't notice Rafe. The pistol was still in his hand. As Rafe watched, the man raised the gun and stared down the barrel toward the stage. He seemed unsure, as though taking a practice aim.

Rafe sprang on him. Seizing the hand holding the revolver, he forced it toward the floor. He expected to hear a shot, but there was none.

The stranger recovered and swung the gun toward him, landing a backhanded swipe across the forehead. Rafe's helmet flew off, and he stumbled backward. Now the stranger was leveling the revolver directly at him.

Rafe rushed forward, grabbing the barrel with both hands. The men struggled chest to chest, their sweaty faces inches apart. Bit by bit, the stranger managed to turn the barrel of the pistol toward Rafe's temple. His finger curled around the trigger. Then Rafe abruptly let go, and the stranger stumbled.

While the man was still off balance Rafe landed a vicious hook to the side of his head. His eyes lost their focus. Rafe followed with an uppercut. The stranger fell, and the pistol crashed to the floor.

Rafe was standing over him, still dazed, when he heard the rustle of curtains behind him. Commissioner Roosevelt with two patrolmen.

The commissioner picked up the revolver. "Officers, take that man to headquarters!" he ordered. They slipped past Rafe and dragged the stranger out by his arms.

Mr. Roosevelt gave a toothy grin. "Fine work, old boy," he told him.

Normally, Rafe would have basked in the commissioner's praise, but tonight he just pushed past him. As he raced toward the stairs, he noticed Riis and Minnie standing to one side. He could see the concern on Minnie's face, but without slowing, he made for the roof.

Dutch was cowering under a table in the middle of the rooftop terrace when he heard the metal door scrape open. Gallagher slammed it shut and wedged a chair under the knob. The boy began shaking as he watched him work his way across the floor.

"Come here, Dutch," he called. "I'm not going to hurt you. I just need to ask you some questions about the other night, is all. I'm not mad. Come on out and we'll have a little talk."

Peeking from under the table, Dutch saw a pistol in Gallagher's hand.

Bryan's voice wafted through an open skylight. "The United States should be an example in all that is good. . . ."

Gallagher was working his way across the terrace now, searching under each table as he went. Dutch gauged the distance to the door. Could he run for it, pull the chair away, and make it out before he got a bullet in the back? His legs felt weak. Could he trust them to carry him at all?

He searched under the table for anything he could use as a weapon, a loose chair leg, a forgotten bottle, but the sweepers had done their work too well. Creeping from under the table, he inched toward the far corner. Then his foot hooked on a chair, and the clatter echoed across the empty space. He pulled himself under another table and held his breath. Through the skylight he could hear the huge crowd applauding something that Bryan had said.

Before long, Gallagher stopped beside Dutch's table. "Come out, son," he whispered. "I promise, I won't hurt you."

Dutch didn't budge, and Gallagher reached under the apron and flicked the lightweight table clear over Dutch's head.

It landed behind him with a crash. Dutch saw that Gallagher's suit was rumpled and soaked with sweat. He was red-faced, his eyes creased in hatred. His revolver was pointed at Dutch's chest. "You little bastard," he said. "Get up."

Dutch froze, and Gallagher eased back the pistol's hammer. "Get up," he told him again.

Shakily, Dutch pulled himself upright. When he was on his feet, Gallagher flicked his wrist and slapped him with the barrel of the gun. Dutch fell backward. There was a searing pain across his cheek, and when he touched the spot, his fingers came away covered in blood.

"You've been nothing but a thorn in my side, you little son of a bitch. Even tonight, you nearly ruined everything." He cocked his head, as though listening for something below. "You couldn't leave well enough alone." He leveled the pistol at the boy's chest. "Turn around," he said. Dutch did as he was told. "Now walk."

"Columbia," Bryan was droning, "her hands bound fast with fetters of gold . . ."

They threaded their way through tables and chairs. Then they climbed a few steps and reached the stone columns near the edge of the roof. Dutch stopped, but Gallagher yelled, "Move!" Now they were next to the parapet overlooking the street.

"Climb up!" Gallagher told him.

Dutch was refiguring the odds of making a run for it. His eyes darted from side to side, searching for the most likely escape route. His muscles tensed to flee. He was struggling to hold back tears.

Before he could move, there was a banging from across the terrace, and a deep voice called through the door, "Gallagher! Open up!"

"Climb!" Gallagher told him.

Dutch wavered, still searching for a way out.

"Dutch, it's Rafe! Open the door!" Then the banging grew louder, as though Rafe was putting his broad shoulder into it.

With his back against the parapet now, Dutch dared to glance down and saw the crowd milling on the street, four stories below.

"Dutch! Dutch!" It was Rafe again.

"Rafe, help!" he called.

"Gallagher, open up!"

Gallagher kept moving closer. "If only you didn't try to run from me. If only you didn't climb up on that low wall. I told you to come down, but you wouldn't. Then you just slipped. I reached out and tried to catch you, but you were gone. It's a shame, really."

Gallagher was within a foot now. He stuck out a hand to grab the boy, but Dutch dodged to his left.

There was more banging on the metal door. Dutch wondered if people in the auditorium could hear. It had been months since he had really prayed. Now he murmured, "Please, Mama, please."

Gallagher heard the banging, too. Deciding he could wait no longer, he made a stab with his left hand, the one without the pistol, and shoved Dutch's shoulder toward the parapet. When Dutch spun to dodge him, Gallagher slipped to one side. He was off balance now, his heavy body pitched toward the roof's edge. Dutch bent and gripped the man's legs in both hands. He was surprised at how effortlessly they lifted and slipped away.

Seconds later, when the door burst open, Rafe and the others—Roosevelt, Riis, and Minnie—were puzzled to find the boy alone, trembling in a corner with a bewildered expression on his bloodied face.

As Rafe approached the edge of the building, he became aware of shouts on the street below. Bending over the parapet, he saw the crowd gathered around a man's twisted body.

Dutch ran to Rafe and threw his arms around his waist. Then he blurted what he'd been trying to tell him all day. "It was Gallagher in the alley that night. Gallagher with the body. He had a gun. He was trying to kill me."

Rafe didn't grasp everything he was saying, but he believed him instantly. His first concern was to protect Dutch, to get him off the roof before more police arrived. Turning to the others, he said, "The boy was never here, understand?" It wasn't quite by the book, but one thing Rafe had learned over the past week was that *law* wasn't always synonymous with *justice*.

He looked toward Mr. Roosevelt, expecting an argument. But the commissioner nodded, then turned to Riis. "Not a word of this in the *Sun*," he said.

ELEVEN

Friday, August 21

"LOOKS LIKE RAIN." Rafe was standing at the commissioner's open window, watching a band of violet clouds creep in from the west.

"It's been threatening all day," Minnie called from her desk.

He glanced at the clock on the mantel. Nearly six o'clock. Time for the commissioner to be getting back.

"I don't think it even hit seventy degrees this afternoon," Rafe answered. It had been a week since the hot wave broke. The night after Bryan's speech, around midnight, a rumble of thunder had rolled up from the south, and by 3 a.m. the long-awaited rain had arrived. Showers had fallen through the morning and afternoon, holding temperatures to the low eighties. Yesterday, according to the *Sun*, the city had reached a low of fifty-seven, a record for the date, with a high of only seventy-one. Today had been more or less the same. Fall appeared to have come early to New York, and it seemed a luxury now when Rafe slipped on his woolen uniform in the morning. Still, they said that more than a thousand people had died in New York and Brooklyn because of the ten-day hot wave.

Rafe heard Mr. Roosevelt's voice in the anteroom. He set a folder on the commissioner's desk, next to his travel case and under the file of letters that Minnie had left for him to sign. He reached the door just as the commissioner was coming through. They stood awkwardly for a second, then Rafe stepped aside. "I've left your itinerary for you," he told him.

Jacob Riis appeared behind the commissioner. "Jake's going to see me to the depot," Mr. Roosevelt said.

Rafe went back to his desk, and in a few minutes Mr. Roosevelt and Riis emerged from the office. The commissioner handed the folder of correspondence to Minnie then stood in the doorway, bag in hand. "I'll see you both in three weeks," he said.

"Have a good trip," Minnie said. "I hope your speeches go well."

"It's the hunting I'm looking forward to," he answered. "North Dakota should be outstanding this time of year." He seemed to hesitate, then extended his hand toward Rafe.

"Good travels," Rafe told him.

The commissioner pushed his wide-brimmed black hat onto his head and was gone.

Rafe sat watching the empty doorway.

"I hope Mr. McKinley appreciates what Mr. Roosevelt is doing for him," Minnie said.

"I hope Mr. McKinley appreciates what you've done for him," he told her. "Typing all those speeches the commissioner is going to give for his campaign." Despite Gallagher's efforts, the sages were predicting a Republican victory. "If McKinley gets elected and takes the commissioner to Washington, maybe he'll ask you to go with him."

Minnie smiled. "I can just see Mama in Washington, can't you?"

"I've never met your mother," he reminded her.

"No, of course not." He felt a little wounded by the certainty in her tone. She went on, "But it would be strange here without Mr. Roosevelt." The prospect seemed more likely every day.

"Would you stay on, with a new commissioner?" he asked.

"If they'll have me."

He let his gaze linger on her delicate features and raven hair. "They'd be fools to let you get away."

"What about you? Will you go to Washington if he asks?"

Rafe shook his head. "All my family are here, too." This wasn't the time to go into other reasons he might want to stay.

"What about all his reforms? I wonder if the rest of the board will keep them up, or if everything will go back to the corrupt way it was."

Rafe doubted that all Mr. Roosevelt's innovations would outlast him. Yes, the commissioner could introduce civil service exams and he could fire cops caught taking bribes, but over the past two weeks Rafe had learned that, no matter what they said, the powerful still looked after themselves and the rest of their kind. As Mr. Roosevelt had shown in trying to scotch the Mann investigation, even he wasn't above cutting corners when it suited his interests. Even so, Rafe still admired the man for his probing intelligence, his superhuman energy, and his sincere desire to help the less fortunate, and he figured a little scheming was to be expected from any politician. He admitted the department would be the poorer when the commissioner left.

"What about you?" Minnie asked. "Still hoping to be the force's first Jewish detective?"

He couldn't tell if she was teasing. "I suppose." He reckoned that policing was still worthwhile, but he no longer thought of it as a mitzvah.

"Well," she said, "you shouldn't have any trouble getting on the list for the detective exam now, whether the commissioner leaves or not."

He wasn't so sure. If the commissioner left, who would stand up for him and the few other Jewish officers on the force?

As if reading his mind, Minnie said, "They wouldn't dare fire you. Once again you're a hero, the man who saved William Jennings Bryan from an assassin."

Rafe had to agree that he'd come out well in the Bryan affair. Logic and perseverance had seen him through, along with a bit of nerve and a pinch of luck. The next morning, Jacob Riis had published a dramatic, flattering story in the *New York Sun*, making the second time that Rafe had found himself a genuine newspaper hero.

"My father appreciated the piece," he said, smiling. "He hung it in the meat market and points it out to all his customers. I guess he finally accepts I won't be going back there after all."

"And you're the one who solved the Mann case," Minnie said. Rafe could hear the pride in her voice.

"Well, that was a little more complicated," he reminded her. After that night in the Garden, they'd brought in Gallagher's friend Jimmy Walsh, and he'd cracked like a two-minute egg. Sitting in the commissioner's office, he'd poured out his confession so fast that Minnie's pencil could barely keep up. First, he described how Gallagher had recruited him to help with the Bryan business. Gallagher knew that he and Walsh were of the same mind on the immigrants, and he assumed that Jimmy would welcome a once-in-a-lifetime chance to make history with him. Jimmy went along for a while, even buying the pistol, but after Kavanaugh died, he panicked and told Gallagher he'd had enough. But Gallagher wouldn't take no for an answer. Even now, Jimmy didn't know exactly why Gallagher was so insistent. He didn't really need anyone other than Hofmann, his stooge and shooter. Rafe's best guess was that Gallagher only wanted somebody to confide in, to listen to his political rants. More than anything, it seemed, he wanted an audience.

Then Walsh admitted that he'd gotten to bragging one night, telling his brother-in-law, Eammon Kavanaugh, about this crazy idea that another detective had hatched. True, the pair had made some good money passing police gossip to *Town Topics*, but how was Walsh to know that Kavanaugh would tell Mann all about the terror plot, including how he'd heard about it? Mann went to Walsh for confirmation, and he denied everything, of course, but the publisher couldn't let it rest.

So Walsh had no choice but to go to Gallagher and confess. Gallagher was furious when he heard about Kavanaugh and Mann, and he insisted they go have a little talk with the publisher. Working the overnight shift that Monday evening, Gallagher borrowed a plain black brougham from the police stables and, with him driving and Walsh riding inside, they pulled up in front of Mann's office. When Mann finally came out around one o'clock in the morning, Jimmy called him over and said he had more information for him. Mann got in, and they drove off. Rafe nodded when he heard that part; it jibed with what Harold Vynne had told him.

There was no traffic at that hour, and soon enough they were having a chat on a deserted street down under the Brooklyn Bridge. Mann said he hadn't yet told his staff about the Bryan plot, but he insisted it was a story too good to ignore. He wouldn't listen to them, talked to them like they were his Irish servants. Before Walsh could stop him, Gallagher gripped a big nightstick he'd lifted from the Mystery Chamber and swung it at Mann like a baseball bat. A single, fatal blow, just as Coroner Tuthill had said.

Walsh was in a panic and wanted to leave the body there, but Gallagher said it was better to drop it somewhere in their own Fourth Precinct, so he could follow the investigation, maybe even handle it himself. He knew just the place, he said. When they got to Rose Street, Walsh pulled the brougham around the corner while Gallagher dragged the body down the alley, wrapped in a horse blanket they'd found in the carriage. It was all going perfectly until Dutch turned up.

The next day, Walsh told them, Gallagher wrote the phony note about terrorists in the police department, to get the commissioner's attention. Then he left him the note about the Bryan plot, to support the accusations he was planning to make against Hofmann and Smolenski. Of course, neither could be allowed to live to contradict Gallagher's lies. The Pole would hang himself, and Hofmann would die on the roof, shot by Gallagher in the act of escaping.

Then he began to cover his tracks. Gallagher didn't know whether the newsboy had seen his face, he told Walsh. Not to worry, he said, he'd take care of the urchin later. But he warned him, if Walsh ever breathed another word about Mann—no, if he so much as had another thought about Mann—it would be the last thought he ever had. With Mann and Walsh no longer threats, Gallagher only had to worry about Kavanagh. And so he followed him out of his favorite gin mill that night and helped him under the wheels of the Third Avenue El. What else were the boys at the precinct going to conclude except that he'd taken his own life, just another man driven mad by the financial crash or the hot wave or both?

But Gallagher hadn't counted on Rafe, whom he'd started calling "the wondering Jew." Rafe winced when he heard that one. "Who appointed him the solver of unsolved mysteries?" he'd complained to Walsh. "Mysteries that nobody else even thinks are mysteries?" Before Rafe got involved, Mann's death was open and shut. Mr. Roosevelt was happy to believe the publisher was killed by a robber, as long as *Town Topics* left him and other prominent Republicans alone. But Gallagher did have one reason to be grateful to Rafe. He'd led him to the publisher's apartment, where he'd followed him on the night after Mann's death.

Gallagher told Walsh how the next morning he crept into the apartment himself, to make sure that Mann hadn't left behind any notes about the terror plot. Rafe surprised him, and he knocked him over the head and found the notebook in his pocket. Gallagher recognized it for what it was, and after he was finished with the business at the Garden, he thought maybe he would team up with somebody from *Town Topics* and get into the blackmail line himself. He may not have his own magazine to publish the gossip in, but he knew half a dozen reporters in New York who would be happy to help him out, for a consideration.

The final loose end was Dutch, who had seen him in the alley with Mann's body that night. Gallagher managed to get the newsboy's name from Pop Heig, but he couldn't keep his hands on him. On the roof of the Garden, the boy escaped him for the last time.

❧

Walsh pleaded guilty to his part in the terror plot, and since there would be no charges brought in Mann's murder, the public would never hear about the leather notebook, which had been found in Gallagher's pocket. The commissioner had taken possession of it, and Rafe understood that it would never be released. Riis knew enough to piece together some parts of the story, but he would never write it up, as another favor for his dear friend Theodore. Of course, the commissioner was outraged to learn that two of his detectives had been involved in the terror plot. But at least the blackmail threat died with Mann and Gallagher, and the department did get some outstanding publicity for foiling the Bryan assassination. As an accessory, Walsh was looking at a good long stay in Sing Sing. For the immigrant Hofmann, the district attorney was asking for life.

The commissioner was also insisting on silence over Dutch's role in solving the case. "Imagine what the papers would make of that," he said, "a newsboy stepping in where New York's Finest had failed." He'd never get to Washington that way. No, as far as the public was concerned, Mann was killed by an unknown robber. But with Gallagher's death, Mann had received a measure of justice. Not from the courts, Rafe figured, but from *Hashgochoh Protis*, divine providence.

And so Dutch was never identified as the newsboy who had led Gallagher on the wild chase through Madison Square Garden. The child was made to promise he would never utter a word about what had happened on the roof, not even to Grady. That was fine with Dutch; he seemed only too eager to put it all out of his mind. So the official version, dutifully published in the *New York Sun*, was that Detective Gallagher had slipped to his death while being pursued by Officer Raphael, who had chased him to the roof after subduing the anarchist Jakob Hofmann.

"Still, it's a shame Dutch got nothing out of it," Rafe said to Minnie now.

"No one will ever know what a little hero he is," she agreed. "But in his case, that's a blessing. Keeping him out of that mess was the kindest thing you and the commissioner could have done for the boy."

It wasn't the first time that Minnie had expressed an aversion to public scrutiny. She had never enjoyed her notoriety as the department's first female stenographer, and she couldn't imagine that Dutch might benefit from the publicity. But Rafe thought that maybe the boy deserved some lionizing. After all, if Rafe hadn't been recognized for running into that burning tenement, he would never have been invited to take the police exam, and he'd still be passing his days plucking chickens in his father's butcher shop. Maybe a story in the *Sun* would have changed Dutch's life as well. Far from feeling he'd done Dutch a kindness, Rafe was afraid he'd betrayed him.

As they straightened their desks for the night, Minnie said, "You mentioned Dutch is coming by this evening, didn't you? Are you going to take him for some supper?"

Rafe nodded. Even with all that had happened to the boy over the past two weeks, there had been worse to come.

The day after Bryan's speech, Rafe had finally gone downstairs and begun the search for Dutch's mother, Anna Maier. He started with the arrests for prostitution, but no one by that name or description had been brought in. One report in the accident files drew his attention though. A little after 1 p.m. on May 5, the day Dutch had said she'd disappeared, a team had broken away from its driver on First Avenue, in Dutch's old neighborhood. A woman had been run down crossing the street. She'd been brought to Bellevue Hospital but had been dead on arrival. He read her description. Tall and blonde and wearing a gray dress, just as Dutch had said. In her pockets were found a house key, eight pennies, and a white handkerchief with an embroidered violet. Rafe opened his desk drawer, where he had placed the handkerchief he'd found in the alley off Rose Street. It too was embroidered with a pale-blue violet.

Rafe returned to the morgue and pulled the record of the woman's death. Since there had been no identification, and since the body hadn't been claimed within forty-eight hours, she had been buried in the potter's field on Hart Island. Her fate had merited only a couple of lines on the inside pages of the New York papers, with all the other small daily tragedies of a great metropolis.

Rafe knew he had to be the one to tell the boy. After spiriting Dutch away from Madison Square Garden, he had thought about taking him to his own family's tenement on Allen Street. But he knew his father wouldn't tolerate another soul in the cramped apartment. So he'd gone with Dutch to the Newsboys Lodging House, where he'd had a word with Pop Heig to make sure he'd take the boy back. Dutch hadn't resisted. It seemed that roughing it had lost its romance.

When Dutch got back to the lodging house from selling his papers late one afternoon, Rafe was waiting. He pulled the boy into the second-floor reading room, closed the door, and sat him down at one of the tables.

"Are you going to arrest me?" Dutch asked.

Rafe wished it was only that. He told him, as simply and matter-of-factly as he could. The boy tried to take it stoically, but before it was over, he had climbed into Rafe's lap and buried his face in his chest.

"Dutch," Rafe asked him gently, "remember when we had lunch that day and you asked me about losing something that someone gave you, whether it meant you would never see them again?"

Dutch rubbed his eyes.

"Was this what you lost?" Rafe asked. And he reached into his pocket and pulled out a woman's white handkerchief.

On this cool Friday evening, Rafe and Minnie were still hashing over the case when Dutch appeared in their doorway. His clothes were still tatty, but now they were clean. His curly blond hair was freshly cut, and on his feet were a pair of shiny brown lace-ups. The cut on his cheek from Gallagher's pistol was fading, and his features were fuller than a week ago, but even Pop Heig's unlimited seconds couldn't hide a change in his expression. The first time he had seen Dutch, that night on the Lower East Side with the commissioner and Jacob Riis, Rafe had thought the boy looked younger than his ten years; now he thought he looked, if not older exactly, more mature.

"Dutch, has it started to rain yet?" Minnie asked.

He shrugged.

"Tell me, how's Grady doing? Rafe says he's still on his corner every morning, cast and all."

"'A man's got to eat,'" Dutch said. They understood he was quoting his friend and mentor.

"Is he staying with you at the lodging house these days?"

"Naw, he's trying to save up some money. Says he wants to go out west."

Rafe asked, "You mean with the Children's Aid Society? Remember, we talked about that."

Dutch shook his head. "The orphan train? Grady says that's for suckers. Who knows who you'll end up with? What if they're mean, or they make you sleep in a barn or something? He says if he goes, he's going on his own. Who knows, maybe I'll go with him."

"Are you saving up, too?" Minnie asked.

"Sure. I got eighty cents in the last week alone." He turned to Rafe. "You ready to go? I'm hungry."

Rafe stood up from his desk. "What do you feel like?"

"How about a frankfurter? There's a place around the corner."

"I know the one," Rafe said. He put his hand on the boy's shoulder and edged him toward the door.

"Wait a minute," Minnie said. "I'll go down with you." She slipped the cloth cover over her typewriter and pinned on her hat. With Dutch walking between them, they made their way down the wide staircase, through the lobby, and out the heavy front door. At the bottom of the building's granite steps, Rafe heard the words come from his mouth, as though emanating from someone else: "Why don't you join us?"

She threw him a look over the top of Dutch's head. Then she smiled. "Thanks, I think I will."

Dutch glanced up from one to the other, then took both their hands. They walked like that to the end of the block and rounded the corner in the cool night air.

AUTHOR'S NOTE

A LTHOUGH THIS IS a work of fiction, many of the characters and situations portrayed are based on actual persons and events. For readers curious about where history leaves off and invention begins, I offer the following notes.

Besides national figures such as Theodore Roosevelt, J. P. Morgan, William Jennings Bryan, William McKinley, Mark Hanna, Jacob Riis, Johann Most, Emma Goldman, and Robert DeCourcy Ward, various New York City officials mentioned were also actual persons, such as police commissioners Andrew Parker, Frederick Grant, and Avery Andrews; police chief Peter Conlin; police captain William O'Brien; police superintendent Thomas Byrnes; morgue superintendent Captain White; and coroner Theodore K. Tuthill. The other characters listed below—Otto Raphael and his family, Minnie Gertrude Kelly, William d'Alton Mann, Harold Vynne, and Pop Heig—were also real people. Aside from the few exceptions noted here, all actual persons' biographical facts are as accurate as I could make them, until August 9, 1896, the day the book begins. In regard to characters' personalities and motivations, I have fabricated freely.

Otto Raphael (for whom I, not Theodore Roosevelt, coined the nickname "Rafe") and his father, Raphael Raphael, did rush into a burning building to save the tenants, and Otto did join New York's Finest at the invitation of Commissioner Roosevelt, becoming one of the first Jewish officers on the force. He was a patrolman, not Roosevelt's assistant. He worked in the police department for many years, and today the NYPD's Shomrim Society, a Jewish fraternal and charitable organization, presents an annual award bearing his name.

Minnie Gertrude Kelly was hired by Theodore Roosevelt as the first woman stenographer on the NYPD. The only liberty I have taken in her case is to give her a quirky sense of humor and the ability to ride a bicycle; according to a newspaper story from the time, she was a serious, old-fashioned girl who eschewed the biking craze then sweeping America. But in light of the rest of her biography, I doubt there was much old-fashioned about her. She also had a long career on the New York City police force.

William d'Alton Mann was the inventor of the boudoir railroad car (a competitor to the Pullman) and publisher of *Town Topics*, and he did make a fortune blackmailing many of New York's most prominent citizens, including J. P. Morgan. Although there is no evidence that he tried to blackmail Theodore Roosevelt, in 1904, when Roosevelt was president, Mann published a particularly nasty account in his "Saunterings" column, attacking Alice Roosevelt's behavior during her debut at Newport. The piece sparked a bitter public feud between that magazine and *Collier's*, which eventually led to Mann's acquittal on charges of perjury but the exposure of his blackmailing. Although many powerful persons would no doubt have relished Mann's early demise, he died of natural causes, at the age of eighty.

Harold Vynne was William d'Alton Mann's son-in-law and an editor at *Town Topics*. He died of alcoholism in 1903, at the age of forty.

Rudolph "Pop" Heig was the beloved superintendent of the Newsboys Lodging House for twenty-three years, before retiring due to ill health in 1910.

Dutch and Grady are fictitious, although they are representative of the estimated fifteen thousand homeless children living in New York City at the time, many of whom survived by selling newspapers.

Some characters' dialogue has been taken, either verbatim or paraphrased, from their writings, newspaper reports, and other published sources. The speech made by the fictional Smolenski was adapted from an actual anarchist address of the time. William Jennings Bryan and Arkansas Senator James Kimbrough Jones did speak the words I have attributed to them at Madison Square Garden on August 12, 1896, but I have compressed both addresses.

All statistics from the heat wave (or "hot wave," as it was called at the time), including temperatures reached, rainfall (or lack thereof), and victim tolls, are part of the historical record. In New York City and Brooklyn, which wouldn't be incorporated into Greater New York until two years later, the ten-day heat wave is thought to have claimed some thirteen hundred victims.

After his election in November 1896, William McKinley decided that Theodore Roosevelt was too impulsive to be trusted as secretary of the navy. But he did name him assistant secretary, in which role he played an important part in preparations for the Spanish-American War, sometimes without the knowledge of his superiors. When war was declared, in April 1898, Roosevelt resigned his post and cofounded the legendary cavalry regiment known as the Rough Riders. Returning from Cuba a certified hero, he was elected governor of New York that fall. Two years later, during his bid for reelection, McKinley chose Roosevelt as his running mate, over the strident objections of his longtime adviser Mark Hanna. "Don't you realize," Hanna railed at the Republican convention, "that there's only one life between that madman and the White House?" His warning proved prescient, and on September 14, 1901, after McKinley was assassinated by an anarchist in Buffalo, Roosevelt was sworn in as the nation's twenty-sixth president.

I would like to thank the authors of several books that were particularly helpful in my research: *Crying the News: A History of America's Newsboys*, by Vincent DiGirolamo; *Commissioner Roosevelt: The Story of Theodore Roosevelt and the New York City Police, 1895–1897*, by H. Paul Jeffers; *Hot Time in the Old Town: The Great Heat Wave of 1896 and the Making of Theodore Roosevelt*, by Edward P. Kohn; *The Man Who Robbed the Robber Barons*, by Andy Logan; *New York's News Boys: Charles Loring Brace and the Founding of the Children's Aid Society*, by Karen M.

Staller; *Morgan: American Financier*, by Jean Strouse; and *Island of Vice: Theodore Roosevelt's Quest to Clean Up Sin-Loving New York*, by Richard Zacks.

Three books published in the period were also helpful, *Darkness and Daylight: Or, Lights and Shadows of New York Life*, by Helen Campbell; *How the Other Half Lives: Studies Among the Tenements of New York*, by Jacob Riis; and *Theodore Roosevelt: An Autobiography*. Also indispensable were the New York Public Library's online collection of period fire insurance maps and the Library of Congress's extensive online newspaper archive, Chronicling America. In my effort to avoid words and expressions that hadn't been coined by 1896, I often consulted the excellent Online Etymology Dictionary (etymonline.com). For readers interested in learning more about newsboys and the Newsboys Lodging House, a wealth of additional information is available at the website No. 9 Duane Street (nineduane.queenitsy.com), from which I have drawn extensively. Of course, any errors and oversights are entirely my own.

In a more personal vein, I offer a belated but heartfelt thanks to the late Carl Smith, of Troy, New York, who many years ago regaled a five-year-old boy with stories of the American Revolution, igniting a lifelong love of history.

Thanks to A. J. Jones for kindly sharing your expertise on the sweet science of boxing.

Thanks to Cal Barksdale, executive editor of Arcade Publishing, for your enthusiasm, professionalism, and astute editorial contributions. You have made the book better in innumerable ways, both great and small, and I am deeply grateful.

Thank you to my longtime agent, Deirdre Mullane, of Mullane Literary Associates, for your continuing encouragement and perseverance, especially in the case of the present book.

Thank you to my dear friend Miriam Schneir for your careful, informed reading of the manuscript. I am in your debt, not least of all for the gift of your friendship.

Thanks and love to my great-nephew Nick Miller. You're an inspiration.

Love to my sister, Marlene Helferich Bergendahl, and thanks for your unflagging encouragement of this and all my writing.

I also owe a great debt to my brother, William H. Helferich III, whose decency, generosity, and love have been a model to me throughout my life.

As always, my deepest love and gratitude go to my wife of forty-four years (and fellow writer), Teresa Nicholas. For two decades, since the start of my writing career, you have been my invaluable first reader and sounding board, but with no other book have I relied on your judgment as much as with this one. Thank you for everything.